betrothed

(book #6 in the vampire journals)

morgan rice

ISBN: 978-0-9829537-7-8

Also by Morgan Rice

turned
(book #1 in the Vampire Journals)

loved
(Book #2 in the Vampire Journals)

betrayed
(Book #3 in the Vampire Journals)

destined
(Book #4 in the Vampire Journals)

desired
(Book #5 in the Vampire Journals)

FACT:

In Shakespeare's London, a common form of entertainment was "bear baiting." A bear would be tied to a pole while a pack of wild dogs was unleashed. Bets would be placed to see who won. The "bear baiting" stadium was right near Shakespeare's theatre. Many of the rough bear baiting crowd would then go and watch a Shakespeare play.

In Shakespeare's time, the crowd that went to see his plays was not elitist or sophisticated. On the contrary. The majority of people who went to see his plays were rough, crude people, commoners who came for entertainment and had to only pay a penny to get in. For that price, they had to stand on the ground throughout the whole play—and thus became known as the "groundlings."

Shakespeare's London was civilized—but it was also barbaric. It was common to see executions and public torture of criminals in the streets. The entrance to its most famous roadway—the London Bridge—was often adorned with pikes, on which sat the severed heads of criminals.

The Bubonic Plague (also known as the Black Death) killed millions in Europe, and struck London repeatedly throughout the centuries. It spread in places with poor sanitation and massive crowds, and hit Shakespeare's theater district the hardest. It would take centuries until it was discovered that the carrier of the plague was fleas, hosted by rats.

"Come, gentle night, come, loving, black-brow'd night,
Give me my Romeo; and, when he shall die,
Take him and cut him out in little stars,
And he will make the face of heaven so fine
That all the world will be in love with night
And pay no worship to the garish sun."

--William Shakespeare, *Romeo and Juliet*

CHAPTER ONE

London, England
(September, 1599)

Caleb awoke to the sound of bells.

He sat bolt upright and looked all around, breathing heavily. He had been dreaming of Kyle, chasing him, of Caitlin, holding out a hand for help. They had been in a field filled with bats, against a blood-red sun, and it had seemed so real.

Now, as he looked around the room, he tried to determine whether it was all real, or if he was truly awake and back in time. After several seconds of listening to his own breathing, of feeling the cool dampness in the air, of listening to the quiet, to his own heartbeat, he realized that it was all a dream. He was truly awake.

Caleb realized he was sitting upright inside an open sarcophagus. He looked around the dim, cavernous room and saw that it was filled with sarcophagi. There were low, arched ceilings and narrow slits for windows, through which streamed the smallest amount of sunlight. It was just enough to see by. He squinted at the glare, reached into his pocket, and applied his eyedrops, glad to find them still there. Slowly, the pain receded, and he relaxed.

Caleb jumped up and onto his feet in one motion, spinning around the room, taking stock in all directions. He was still on guard, not wanting to get attacked or ambushed before he'd had a chance to get his bearings. But there was nothing, and no one, in the room. Just silence. He noticed the ancient stone floors, walls, the small altar and cross, and guessed that he was in the lower crypt of a church.

Caitlin.

Caleb spun around the room again, searching for any sign of her. He felt a sense of urgency as he hurried to the sarcophagus nearest him. With all his might, he scraped back the lid.

His heart lifted at the hope of finding her. But he was crestfallen to find it empty.

Caleb hurried through the room, going from one sarcophagus to the next, pushing back each lid. But they were all empty.

Caleb felt a sense of growing desperation as he pushed back the final lid in the room, with so much force that it crashed to the ground and shattered into a million bits. But he already had a sinking feeling he would find it, like the others, to be vacant—and he was right. Caitlin was nowhere in this room, he realized, breaking out into a cold sweat. Where could she be?

The thought of coming back in time without her sent a chill up his spine. He cared more for her than he could say and without her by his side, his life, his mission, felt purposeless.

He suddenly remembered something, and reached into his pocket, checking to see if it was still there. Thankfully, it was. His mother's wedding ring. He held it up to the light, and admired the six-carat sapphire, perfectly cut, mounted on a band of diamonds and rubies. He had never been able to find the right moment to propose to her. This time, he was determined to.

If, of course, she had come back at all.

Caleb heard a noise and spun towards the entrance, sensing motion. He hoped beyond hope that it was Caitlin.

But he was surprised to find himself looking down, as the person turned the corner, and to see that it wasn't a person at all. It was Ruth. Caleb was overjoyed to see her there, to see that she had survived the trip back in time.

She walked towards Caleb, her tail wagging, her eyes lighting with recognition. As she got closer, Caleb knelt down and she ran into his arms. He loved Ruth, and he was surprised at how much she had grown: she seemed to be twice the size, and a formidable animal. He was also encouraged to find her here: maybe it meant that Caitlin was here, too.

Ruth suddenly turned and ran out the room, disappearing around the corner. Caleb was baffled by her behavior, and he hurried off after her, to see where she went.

He found himself entering another vaulted chamber, this one also littered with sarcophagi. He could see at a glance that they were all already opened, and empty.

Ruth kept running, whining, and ran out this room, too. Caleb started to wonder whether Ruth was leading him somewhere. He sped up after her.

After tearing through several more rooms, Ruth finally stopped in a small alcove at the end of the corridor, dimly lit by a single torch. Inside, sat a lone, marble sarcophagus, intricately designed.

Caleb approached it slowly, holding his breath, hoping, sensing, that Caitlin could be inside.

Ruth sat down beside it, and stared up at Caleb. She whined frantically.

Caleb knelt and tried to push back its stone lid. But this one was much heavier than the others, and it hardly budged.

He knelt and pushed harder, using all his might, and finally, it began to budge. He kept pushing, and moments later, the lid came off completely.

Caleb was flooded with relief to find Caitlin lying there, still as could be, her hands neatly folded across her chest. But his relief turned to concern as he studied her, and saw that she was paler than he had ever seen. There was no color in her cheeks whatsoever, and her eyes did not even react to the torchlight. He looked more closely and noticed that she didn't appear to be breathing.

He leaned back in horror. Caitlin appeared to be dead.

Ruth whined louder: now he understood.

Caleb leaned in and placed both hands firmly on her shoulders. He shook her gently.

"Caitlin?" he said, hearing the worry in his own voice. "CAITLIN!?" he called louder, as he shook her with more force.

But she didn't respond, and his entire body went cold as he imagined what his life would be like without her in it. He knew there was a danger to time travel, and that not all vampires survived every trip. But he had never really contemplated the reality of dying on the trip back. Had he made a mistake to keep encouraging her on the search, on the mission? Should he have just let it go, have settled with her in the last time and place?

What if he had lost everything?

Ruth jumped into the sarcophagi, standing with all four paws on Caitlin's chest, and began licking her all over her face. Minutes passed, and Ruth never stopped licking, whining as she did.

Just as Caleb leaned over, ready to pull Ruth off, he stopped. He was shocked as Caitlin began to open an eye.

Ruth howled, ecstatic, as she jumped off of Caitlin and ran in circles. Caleb leaned in, equally ecstatic, as Caitlin finally opened both eyes, and began to look around.

He hurried over and grabbed one of her ice-cold hands, warming it between his.

"Caitlin? Can you hear me? It's me, Caleb."

Slowly, she began to sit up, and he helped her, reaching in, gently placing a hand behind her neck. He was so happy to see her blinking, squinting. He could see how disoriented she was, as if awoken from a deep, deep sleep.

"Caitlin?" he asked again, softly.

She looked at him blankly, her brown eyes as beautiful as he'd remembered. But something, he could tell, was wrong. She was still unsmiling, and as she blinked at him, her eyes held the look of a stranger.

"Caitlin?" he asked again, worried this time.

She stared right at him, her eyes wide open, and he saw, with a sudden shock, that she didn't recognize him.

"Who are you?" she asked.

Caleb's heart fell. Was it possible? Had the trip wiped out her memory? Had she really forgotten him?

"Caitlin," he prodded again, "it's me. Caleb."

He smiled, hoping maybe that would help her remember.

But she didn't smile back. She just stared at him, with a vacant look, blinking several times.

"I'm sorry," she finally said. "But I have no idea who you are."

CHAPTER TWO

Sam woke to the sound of screeching birds. He opened his eyes and saw, high up overhead, several huge vultures circling. There must have been a dozen of them, and they circled lower and lower, seemingly right over him, as if watching him. As if waiting.

He suddenly realized they assumed he was dead, and were waiting for their chance to swoop in and eat him.

Sam jumped to his feet, and as he did, the birds suddenly flew off, as if startled that the dead could rise again.

He looked around, trying to get his bearings. He was in a field, in the midst of rolling hills. As far as he could see, there were more hills, covered in grass and odd bushes. The temperature was perfect, and there was not a cloud in the sky. It was very picturesque, and there was not a single building in sight. It appeared he was in the middle of nowhere.

Sam tried to figure out where he was, what time period, and how he'd arrived. He desperately tried to think back. What had happened before he'd gone back in time?

Slowly, he remembered. He had been in the Notre Dame, in Paris, in 1789. He had been fighting off Kyle, Kendra, Sergei and their people, keeping them at bay so that Caitlin and Caleb could escape. It had been the least he could do, and he owed her that much, especially after endangering her with his reckless romance with Kendra.

Vastly outnumbered, he had used his shape-shifting power, and had managed to confuse them just enough to wreak considerable damage, wiping out many of Kyle's men, incapacitating the others, and managing to escape with Polly.

Polly.

She had been by his side the whole time, had fought valiantly, and the two of them, he remembered, had been quite a force together. They had escaped through the ceiling of the Notre Dame, and had gone searching for Caitlin and Caleb in the night. Yes. It was all starting to come back....

Sam had found out that his sister had gone back in time, and he knew, on the spot, that he had to go back, too, to make wrongs right, to find Caitlin again, to apologize, and to protect her. He knew she didn't need it: she was a better warrior than he was now, and she had Caleb.

But she was his sister, after all, and the impulse to protect her was something he could not turn off.

Polly had insisted on coming back with him. She, too, was intent on seeing Caitlin again, and on explaining herself to her. Sam hadn't objected, and they had gone back together.

Sam looked around again now, staring out at the fields, wondering.

"Polly?" he called out, tentatively.

No response.

He walked towards the edge of a hill, hoping to get a view of the landscape.

"Polly!?" he called out again, louder this time.

"Finally!" came a voice.

As Sam looked out, Polly appeared, walking up over the horizon, rounding a hill. She carried an armful of strawberries and was eating one, her mouth full as she spoke. "I've been waiting for you all morning! Gosh! You really love to sleep, don't you!?"

Sam was delighted to see her. Seeing her, he realized how alone he had felt coming back, and how happy he was to have some companionship. He also realized, despite himself, how much she had grown on him. Especially after his fiasco with Kendra, he appreciated being around a normal girl, appreciated Polly more than she knew. And as she got closer, and as the sun lit up her light brown hair and blue eyes, her translucent white skin, he was surprised, once again, by her natural beauty.

He was about to respond, but as usual, she didn't let him get a word in.

"I woke up not ten feet from you," she continued, as she approached, eating another strawberry, "and I shook you and shook you, but you wouldn't wake! So I went off and did some gathering. I'm anxious to leave this place, but I figured I'd not leave you to the birds before I went. We have to find Caitlin. Who knows where she is? She could need our help right now. And all you do is sleep! After all, what did we come back for if we're not going to get up and go and—"

"Please!" Sam called out, breaking into a laugh. "I can't get a word in!"

Polly stopped and stared at him, looking surprised, as if she had no idea she were speaking so much.

"Well then," she said, "speak!"

Sam stared back at her, distracted by how blue her eyes looked in the early morning light; finally having a chance to speak, he froze up, forgetting what he was about to say.

"Uh…" he began.

Polly threw up her hands.

"Boys!" she exclaimed. "They never want you to talk—but they never have anything to say themselves! Well, I can't wait around here anymore!" she said, and hurried off, strutting through the fields, eating another strawberry.

"Wait!" Sam called out, hurrying to catch up with her. "Where are you going?"

"Why, to find Caitlin, of course!"

"You know where she is?" he asked.

"No," she said. "But I know where she *isn't*—and that's in this field! We need to get out of here. Find the closest city, or buildings, or whatever, and figure out what time we're in. We have to start somewhere! And this is not the place!"

"Well, don't you think I want to find my sister, too!?" Sam called out, exasperated.

Finally, she stopped and turned, facing him.

"I mean, don't you want company?" Sam asked, realizing as he said it, how much he wanted to look for Caitlin with her. "Don't you want to search together?"

Polly looked back at him with her large blue eyes, as if summing him up. He felt as if he were being scrutinized, and he could see she looked unsure. He couldn't understand why.

"I don't know," she finally said. "I mean, you handled yourself pretty well back there in Paris—I do have to admit. But..."

She paused.

20

"What is it?" he finally asked.

Polly cleared her throat.

"Well, if you must know, the last—um—boy—I spent any time with—Sergei—turned out to be a liar and a con-man, who tricked and used me. I was too stupid to see it. But I'm never going to fall for anything like that again. And I'm not ready to trust anybody of the male race—not even you. I just don't want to spend any time with any more boys right now. Not that you and I—not that I'm saying that we're—not that I think of you that way—as anything more than a friend—than an acquaintance—"

Polly began stammering, and he could see how nervous she had become, and couldn't help smiling inwardly.

"—but it's just that, regardless, I'm sick of boys. No offense."

Sam smiled broadly. He loved her candor, and her spunkiness.

"None taken," he answered. "The truth be told," he added, "I'm sick of girls."

Polly's eyes opened wide in surprise; that clearly wasn't the response she'd been expecting.

"But it occurs to me that we have a better chance of finding my sister if we search together. I mean—just—" Sam cleared his throat, "—just professionally speaking."

Now it was Polly's turn to smile.

"Professionally speaking," she repeated.

Sam reached out his hand, formally.

"I promise, we'll just be friends—nothing more," he said. "I've sworn off of girls forever. No matter what."

"And I've sworn off of guys forever. No matter what," Polly said, still examining his hand, as it dangled in the air, unsure.

Sam left his hand out patiently, waiting.

"Just friends?" she asked. "Nothing more?"

"Just friends," Sam said.

She finally reached out and shook on it.

And as she did, Sam couldn't help noticing that she held his hand just the slightest bit too long.

CHAPTER THREE

Caitlin sat up in the sarcophagus, and stared back at the man before her. She knew she recognized him from somewhere, but could not place where. She stared at his large, brown, concerned eyes, his perfectly chiseled face, his cheekbones, his smooth skin, his thick, wavy hair. He was gorgeous, and she could sense how much he cared for her. She felt deep down that this was an important person to her, but for the life of her, she could not remember who it was.

Caitlin felt something wet in her palm, and looked down to see a wolf sitting there, licking her. She was surprised at how caring it was towards her, as if it had known her forever. It had beautiful white fur, with a single grey streak running down the middle of its head and back. Caitlin felt she knew this animal, too, and that at some point in her life she'd had a close connection to it.

But try as she did, she could not remember how.

She looked around the room, trying to take in her surroundings, hoping it might jog her memory. The room slowly came into focus. It was dim, lit only by a torch, and in the distance, she saw adjoining rooms, filled with sarcophagi. It had a low, vaulted ceiling, and the stones looked ancient. It looked like a crypt. She wondered how she had gotten here—and who these people were. She felt as if she had been awakened from a dream that would not end.

Caitlin closed her eyes for a moment, breathing deeply, and as she did, a collection of random images suddenly flashed through her mind. She saw herself standing in the Roman Colosseum, fighting off multiple soldiers on its hot, dusty floor; she saw herself flying over an island in the Hudson River, looking down at a sprawling castle; she saw herself in Venice, on a gondola, with a boy she did not recognize, but who was also beautiful; she saw herself in Paris, walking along a river with a man who she recognized as the same man across from her. She tried to focus on that image, to hold onto it. Perhaps it would help her remember.

She saw the two of them again, this time in his castle, in the countryside of France. She saw them riding horses on the beach, then saw a falcon, circling high above them, dropping off a letter.

She tried to zoom in on his face, to remember his name. It seemed to be coming back to her; it was so close. But her mind kept flashing something new, and it was so hard to hold onto anything. Lifetime after lifetime flashed before her in an endless snapshot of images. It was as if her memory were repopulating itself.

"Caleb," came a voice.

Caitlin opened her eyes. He was leaning in close, reaching out a hand, holding her shoulder.

"My name is Caleb. Of the White Coven. Don't you remember?"

Caitlin's eyes closed again, as her mind was jogged by his words, his voice. *Caleb*. The name rang like a bell in her brain. It felt like an important name to her.

White Coven. That, too, rang a bell. She suddenly saw herself in a city she knew to be New York City, in a cloister at the northern end of the island. She saw herself standing on a large terrace, looking out. She saw herself arguing with a woman named Sera.

"Caitlin," came the voice again, more firmly. "Don't you remember?"

Caitlin. Yes. That was her name. She felt certain of it now.

And Caleb. Yes. He was important to her. He was her…boyfriend? He felt like more than that. Fiancé? Husband?

She opened her eyes, and stared at him, and it was all starting to flood back. Hope filled within her, as slowly, bit by bit, she was starting to remember everything.

"Caleb," she said back, softly.

His eyes suddenly filled with hope, watering. The wolf whined beside her licked her cheek, as if encouraged. She looked over at her, and suddenly remembered her name.

"Rose," she said, then realized that wasn't right. "No. Ruth. Your name is Ruth."

Ruth leaned in closer, licking her face. Caitlin couldn't help but smile, and stroked her head. Caleb broke into a relieved grin.

"Yes. Ruth. And I am Caleb. And you are Caitlin. Do you remember now?"

She nodded. "It's coming back to me," she said. "You are my…husband?"

She watched as his face suddenly turned red, as if he were embarrassed, or shamed. And at that moment, she suddenly remembered. No. They were not married.

"We are not married," he said, apologetic, "but we are together."

She was embarrassed, too, as now she started to remember everything, as it all started flooding back to her.

She suddenly remembered the keys. Her father's keys. She reached down, into her pocket, and was reassured to feel them there. She reached into another pocket and felt her journal, still there. She was relieved.

Caleb reached out a hand.

She took it, and let him pull her up and out of the sarcophagus.

It felt so good to be standing, to stretch her aching muscles.

Caleb reached out and brushed the hair back out of her face. His soft fingers felt so good as they brushed her temple.

"I'm so glad you're alive," he said.

He embraced her, hugging her tight. She hugged him back, and as she did, more memories flooded through her. Yes, this was the man she loved. The man she hoped, one day, to marry. She could feel his love coursing through her, and she remembered that they had gone back in time together. They had last been in France, in Paris, and she had found the second key, and they had both been sent back. She had prayed that they would come back together this time. And as she held him tighter, she realized that her prayers had come true.

Finally, this time, they were together.

CHAPTER FOUR

"I see you two have found each other," came a voice.

Caitlin and Caleb, in the midst of their embrace, both spun at the voice, startled. Caitlin was shocked that anyone could have snuck up on them so quickly, especially given their alert vampire senses.

But as she stared back at the woman standing before them, she realized why: this woman too, was a vampire. Dressed in all white, wearing a hood, the woman lifted her chin and stared back with piercing blue eyes. Caitlin could detect a sense of peace and harmony coming off of her, and she let down her guard. She felt Caleb let down his guard, too.

The woman broke into a wide smile.

"We've been waiting for you for quite some time," she said, in a gentle voice.

"Where are we?" Caitlin asked. "What year is it?"

The woman only smiled back.

"Come this way," she said, turning her back, and heading back out through the low, arched doorway.

Caitlin and Caleb exchanged a look, then followed her out the doorway, Ruth at their side.

They walked down a stone corridor, twisting and turning, and it led to a set of narrow stairs, lit only by a torch. They were close behind the woman, who simply kept walking, as if assuming they would follow.

Caitlin felt a desire to ask more questions, to press her on where they were; but as they reached the top of the staircase, the room suddenly opened up into a magnificent sight, taking her breath away, and she realized they were inside an enormous church. At least that part of the question was answered.

Caitlin once again regretted not having listened more carefully in her history and architecture classes, regretted not being able to tell at first sight exactly what church this was. She thought back to all the magnificent churches she'd visited—the Notre Dame in Paris, the Duomo in Florence—and couldn't help thinking that this reminded her somewhat of them.

The nave of the church stretched for hundreds of feet, had a tiled, marble floor, and had walls adorned with dozens of carved, stone statues. It had soaring, vaulted ceilings, climbing hundreds of feet high. High up were rows and rows of arched stained-glass, flooding the church with a soft, multicolor light. At its far end was a huge, circular piece of stained glass, filtering light into an enormous, gilded altar. Spread out before that were hundreds of small, wooden chairs for worshipers.

But now, the church was empty. It seemed as if they had the entire place to themselves.

They walked across the room, following the vampire, and their footsteps echoed, reverberating in the huge, empty hall.

"What church is this?" Caitlin finally asked.

"Westminster Abbey," came the woman's voice, as she continued walking. "The coronation seat of Kings and Queens for thousands of years."

Westminster Abbey, Caitlin thought. She knew that was in England. London, in fact.

London.

The idea of being here hit her like a wave of bricks. It was overwhelming, awe-inspiring. She had never been here before, and had always wanted to go. She had had friends who had gone, and had seen pictures online. It made sense to her that they were here, given this city's long medieval history. This church alone was thousands of years old—and she knew that this city had a lot more like it. But she still didn't know the year.

"And what year is it?" Caitlin asked, nervous.

But their guide walked so quickly, she had already crossed the huge chapel and ducked through another arched door, forcing Caitlin and Caleb to hurry to keep up.

As they entered, Caitlin was surprised to find herself in a cloister. There was a long, stone corridor, with stone walls and statues on one side and on the other, open arches. These arches were open to the elements, and through them, she could see a small, peaceful courtyard. It reminded her of so many other cloisters she had been to; she was starting to see the pattern of their simplicity, their emptiness, the arched walls, the columns, the well-cared for courtyards. They all felt like a shelter from the world, like a place for prayer and silent contemplation.

The vampire finally stopped and faced them. She stared back at Caitlin with her large, compassionate eyes, and looked otherworldly.

"We are at the turn-of-the-century," she said.

Caitlin thought for a moment. "What century?" she asked.

"The sixteenth, of course. It is 1599."

1599, Caitlin thought. The idea was overwhelming. Once again, she wished she'd read her history more closely. Previously, she

31

had gone from 1791 to 1789. But now she was in 1599. Nearly a 200 year leap.

She recalled how many things had seemed primitive even in 1789—the lack of plumbing, the occasional dirt road, the people rarely bathing. She couldn't even comprehend how much more primitive things could be two hundred years further back. Surely, it would be far less recognizable than any other time. Even London would probably be barely recognizable. It made her feel isolated, alone, in a distant world and place. If it weren't for Caleb's being there, by her side, she would have felt completely alone.

But at the same time, this architecture, this church, these cloisters—it all felt so recognizable, so familiar. After all, she was walking in the same exact Westminster Abbey that existed in the 21st century. Not only that, this building, even as it was now, was already ancient, had already been around for centuries. At least that gave her a touch of comfort.

But why had she been sent back to this time? And this place? Clearly, it had some great significance for her mission.

London. 1599.

Was this the time that Shakespeare had lived? she wondered, her heart suddenly beating faster, as she imagined, just maybe, having the chance to actually get a glimpse of him, in the flesh.

They walked silently down corridor after corridor.

"London in 1599 is not as primitive as you think," their guide said, glancing at her with a smile.

Caitlin felt embarrassed that her thoughts had been read. As always, she knew she should have been more vigilant in guarding them. She hoped that she had not offended this vampire.

"No offense at all," she replied, reading her thoughts again. "Our time is primitive in many technological ways that you are accustomed to. But we are, in other ways, more sophisticated than even your modern time. We are extremely knowledgeable, and scholarly, and books rule the day. A people of primitive means, maybe, but with a very sharp intellect.

"More importantly, this is a crucial time for the vampire race. We stand at a crossroads here. You have arrived at the turn of the century for a reason."

"Why?" Caleb asked.

The woman smiled at them before entering yet another door.

"The answer to that is one that you will have to find out for yourself."

They entered another magnificent room, with soaring ceilings, stained glass, marble floors, adorned with enormous candles, and carved statues of kings and saints. But this room was different than the others. It had sarcophagi and effigies placed carefully throughout, and at the center sat an enormous tomb, dozens of feet high, and covered in gold.

Their guide walked right up to it, as they followed. She stopped before it, and turned to them.

Caitlin looked up at the magnificent tomb: it was large, imposing. It was itself a magnificent work of art, plated in gold, adorned with intricate carvings. She also felt an energy coming off of it, as if it held some importance.

"The tomb of Saint Edward the Confessor," the vampire said. "It is a holy place, a place of pilgrimage for our kind for hundreds of years. It is said that if one prays by its side, one will receive miraculous healings for those who are sick. See the stone, by your feet: it has been worn from all the people kneeling here over time."

Caitlin looked down, and saw that, indeed, the marble platform had slight impressions around its edges. She marveled at how many people must have knelt here throughout the centuries.

"But in your case," she continued, "it holds even more significance."

She turned and looked directly at Caitlin.

"Your key," she said to Caitlin.

Caitlin was baffled. Which key was she referring to? She reached into her pockets, and felt again the two keys that she had found thus far. She wasn't sure which one the woman wanted.

She shook her head. "No. Your other key."

Caitlin thought, puzzled. Had she forgotten some other key?

Then, as she glanced at the base of her throat, she realized. Her necklace.

Caitlin reached down, and was amazed to realize it was still there. She gingerly removed it, and held the delicate, antique silver cross in her palm.

The vampire shook her head.

"Only you can use it."

She reached out and gently took Caitlin's wrist, and guided it towards the smallest of keyholes, at the base of the pedestal.

Caitlin was amazed. She never would have even noticed that keyhole otherwise. She inserted the key, turned it, and there was a gentle click.

She looked up, and saw that a tiny compartment had open in the side of the tomb. She looked at the vampire, and she nodded solemnly back.

Caitlin reached up and slowly pulled out a long, narrow compartment. Inside, she was shocked to discover, was a long, golden scepter, its head adorned with rubies and emeralds.

She reached in and extracted it, and was amazed at how heavy it felt, at how smooth the gold was in her hands. It must have been three feet long, and made of solid gold.

"The holy scepter," the nun said. "It was your father's, once."

Caitlin looked at it with a new sense of awe and respect. She felt electrified holding it, and felt closer to her father than ever.

"Will this lead me to my father?" she asked.

Their guide simply turned and headed out the chamber. "This way," she said.

Caitlin and Caleb followed her through another door, and down several more corridors, passing the medieval courtyard of another cloister. As they walked, Caitlin was surprised to see several other vampires, dressed in white robes and hoods, walking through the halls. Most looked down, as if lost in prayer. Some swung incense decanters. A few who passed nodded their way, and continued on in silence.

Caitlin wondered how many vampires lived here, and if they belonged to her father's coven. She had never realized that Westminster Abbey was a cloister, in addition to a church. Or that it was a resting place for her kind.

They finally entered another room, this one smaller than the others, but with high, vaulted ceilings, and natural light pouring in. This room had stark, stone floors, and in its center sat one remarkable piece of furniture: a throne. Mounted high up on a pedestal, at least fifteen feet high, sat the wooden throne, a chair which was extra wide, with arms that sloped upward, and a back that angled on a triangle, coming to a point in the middle. Beneath it, on its corners, sat two golden lions, designed to look as if they were holding up the chair.

Caitlin examined it in awe.

"King Edward's chair," said the vampire. "The coronation throne for kings and queens for thousands of years. A very special piece of furniture—not only for its place in history, but because it holds one of the keys for our kind."

She turned and looked at Caitlin. "We have been guarding this throne for thousands of years. Now that you are here, and now that you have unlocked the scepter, it is time for you to take your rightful place."

She gestured for Caitlin to ascend the throne.

Caitlin looked back at her, shocked. What right did she, a simple girl, have to ascend such a regal throne—a throne that had been sat on by kings and queens for thousands of years? She didn't feel right going anywhere near it, much less ascending its huge pedestal and sitting on it.

"Please," prodded the vampire. "You are entitled. You are The One."

Caleb nodded at her, and Caitlin slowly, reluctantly, climbed up on the huge pedestal, carrying the scepter. When she reached the top, she turned and delicately eased herself into the throne.

It was made of hard wood, and didn't give. As she leaned back on it, she rested her hands on his arms, and could feel its power. She could feel the thousands of years of royalty, who had received their crowns in this very spot. It felt electrically charged.

As she looked out the room, fifteen feet higher than everyone else, she felt as if she towered over it, over the world. It was an awe-inspiring feeling.

"The scepter," said the vampire.

Caitlin looked down at her, puzzled, unsure what she wanted her to do with it.

"In the arm of the throne, you will find a small hole. It is meant to hold it."

Caitlin looked down, closely, and this time saw a small hole, just wide enough to fit its exact diameter. She reached up and slowly inserted the scepter into the hole.

It sank all the way down until only its head sat above the arm.

Suddenly, there was a soft click.

Caitlin looked down and was amazed to see a tiny compartment open at the base of one of the lions' heads. Inside, sat a small, gold ring. She reached down and took it out.

She held it up, staring.

"The ring of destiny," said the vampire. "It is meant only for you. A gift from your father."

Caitlin stared in awe, holding it up to the light, watching the jewels sparkle as she moved it.

"Place it on the ring finger of your right hand."

Caitlin slid it on, and as she felt the cool metal, a vibration went right through her. She could feel the power coming off of it.

"It will lead the way."

Caitlin examined it. "But how?" she asked.

"You need only inspect it," the vampire said.

Caitlin was at first puzzled, but then examined the ring more closely. As she did, she noticed a fine, delicate engraving all around the band. Her heart beat faster as she began to read it. She felt immediately that it was a message from her father.

Across the Bridge, Beyond the Bear,
With the Winds or the sun, we bypass London.

Caitlin read the riddle again, then read it aloud, so that Caleb could hear it.

"What does it mean?" she asked.

Their guide only smiled back.

"This is as far as I'm allowed to take you. The rest of the journey is yours to discover." Then she leaned in close. "We are counting on you. Whatever you do, don't let us down."

CHAPTER FIVE

Caitlin and Caleb walked out the enormous arched doors of Westminster Abbey, into the morning light, Ruth at their heels. They both instinctively squinted and raised their hands to the light, and Caitlin was grateful that Caleb had given her the eyedrops before they'd exited. It took her a few moments for her eyes to adjust. Slowly, the world of 1599 London came into focus.

Caitlin was amazed. Paris in 1789 had not been all that different from Venice in 1791. But London in 1599 was a world apart. She was shocked at the difference 190 made.

Before her, London was spread out. But it was not a bustling, metropolitan city. Rather, it felt more like a large, rural town, with large, empty lots, still in development. There were no paved roads—everywhere was dirt—and while there were many buildings, there were far more trees. Nestled amidst the trees were crudely laid out blocks and rows of houses, many of them uneven. The houses were all built of wood, with huge, thatched, straw roofs. She could see at a glance how combustible this city was, with most everything built of wood, and with all that straw sitting atop houses, and realized how susceptible it was to fire.

She could see right away that the dirt roads made passageway tricky. Traveling by horse seemed to be the preferable way, and the occasional horse, or horse and carriage, went by. But that was the exception. Most people walked—or rather, stumbled. The people who walked down the muddy streets all seemed to struggle to get their footing.

She spotted excrement lining the streets, and was struck by the stench, even from here. The occasional cattle walking by didn't help. If she had ever considered going back in time to be romantic, this sight certainly gave her pause.

What's more, in this city she didn't see people strolling in their finery, carrying parasols, showing off the latest fashions, as they had in Paris and Venice. Rather, they were all dressed more simply, with much more outdated clothing, men wearing either simple farming clothing, much like rags, and only a few wearing white britches up to their thighs, with short tunics that looked like skirts. The women, for their part, were still covered in so much material, they struggled to navigate the streets as they grabbed the hems of their skirts and held them as high as they could—not just to keep them away from the mud and excrement, but also from the rats, which Caitlin was shocked to see scurrying out in the open.

Still, despite everything, this time was clearly unique—and, at least, relaxed. She felt as if she were in a large country village. There was no fast-paced bustle of the 21st century. There were no cars racing by; there was no sound of construction. No horns, buses, trucks, machinery. Even the sound of the horses were muted, their feet sinking into the dirt. Indeed the only sounds that could be heard, aside from the vendors calling out, were the sounds of church bells, ringing ever presently, like a chorus of bombs, throughout the city. This was clearly a city dominated by churches.

The only thing hinting at the built-up future to come were, paradoxically, the ancient churches—rising high over the rest of the humble architecture and dominating the skyline, their steeples rising impossibly high. Indeed, the building they were exiting from, Westminster Abbey, towered over all the buildings in sight. She could already tell that its steeple, was a beacon for the entire city to get its bearings by.

She looked at Caleb, and saw him surveying the scene, equally amazed. She reached out and was happy to feel him place his hand in hers. It felt so good to feel his touch again.

He turned and looked at her, and she could see the love in his eyes.

"Well," he said, clearing his throat, "it's not exactly the Paris of the 18th century."

She smiled back. "No, it's not."

"But we're together, and that's all that matters," he added.

She could feel his love, as he looked deeply into her eyes, and for a moment, was distracted from their mission.

"I'm so sorry for what happened in France," he said. "With Sera. I never meant to hurt you. I hope you know that."

She looked at him, and could tell that he meant it. And to her surprise, she felt that she could now easily forgive him. The old Caitlin would have held a grudge. But she felt stronger than she ever had, and truly capable of letting it go. Especially since he had come back for her, and especially since it was clear he had no feelings for Sera.

Even more, she now, for the first time, realized her own mistakes in the past, her rushing to judgment too quickly, her not trusting him, her not giving him enough space.

"I'm sorry, too," she said. "This is a new life now. And we're here together. That's all that matters."

He squeezed her hand, and as he did, she felt a thrill running through her.

He leaned in and kissed her. She was surprised, and thrilled at the same time. She felt the electricity running through her, and kissed him back.

Ruth started whining at their feet.

They both broke away, looked down and laughed.

"She's hungry," Caleb said.

"So am I."

"Shall we see London?" he asked with a grin. "We could fly," he added, "that is, if you're ready."

She arched her shoulders back, and felt her wings there, and felt that she was, indeed, ready. She felt restored from this trip back. Maybe she was, finally, getting used to time travel.

"I am," she said, "but I'd like to walk. I'd like to experience this place, for the first time, like everybody else."

And it's also more romantic, she thought to herself, but didn't say.

But he looked down and smiled at her, and she wondered if he'd read her thoughts.

He reached out his hand with a smile, she took it, and the two of them set off down the stairs.

*

As they walked out of the church, Caitlin spotted a river in the distance, and a wide road about fifty yards off of it, with a crudely carved wooden sign that read "King Street." They had a choice to turn left or right. The city seemed more condensed to the left.

They turned left, heading north, up King Street, parallel to the river. As they went, Caitlin was amazed by the sights and sounds, taking it all in. To their right were a series of grand, wooden houses, great estates, built in the Tudor manor, with a white stucco exterior, brown framing, and culminating in a thatched roof. To their left, she was amazed to see, were rural parcels of farmland, with the occasional small, humble house, and sheep and cows dotting the landscape. London of 1599 was fascinating to her. One side of the street was cosmopolitan and wealthy, while the other was still populated by farmers.

The street itself was also a thing of wonder. Their feet nearly stuck in the mud as they walked, the dirt made even softer by all the foot and horse traffic. This in itself was bearable, but interlaced all throughout the dirt was excrement, from the packs of wild dogs, or, thrown out the windows, from humans. Indeed, as they went, shutters opened sporadically, and pails appeared, with old women throwing out waste from households. It smelled far worse than Venice or

Florence or Paris. She almost gagged at times, and wished she had one of those small perfume pouches to bring to her nose. Luckily, at least, she still wore the practical sparring shoes that Aiden had given her back in Versailles. She couldn't imagine ever walking down this street in heels.

Yet, intermixed with this strange mix of farmland and grand estates, was also the occasional feat of architecture. Caitlin was amazed to see, here and there, some buildings she actually recognized from pictures from the 21st century, ornate churches, and an occasional palace.

The road came to an abrupt halt in a large, arched gateway, several guards standing before it in uniform, standing at attention, holding lances. The gate was open, though, and they walked through.

A sign etched into stone read "Whitehall Palace," and they continued through its long, narrow courtyard, then through another arched gate and out the other side, and back onto the main road. They soon approached a circular intersection with a sign that read "Charing Cross," and a large vertical monument in its center. The road forked to the left and to the right.

"Which way?" she asked.

Caleb seemed as overwhelmed as she did. Finally, he said, "My instincts tell me to stay close to the river, and fork to the right."

She closed her eyes, and tried to feel it, too. "I agree," she said, then added, "Do you have any idea exactly what it is we are looking for?"

He shook his head. "Your guess is as good as mine."

She looked down at her ring, and read the riddle aloud once again.

Across the Bridge, Beyond the Bear,
With the Winds or the sun, we bypass London.

It didn't ring any bells for her, and it didn't appear to ring any for Caleb either.

"Well, it mentions London," she said, "so I feel like we're on the right track. My instinct tells me that we have to proceed further, deeper into the city, and that we'll know it when we see it."

He agreed, and she took his hand, and they forked right, heading parallel to the river, following a sign that read "The Strande."

As they continued along this new street, she noticed that the area was getting more and more dense, with more houses built close to each other, on both sides of the street. It felt like they were getting closer to the center of town. The streets were becoming more crowded, too. The weather was perfect—it felt like an early fall day to her, and the sun shone steadily. She briefly wondered what month it was. It amazed her how she had lost track of time.

At least it wasn't too hot. But as the streets became more and more filled with people, she was beginning to feel claustrophobic. They were definitely approaching the center of a huge, metropolitan city, even if it didn't have the modern-day sophistication. She was surprised: she had always imagined the old times to have less people, to be less crowded. But if anything, the opposite was true: as the streets became more and more packed, she couldn't believe how crowded it was. It reminded her of being back in New York City in the 21st century. People elbowed and jostled and didn't even look back to apologize. They also stank.

Adding to the scene, on every corner were street peddlers, aggressively trying to sell their wares. In every direction, people shouted out, in funny British accents.

And when the voices of the peddlers died down, other voices dominated the air: those of preachers. Everywhere, Caitlin saw makeshift platforms, stages, soapboxes, pulpits, on which preachers stood and preached their sermons to the masses, shouting to be heard.

"Jesus says REPENT!" yelled one minister, standing there with a funny top hat and a stern gaze, looking down at the crowd in a sweeping gaze. "I say that ALL THEATRES must be shut down! All idle time must be FORBIDDEN! Return to your houses of worship!"

It reminded Caitlin of the people who preached from street corners in New York City. In some ways, nothing had changed.

They came to another gateway, right in the middle of the street, with a sign that read "Temple Barre, City Gate." Caitlin was amazed that cities actually had gates. The large, imposing gate was open, for people to pass right through, and Caitlin wondered if they closed it at night. On either side stood more guards.

But this gate was different: it seemed to also be a gathering place. A large crowd huddled around it, and way up high, atop a small platform, a guard stood holding a whip. Caitlin looked up and was amazed to see that a man, chained and barely clothed, was tied to a whipping post. The guard reached back and lashed him again and again, and the entire crowd oohed and aahed at the sight.

Caitlin surveyed the faces of the crowd, and couldn't believe how indifferent they seemed, as if this were an ordinary, everyday occurrence, as if it were a popular form of entertainment. She felt anger well up inside her at the barbarism of this society, and she nudged Caleb. He was also riveted to the scene, and she took his hand and hurried through the gate with him, forcing herself not to look. She feared that if she dwelled on it too much, she would be unable to stop herself from attacking the guards.

"This place is barbaric," she said, as they gained distance from the grizzly sight and the sounds of the whip grew fainter.

"Terrible," he agreed.

As they continued onward, she tried to put the image out of her head. She forced herself to focus her attention elsewhere. She looked up at a street sign, and saw that the name of the street they were walking on had changed, to "Fleet Street." As they walked, the streets became even more crowded, more condensed, and the buildings and numerous rows of wooden houses were built even closer to each other. This street was also lined with various stores. One sign read: "Shave for a Penny." Before another shop dangled a blacksmith's sign, with a horseshoe hanging in front of it. Another sign read, in large letters, "Horse Saddles."

"Need a new horseshoe, Miss?" a local shopkeeper asked Caitlin as they walked by.

She was caught off guard. "Um…no thanks," she said.

"How about you, Sir?" persisted the man. "Want a shave? I've got the cleanest blades on Fleet Street."

Caleb smiled back at the man. "Thank you, but I'm okay."

Caitlin looked at Caleb, and realized how clean-shaven he looked, all the time. His face was so smooth, it looked like porcelain.

As they continued down Fleet Street, Caitlin couldn't help noticing how the crowd had changed. It became more seedy here, with several people openly drinking from flasks and glass bottles, stumbling about, laughing too loudly, and openly leering at women.

"GIN HERE! GIN HERE!" yelled out a boy, hardly older than ten, holding a crate filled with small green bottles of gin. "GET YOUR BOTTLE! TWO FARTHINGS! GET YOUR BOTTLE!"

Caitlin got jostled again, as the crowd grew increasingly thick. She looked over and saw a group of women, with too much makeup, dressed in heavy clothing with tons of fabric, and with their shirts pulled down low, revealing most of their breasts.

"Want a good time?" one of the women yelled out, clearly drunk, wobbling on her feet. She approached a passerby, who roughly pushed her off.

Caitlin was amazed at how rough this part of town was. She felt Caleb instinctively come closer, putting his hand around her waist, and she could feel his protectiveness. They picked up their pace and continued quickly through the crowd, and Caitlin looked down and checked that Ruth was still by their side.

The street soon ended in a small foot bridge, and as they walked over, Caitlin looked down. She saw a large sign that read "Fleet Ditch," and was amazed at the sight. Below them was what looked like a small canal, maybe ten feet wide, completely flowing with murky water. Amidst this water bobbed all sorts of garbage and refuse. As she looked up, she saw people urinating into it, and saw others throwing pots of excrement, chicken bones, household refuse, and all sorts of debris. It looked like an immense, flowing sewer, carrying all the waste of the city downstream.

She looked to see where it lead, and saw that, far off in the distance, it led into the river. She turned her head away at the smell. It was probably the worst thing she had ever smelled in her life. Toxic gases rose up, and made the awful smell of the streets seem like roses in comparison.

They hurried over the bridge.

As they crossed to the other side of Fleet Street, Caitlin was relieved to see that the street finally opened up, and became a little less condensed. The smell, too, faded. And after the horrific smell of Fleet Ditch, the everyday street smells no longer bothered her. She realized that

that was how people lived happily with these conditions: it was all about what you got used to, in context of the time you lived.

As they walked, the neighborhood became nicer. They passed a huge church on the left, and etched into the stone edifice, in neat calligraphy, were the words: "Saint Paul's." It was a massive church, with a beautiful ornate façade, reaching high into the sky, towering over all the buildings around it. Caitlin marveled at how beautiful its architecture was, that such a building could still fit in perfectly in the 21st century. It felt so out of place, towering above all the small wooden architecture around it. Caitlin was beginning to see just how much churches dominated the urban landscape of this time, and just how important they were to its people. They were literally omnipresent. And their bells, so loud, were always ringing.

Caitlin paused before it, studying its ancient architecture, and couldn't help but wonder if perhaps some clue lay for them inside.

"I wonder if we should go in?" Caleb asked, reading her mind.

She studied her ring's inscription once again.

Across the bridge, Beyond the Bear.

"It mentions a bridge," she said, thinking.

"We just crossed a bridge," Caleb answered.

Caitlin shook her head. It didn't feel right to her.

"That was just a foot bridge. My instinct tells me this is not the place. Wherever it is we need to go, I don't feel it is here."

Caleb stood there and closed his eyes. Finally, he opened them. "I don't feel anything either. Let's move on."

"Let's get closer to the river," Caitlin said. "If there's a bridge to be found, I assume it would be by the river. And I wouldn't mind some fresh air."

She spotted a side road leading down to the riverfront, with a crudely marked sign that read "St. Andrews Hill." She took Caleb's hand and led him towards it.

They walked down the gently sloping road, and she could see the river in the distance, bustling with boat traffic.

This must be London's famous Thames River, she thought. It had to be. She remembered at least that much from her basic geography class.

This street ended in a building, not taking them all the way down to the river, so they turned left on a street that ran close to the river, parallel to it, only fifty feet away, aptly named "Thames Street."

Thames Street was even more genteel, a world apart from Fleet Street. The houses were nicer here, and to their right, along the riverside, sat more grand estates, with huge plots of land sloping down to the riverfront. The architecture was more elaborate and more beautiful here, too. Clearly this part of town was reserved for the rich.

It felt like a quaint neighborhood, as they passed many twisting and turning side streets with funny names, like "Windgoose Lane" and "Old Swan Lane" and "Garlick Hill" and "Bread Street Hill." In fact, the smell of food was in the air everywhere, and Caitlin felt her stomach growl. Ruth whined, too, and she knew she was hungry. But she didn't see any food for sale.

"I know, Ruth," Caitlin sympathized. "I'll find us food soon, I promise."

They walked and walked. Caitlin didn't know exactly what she was looking for, and neither did Caleb. It still felt as if the riddle could lead them anywhere, and they didn't have any concrete leads. They were getting deeper into the heart of the city, and she still wasn't sure which way to turn.

Just as Caitlin was beginning to feel tired, hungry, and cranky, they came to a huge intersection. She stopped and looked up. A crude, wooden sign read "Grace Church Street." The smell of fish was heavy in the air here.

She stopped in exasperation and faced Caleb.

"We don't even know what we're looking for," she said. "It mentions a bridge. But I haven't seen a single bridge anywhere. Are we just wasting our time here? Should we be thinking about this a different way?"

Caleb suddenly tapped her on her shoulder, and pointed.

She slowly turned, and was shocked at the sight.

Grace Church Street lead down to a massive bridge, one of the biggest bridges she had ever seen. Her heart soared with new hope. A huge sign above it read "London Bridge," and her heart beat faster. This street was wider, a major artery, and people, horses, carts and traffic of all kind funneled onto and off the bridge.

If a bridge was truly what they were looking for, clearly they had found it.

*

Caleb took her hand and led her towards the bridge, merging with the traffic. She looked up, and was overwhelmed at the sight. It was unlike any bridge she had ever seen. Its entrance was heralded by a huge, arched gate, with guards on either side. At its top were multiple spikes, on which sat severed heads, blood dripping from their throats, impaled on the spikes. It was a gruesome sight, and Caitlin averted her gaze.

"I remember this," sighed Caleb. "From centuries ago. This is how they always adorned their bridges: with heads of prisoners. They do it as a warning to other criminals."

"It's horrific," said Caitlin, as she lowered her head, and they walked quickly onto the bridge.

At the base of the bridge, booths and vendors were selling fish, and as Caitlin looked over, she could see boats pulling up, and workers carrying the fish up the muddy banks, slipping as they went. The entryway to the bridge stank of fish, so much so that she had to hold her nose. Fish of every type, some still moving, were laid out on small, makeshift tables.

"Snapper, three pence a pound!" someone yelled out.

Caitlin hurried past, trying to get away from the smell.

As they went, the bridge surprised her again, as she discovered that it was filled with shops. Small booths, vendors, lined the bridge on either side, as foot traffic, livestock, horses and carriages squeezed in the middle. It was a chaotic, crowded scene, with people calling out in every direction, selling their wares.

"Tannery here!" someone yelled out.

"We'll skin your animal!" yelled another.

"Candle wax here! The finest candle wax!"

"Roof thatching!"

"Get your firewood here!"

"Fresh quills! Quills and parchment!"

As they progressed further, there were nicer shops, some selling pieces of jewelry. Caitlin couldn't help but think of the gold bridge in Florence, of her time with Blake, of the bracelet he had bought her.

Momentarily overwhelmed with emotion, she drifted off to the side, held onto the railing, and looked out. She thought of all the lifetimes she'd already lived, all the places she'd been, and felt overwhelmed. Was this all really true? How could one person have lived so many lives? Or would she just wake up from all of this, back in her apartment in New York City, and think that this had all just been the longest, craziest dream of her life?

"Are you okay?" Caleb asked, coming up beside her. "What is it?"

Caitlin quickly wiped back a tear. She pinched herself, and realized that she was not dreaming. It was all real. And that was most shocking of all.

"Nothing," she said quickly, putting on a forced smile. She hoped he hadn't been able to read her thoughts.

Caleb stood beside her, and together, they looked out, right down the middle of the Thames. It was a wide river, and completely congested with traffic. Sailboats of every size navigated their way through, sharing the waters with rowboats, fishermen's boats, and every type of vessel. It was a bustling waterway, and Caitlin marveled at the size of all the different craft and sails, some climbing dozens of feet into the air. She marveled at how quiet the waters were, even with so many vessels in it. There were no sounds of engines, no motorboats. There was just the sound of the canvas flapping in the wind. It relaxed her. The air up here, with the constant breeze, was fresh, too, finally free of smells.

She turned to Caleb and they continued strolling back down the bridge, Ruth at their heels. Ruth started whining again, and Caitlin could feel her hunger, and wanted to stop. But everywhere she looked, she still could not find any food. She was getting hungrier herself.

As they reached the middle of the bridge, Caitlin was shocked, once again, at the sight before her. She didn't think that there'd be anything left to shock her after seeing those heads on the pikes—but this did.

Right there, in the center of the bridge, three prisoners stood up on a scaffold, nooses around their necks, blindfolded, barely clothed, and still alive. An executioner stood behind them, wearing a black hood, slits for his eyes.

"The next hanging is at one o'clock!" he screamed out. A thick and gathering crowd huddled around the scaffold, apparently waiting.

"What did they do?" Caitlin asked one of the crowd members.

"They were caught stealing, Miss," he said, not even bothering to look her way.

"One was caught slandering the Queen!" an old lady added.

Caleb led her away from the gruesome sight.

"Watching executions seems to be a daily sport around here," Caleb commented.

"It's cruel," Caitlin said. She marveled at how different this society was from the modern day, at how much tolerance it had for cruelty and violence. And this was London, one of the most civilized places of 1599. She could hardly imagine what the world was like outside of a civilized city like this. It amazed her how much society, and its rules, had changed.

They finally finished crossing the bridge, and as they stood at its base, on the other side, Caitlin turned to Caleb. She looked at her ring, and read aloud again:

Across the Bridge, Beyond the Bear,
With the Winds or the sun, we bypass London.

"Well, if we're following this correctly, we've just 'crossed the bridge.' Next would be 'Beyond the Bear.'" Caitlin looked at him. "What could that mean?"

"I wish I knew," he said.

"I feel as if my father is close," Caitlin said.

She closed her eyes, and willed a clue to come along.

Just then, a young boy, carrying huge pile of pamphlets, hurried past them, shouting as he went. "BEAR BAITING! Five pence! This way! BEAR BAITING! Five pence! This way!"

He reached out and shoved a flyer into Caitlin's hand. She looked down, and saw, in huge letters, the words "Bear Baiting," with a crude picture of a stadium.

She looked at Caleb, and he looked at her at the same time. They both watched the boy as he began to disappear down the road.

"Bear baiting?" Caitlin asked. "What's that?"

"I remember now," Caitlin said. "It was the big sport of the time. They would put a bear in a circle, and tie him to a stake, and bait him with wild dogs. They take bets on who wins: the bear or the dogs."

"That's sick," Caitlin said.

"The riddle," he said. "'Across the bridge, and Beyond the Bear. Do you think that could be it?"

As one, they both turned and followed the boy, now off in the distance, still shouting.

They made a right at the base of the bridge and walked along the river, now on the other side of the Thames, heading down a street named "Clink Street." This side of the river, Caitlin noticed, was very different from the other. It was less built up, less populated. The houses were also lower here, more crude, this side of the river more neglected. There were certainly fewer shops, and thinner crowds.

They soon came upon a huge structure, and Caitlin could tell, from the bars on the window and the guards standing outside, it was a prison.

Clink Street, Caitlin thought. *Aptly named.*

It was a huge, sprawling building, and as they passed, Caitlin saw hands and faces sticking out of the bars, watching her as she went. Hundreds of prisoners were crowded in there, leering out at her, yelling crude things as they passed.

Ruth growled back, and Caleb came closer.

They walked further, passing a street with a sign that read "Dead Man's Place." She looked to her right and saw another scaffold, with another execution being prepared. A prisoner, shaking, stood on a platform, blindfolded, a noose around his neck.

Caitlin was so distracted, she almost lost sight of the boy, as she felt Caleb grab her hand and guide her further down Clink Street.

As they continued, Caitlin suddenly heard a distant shout and then a roar. She saw the boy, in the distance, turn the corner, and heard another shout rise up. She then was surprised to feel the earth shake beneath her. She hadn't felt anything like that since the Roman Colosseum. She realized that there must be a huge stadium of some sort just around the bend.

As they turned the corner, she was astonished by the sight before her. It was a huge, circular structure, looking like a miniature Colosseum. It was built several stories high, and closed off from view, but in each direction there were arched doors leading into it. She could hear the shouts, louder now, clearly coming from behind its walls.

Before the building milled hundreds of people, some of the most seedy people she had ever laid eyes upon. Some were barely dressed, many had huge bellies sticking out, unshaved and unbathed. Wild dogs roamed amidst them, and Ruth growled, the hairs on her back standing up, clearly on edge.

Vendors pushed carts in the mud, many selling pints of gin. From the looks of the crowd, it seemed most people partook. The crowd jostled each other roughly, and most of them looked drunk. Another roar rose up, and Caitlin looked up and saw the sign hanging over the stadium: "Bear Baiting."

She felt sick to her stomach. Was this society really so cruel?

The small stadium seemed to be part of a complex. There, in the distance, sat another small stadium, with a huge sign which read "Bull Baiting." And there, off to the side, set apart from these two, was another large circular structure—although this one looked different from the others, classier.

"Come see the new Will Shakespeare play in the new Globe Theatre!" yelled out a passing boy, holding a stack of pamphlets. He walked right up to Caitlin, and shoved a pamphlet into her hands. She looked down and it read: "the new play by William Shakespeare: The Tragedy of Romeo and Juliet."

"Will you come, Miss?" the boy asked. "It's his new play, and it's going to be performed for the first time in this brand-new theater: the Globe."

Caitlin looked down at the pamphlet, feeling a rush of excitement. Could this be real? Was this really happening?

"Where is it?" she asked.

The boy chuckled. He turned and pointed. "Why, it's right over there, Miss."

Caitlin looked to where he was pointing, and saw a circular structure in the distance, with white stucco walls and a Tudor wooden trim.

The Globe. Shakespeare's Globe. It was incredible. She was really here.

In front of it, thousands of people were milling about, entering from all directions. And the crowd looked just as rough as the crowd entering the bullbaiting and bearbaiting. That surprised her. She had always imagined Shakespeare theatergoers to be more civilized, more sophisticated. She had never really considered that it was entertainment for the masses—and the crudest type of masses at that. It seemed to be right up there with bearbaiting.

Yes, she would love to see a new Shakespeare play, love to go to the Globe. But she felt determined to fulfill her mission first, to solve the riddle.

A new roar arose from the bearbaiting stadium, and she turned and focused her attention back on it. She wondered if the answer to the riddle lay just beyond its walls.

She turned to Caleb.

"What do you think?" she asked. "Should we see what it's about?"

Caleb looked hesitant.

"The riddle did mention a bridge," he said, "and a bear. But my senses are telling me something else. I'm not quite sure—"

Suddenly, Ruth growled, then took off, sprinting away.

"Ruth!" Caitlin yelled.

She was gone. She didn't even turn back to listen, and she sprinted for all she was worth.

Caitlin was shocked. She had never see her behave that way, even in times of utmost danger. What could possibly pull her so much? She had never known Ruth not to listen.

Caitlin and Caleb broke into a sprint after her at the same time.

But even with their vampire speed, it was slow going through the mud, and Ruth was way faster than them. They watched her turn and weave through the masses, and they had to jostle their way to keep sight of her. Caitlin could see, in the distance, Ruth turn a corner, and sprinted down a narrow alleyway. She picked up speed, as did Caleb, pushing a big man out of her way as she did, and turned down the alleyway, after her.

What on earth could she be after? Caitlin wondered. She wondered if it were a stray dog, or if perhaps she had just reached a tipping point with hunger, and was chasing after a meal. She was a wolf, after all. Caitlin had to remind herself of that. She should have searched harder for food for her, and sooner.

But when Caitlin turned the corner and looked down the alley, she suddenly realized, with a shock, what it was.

There, at the far end of the alley, sat a young girl, maybe eight, in the dirt, cowering, crying, shaking. Towering above her was a large, beefy man, no shirt, his huge belly sticking out, unshaven, his chest and shoulders covered in hair. He wore an angry scowl, revealing his missing teeth, and he reached back with a leather belt and whipped the poor girl in her back, again and again.

"That's what you get for not listening!" the man screamed in a vicious tone, as he raised his belt again.

Caitlin was mortified, and without even thinking, she prepared to burst into action.

But Ruth beat her to it. Ruth had a head start, and as the man reached back his arm, Ruth sprinted and leapt into the air, opening her jaws wide.

She clamped down on the man's forearm and sunk her teeth all the way in. Blood sprayed everywhere, as the man shrieked an unearthly shriek.

Ruth was furious, and would not be appeased. She snarled and shook her head to and fro, tearing more deeply into the man's flesh, and would not let go.

The man swung Ruth to and fro, only able to do so because of his considerable size and because she was still not yet a full-grown wolf. She snarled, and it was a sound scary enough to raise the hair even on the back of Caitlin's neck.

But this man was clearly used to violence, and he swung his big beefy shoulder around and managed to slam Ruth against the brick wall. He then reached over with his other hand and whipped his belt down hard on her back.

Ruth shrieked and yelped. She finally let go, dropping to the ground.

The man, a look of hatred in his eyes, reached back with both hands, ready to bring his belt down with all his might on Ruth's face.

Caitlin sprang into action. Before the man could bring it down, she lunged forward, reaching out with her right hand, grabbing his throat. She drove him back, by the throat, lifting him up, off the ground, higher than her, until she slammed him into a wall, bricks crumbling.

She dangled him there before her, his face turning blue, choking. She was much smaller than he was, but he didn't stand a chance in her iron grip.

Finally, she let him drop. He reached up, scrambling for his belt, and Caitlin leaned back and kicked him hard across the face, breaking his nose.

She then leaned back and kicked him in the chest, a kick so forceful that she sent him flying back several feet. He hit the wall with such force that he left an indent in the bricks, and finally slumped down to the ground, a mess.

But Caitlin could still feel the rage bursting through her veins. She thought of that innocent girl, of Ruth, and she hadn't felt such rage in she didn't know when. She couldn't stop herself. She walked over to him, yanked the belt from his hand, reached back, and cracked him hard, right across his huge belly.

He lurched up, gripping his stomach.

As he sat up, she kicked him hard, right in the face. She connected with his chin, and sent him backwards fast, slamming the back of his head on the ground. Finally, he was unconscious.

But Caitlin still wasn't satisfied. The rage in her wasn't easily summoned these days, but when it was, she couldn't turn it off.

She stepped up, placed a foot on his throat, and prepared to kill this man on the spot.

"Caitlin!" came a sharp voice.

She turned, still pulsing with rage, and saw Caleb standing beside her. He shook his head slowly, with a reprimanding look.

"You've done enough damage. Let him go."

Something about Caleb's voice got to her.

She grudgingly lifted her foot.

In the distance, she spotted a huge tub filled with sewage. She could see the thick dark liquid spilling over its edges, and could smell its stink from here.

Perfect.

She reached down, hoisted the man above her head, even though he easily weighed over 300 pounds, and walked him across the alley. She threw him, headfirst, into the vat of sewage.

He landed with a splash. She saw him stuck, up to his neck, in all the excrement. She enjoyed the idea of his waking up, realizing where he was, and finally, she felt satisfied.

Good, she thought. *It is where you belong.*

Caitlin immediately thought of Ruth. She ran over to her, and examined the belt mark on her back; she was cowering, and slowly regaining her feet. Caleb came over, too, examining her, as Ruth placed her face in Caitlin's lap and whined. Caitlin kissed her on the forehead.

Ruth suddenly shook them off and darted across the alley, to the girl.

Caitlin spun, and suddenly remembered. She hurried over to her, too.

Ruth ran to the girl, though, licking her on her face. The hysterically crying girl slowly stopped, distracted by Ruth's tongue. She sat there in the mud, in her soiled, dirty dress, covered with belt marks on her back, blood oozing through, and looked up at Ruth in surprise.

Her wet eyes opened wide as Ruth kept licking her. Finally, she reached up, slowly, hesitantly, and petted Ruth. She then reached up and gave her a hug. Ruth reciprocated, coming in close.

It was amazing, Caitlin thought. Ruth had detected this girl from blocks away. It was as if the two had known each other forever.

Caitlin came over and knelt down beside the girl, reaching out a hand, and helping her sit up.

"Are you okay?" Caitlin asked.

The girl looked at her in shock, then at Caleb. She blinked several times, as if wondering who these people could be.

Finally, slowly, she nodded yes. Her eyes were open wide, and she looked too afraid to speak.

Caitlin reached out and gently stroked the matted hair from her face. "It's okay," Caitlin said. "He won't hurt you anymore."

The girl looked as if she were about to start crying again.

"I'm Caitlin," she said. "And this is Caleb."

The girl looked at them, still not speaking.

"What's your name?" Caitlin asked.

After several seconds, the girl finally answered: "Scarlet."

Caitlin smiled. "Scarlet," she repeated. "Such a pretty name. Where are your parents?"

She shook her head. "I don't have any parents. He is my ward. I hate him. He beats me every day. For no reason. I hate him. *Please* don't make me go back to him. I don't have anyone else."

Caitlin turned to Caleb, and saw him look at her, both thinking the same thing at the same time.

"You're safe now," Caitlin said. "You don't have to worry anymore. You can come with us."

Scarlet's eyes opened wide in surprise and delight, and she nearly broke into a smile.

"Really?" she asked.

Caitlin smiled back, reached out her hand, and Scarlet took it, as she helped her to her feet. She saw the wounds on her back, still oozing blood, and from somewhere deep within herself, Caitlin suddenly felt a power overcome her. She thought of what Aiden had taught her, of the power of being one with the universe, and deep within herself, she suddenly felt a power surging that she'd never known. She had always felt her power for the rage, but she had never felt a power like this. This was different, a new power, tingling up from her feet to her legs, through her torso, through her arms, to her fingertips.

It was the power to heal.

Caitlin closed her eyes and reached out, and gently placed her hands on Scarlet's back, where the marks were. She breathed deeply, and summoned the power of the universe, summoned all the training Aiden had given her, and focused on sending white light to the girl.

She felt her hands grow very hot, and felt an incredible energy coursing through her.

Caitlin wasn't sure how much time had passed when she opened her eyes again. She looked up, slowly opening them, and saw Scarlet staring back at her, eyes wide in amazement. Caleb stared at her too, also amazed.

Caitlin looked down, and saw that Scarlet's wounds were completely healed.

"Are you a magician?" Scarlet asked.

Caitlin smiled wide. "Something like that."

CHAPTER SIX

Sam flew over the British countryside, Polly at his side, but keeping her distance. Their wings were spread out but they were not close to touching, as they each wanted space from each other. Sam preferred it that way, and he assumed she did, too. He liked Polly, he really did. But after his debacle with Kendra, he wasn't ready to get close to anyone of the opposite sex for a long time to come. It would be a while before he could trust someone again. Even someone who had been close to his sister, as Polly seemed to be.

They had been flying for hours, and as Sam looked down in the morning light, he saw endless stretches of farmland, with occasional small houses, smoke rising from their stone chimneys, even on this beautiful fall day. He saw the occasional person out in their yard, tending to clothing, hanging sheets on strings. There were not many houses, though. This countryside seem so entirely rural, he began to wonder if cities even existed in this time—whatever time and place they were in.

Sam had no idea where to go, and Polly hadn't been much help. They had both used their keen vampire senses to tune in, to try to use their close connection to Caitlin to sense where she might be. They had both intuited that she might be in this general direction, and they had been flying for hours. But since then, they had seen no clues or direct leads. Sam's instincts told him that Caitlin was in a large city. But they hadn't passed anything remotely like a city for hundreds of miles.

Just when Sam was beginning to wonder if they'd chosen the right direction, they rounded a bend, and as they did, he was shocked at what unfolded in the distance. There, on the horizon, sat a sprawling city. He couldn't recognize what city it was, and he wasn't sure that he'd be able to recognize it at all, even up close. His geography was pretty bad, and his history was even worse. It was the result of being moved one too many times, of falling in with the wrong friends, of not paying attention in school. He had been a C student, although he knew he had the potential to get A's. But with his upbringing, it had just been too hard for him to find a reason to care. Now, he regretted it.

"It's London!" Polly called out, in delight and surprise. "Oh my God! London! I can't believe it. We're here! We're *really* here! What an amazing place to be!" she yelled, excitedly.

Thank God for Polly, Sam thought, feeling stupider than ever. He realized there was a lot he could learn from her.

As they got closer and buildings came into view, he marveled at the architecture. Even from this great distance, he could see church steeples rising into the sky, punctuating the city like a field of lances. As they came even closer, he saw just how grand and magnificent all the churches were—and was surprised that they already looked ancient. Beside them, all the other architecture was dwarfed by comparison.

As he began to take it all in, he sensed keenly that Caitlin was here. And the thought of that excited and thrilled him.

"Caitlin's down there!" he yelled out. "I can feel it."

Polly smiled back. "So can I!" she yelled.

For the first time since landing in this time and place, Sam finally felt grounded, felt a strong sense of direction, and of purpose. Finally, he felt as if he were on the right track.

He tried to sense whether she was in any danger. Try as he did, he was coming up blank. He thought of the last time he had seen her, in Paris, right before she'd fled the Notre Dame. She had been with that guy—Caleb—and he wondered if they were still together. He'd only met Caleb once or twice, but he'd liked him a lot. He hoped that Caitlin was with him, and that he was taking care of her. He got a good feeling from their being together.

Polly suddenly dove lower, without warning, getting closer to the rooftops. Either she didn't care about Sam following, or she just assumed that he would. It annoyed Sam. He wished she'd given him some warning, or at least cared enough about him to signal that she was diving down low. And yet, a part of him sensed that she did care. Was she just playing hard to get?

And why did he even care, either way? Didn't he just get through telling himself that he wasn't interested in girls right now?

Sam dove down lower, to her level, and they flew just feet above the city. But he also made a point of veering off to the left, so that they flew even further apart. *Take that*, Sam thought.

As they approached the city center, Sam was blown away. This time and place was so different, so unlike anything he had ever seen or experienced. He was so close the rooftops, he felt as if he could almost reach down and touch them. The majority of buildings were low, just a few stories high, and were built with slanted roofs, topped with what looked like huge piles of hay or straw. Most buildings were painted a bright white, with brown lines framing them. The churches—huge, marble, limestone—rose up out of the landscape, dominating entire blocks, and here and there were a few other large structures that looked like palaces. Probably, he guessed, residences for royalty.

The city was divided by a wide river, over which they now flew. The river was bustling with traffic—boats of all shapes and sizes—and as he looked over at the streets, he saw that they were bustling, too. In fact, he couldn't believe how packed they were. There were people everywhere, hurrying to and fro. He couldn't imagine what they could possibly have to hurry about. It wasn't like they had internet, or e-mails, or faxes, or even phones.

Still, other parts of the city were relatively peaceful. The dirt roads, the river, and all the boats provided a tranquil feeling. There were no racing cars, buses, horns, trucks or motorcycles revving. All was relatively quiet.

That is, until a sudden roar rose up.

Sam turned his head, and so did Polly.

There, off to the side, they spotted a large stadium, built in a perfect circle and rising several stories high. It reminded him of the Roman Coliseum, although much smaller.

From his bird's-eye view, it looked as if there were some sort of large animal in the center of it, running around, with many other small animals running around it. He couldn't quite figure out what it was, but he could see that the stadium was packed with thousands of people, all standing, on their feet, cheering and roaring.

He suddenly felt a tingling in his body as he watched. Not because he could tell what it was. But because he suddenly sensed Caitlin's presence there. Strongly.

"My sister!" he yelled out to Polly. "She's there," he said, pointing. "I feel it."

Polly looked down, and furrowed her brow.

"I'm not so sure," she said. "I don't feel anything."

She turned her head in the other direction, and pointed at the bridge looming before then. "I sense that she's there."

Sam looked, and saw a huge bridge spanning the river. He was surprised to notice that it was covered with shops of all sorts, and even more surprised to see, as they flew over it, that there were several prisoners standing there, on a scaffold, nooses around their necks, hoods around their heads. It looked as if they were about to be executed. And large crowds gathered around them.

"Okay," Sam said, and suddenly dove down low, right for the bridge. He figured he would pre-empt her, and be the first one to dive down this time.

Sam landed on the bridge, not turning around, and moments later, he sensed Polly land several feet behind him. She caught up to him, and the two of them walked side-by-side, keeping their distance, he not looking at her, and she not looking at him either. He was proud that he was keeping their relationship purely professional. There wasn't even a semblance of closeness, which was clearly what they both wanted.

Sam was amazed at the sights on the bridge. It was overwhelming, with so much stimulation coming at him from every direction.

"Tan your leather, son?" a man asked him, holding a piece of rawhide up in his face. The man's breath stank, and Sam dodged out of his way.

"Now where?" Sam asked Polly.

She scanned the bridge, looking everywhere for Caitlin, as did he. But there was no sight of her anywhere.

Polly finally shrugged. "I don't know," she said. "I had sensed her here before, but now...I'm not so sure."

Sam turned and looked off at the horizon, back towards that stadium.

"I sensed her back there," he said. "In that stadium we flew over."

"Okay," Polly said, "let's go that way. But let's walk—just in case she's on the bridge."

As they walked across the bridge, through all the vendors, Polly seemed to cheer up again, to slowly become her jolly self. "Look at the fashions of all these people!" she said. "I mean, look at what they wear! It's amazing, isn't it? I don't think I would ever be caught dead wearing something like that. But I can see the functionality of it. I wonder how these fashions even come to be. I mean, how do they just change from generation to generation? So crazy, isn't it? And I was thinking, if I lived in this time, if I was one of these people, what color would I wear…"

Sam sighed. Polly had begun talking again, and he knew there was no stopping her now. Inwardly, he tuned her out.

As they walked, Sam scanned all the faces on the bridge, looking for any sign of Caitlin. He kept thinking he saw her, for a second, only to be disappointed. At one point, he saw a girl from behind that looked just like her, and grabbed her shoulder.

"Caitlin!" he exclaimed.

But the girl turned, and he was embarrassed to realize it wasn't her; she gave him an odd look and walked away.

Soon they were over the bridge, standing on land, and Sam spotted a huge sign which read "Southwark." He turned right, in the direction of that stadium.

They headed down a street which read "Clink Street," and passed a large prison. They heard another roar, and this time, Sam felt certain that she was there. Caitlin. His sister. Just blocks away.

They increased their pace and as they rounded the bend, Sam was blown away by the sight: before them sat a large stadium, in front of which milled thousands of people—crude, tough looking types—all hurrying in and out.

He stopped and turned to Polly. She stood there, looking amazed.

"I feel that she's in there," he said to her. "Do you want to check it out?"

Polly stared at the crowd, looking appalled.

"These people look like they haven't bathed in a year," she said. "And their fashion leaves much to be desired."

A huge, sweaty man passed by them, not wearing a shirt, hair coming off his arms, and brushed by Polly's arm, leaving sweat on her which she furiously wiped off.

"Gross," she said.

Sam felt repulsed by it, too.

"I don't know," Polly said. "I don't feel that she's in there. And I don't get a good feeling about this place."

Sam scanned the faces. "Do you have any other ideas?" he asked.

He saw Polly close her eyes for several seconds. Finally, she opened them, looking frustrated.

"No," she said.

"Then let's check it out," Sam said. "What do we have to lose?"

Sam was on guard as they walked through the large, open-air archway, into the stadium. It reminded him of entering the Roman Coliseum, but smaller.

The electricity in the air was palpable. Before them, at eye level, was a circular, dirt floor, surrounded by wooden seating, rising steeply for several levels. There was not an empty seat in the packed house, and everyone was on their feet. People were crammed in impossibly close, shoulder to shoulder, leaning over the wooden railings, and screaming at the top of their lungs.

Sam looked down to see what they were screaming about, and saw that there, tied to a post in the center of the dirt floor, was a huge, brown bear, fixed to the post by a ten foot metal chain, clamped to its hind leg. The bear snarled and roared, trying to break free, but to no avail.

The bear ran in circles, back and forth, yanking at the chain with all its might—but it was futile. The crowd seemed to get excited every time the bear tried to break free, shouting and jeering. Sam looked closely, scanning the faces, and he could see that most of them were drunk, in the middle of the day, gripping flasks.

It was crowded down here, too. In the entryway, hundreds of people milled about, shoulder to shoulder, jostling Sam and Polly. While Polly previously had kept her distance from Sam, she inched closer, clearly nervous.

He cleared a space for them both, pushing their way towards the front so that they could get a better look. Sam scanned all the faces intently, trying to see if he could spot Caitlin anywhere. But it was so chaotic, and there was so much energy in the air, he felt his senses being tuned out. He couldn't see her anywhere, and now he was starting to worry if they were in the right place at all. Maybe he had made a mistake coming here. Maybe Polly had been right.

Sam also couldn't figure out why all these people were so excited about watching a bear chained to a post.

And then it happened.

A trumpet sounded, and several trap doors opened all around the sides of the stadium. In a perfect circle, out charged a dozen hunting dogs. They all charged right for the bear. Sam couldn't believe it.

The dogs leapt high into the air, claws and teeth extended, aiming right for the bear. The first dog to reach it sunk its fangs into the bear's hind leg.

The bear wheeled in anger, and knocked the dog off of him with a swipe of his paw. The bear's huge claws tore the dog in half, and the dog fell to the ground, dead.

The crowd roared in approval.

The other dogs attacked the bear from all directions, and he fought back viciously. They did damage, biting and scratching him, but he did much more damage than they, killing or wounding most of the dogs with a single bite.

"PLACE YOUR BETS! PLACE YOUR BETS!" shouted a voice. A man walked past Sam and Polly holding out a pouch filled with coins, and an empty palm. As he went, various people reached over, brushing by Sam, and shoved various size coins into his hand. He stuffed these coins into his pouch, and reached out and gave the people tickets in return.

"Twenty pence on the dogs!" yelled a man, as he thrust a coin into his hand.

"Two pounds on the bear!" called out another man.

The man stopped before Sam and Polly, looking at them, holding out his hand. "Will the young couple be placing a bet?" he asked.

Sam, embarrassed, looked at Polly, and she looked away, equally embarrassed.

"We are *not* a couple," Polly corrected, her face reddening.

But the man didn't seem to care. Realizing they weren't betting, he moved on.

Sam was embarrassed, too. And despite himself, he also felt a little hurt that Polly was so quick to clarify that they were not a couple. Not that they were. She just didn't have to be so forceful about it.

The man moved on, but as soon as he did, another man appeared, carrying a sack over his shoulder. "GIN HERE! GIN HERE! Fifteen pence!"

A huge, drunken man brushed by Sam, and as he did, he bumped Polly roughly, sending her stumbling, as he reached out and grabbed a flask of gin.

Sam felt his temper flare. He turned to Polly, and could see that she was flustered.

"Are you okay?" he asked.

She nodded back, but looked shaken.

"Let's go," she said. "Caitlin's not here. I want to get out of here."

Sam was willing to go, especially since it was clear that Caitlin was nowhere to be found—but he wasn't ready to leave just yet. He was indignant that the man had so rudely jostled Polly, and he didn't feel right about leaving until he'd spoken his mind.

"That'll be fifteen pence," said the vendor to the huge man.

The man suddenly extracted a small knife from somewhere in his garment and held it up to the vendor's throat.

"How about I trade you the flask for your life?" the man responded.

The vendor, wide-eyed, hurried off.

The man turned and began to make his way back.

But Sam stepped sideways, and blocked his path. He bravely stared the man down, right in the eye.

"You owe her an apology," Sam said to him, in a calm, cool rage.

The man, a good foot taller than Sam—and twice as wide—looked down at Sam as if he were joking, then broke out into a menacing laugh.

"Do I?" he asked.

He turned and looked at Polly, and then licked his huge fat lips, practically drooling.

"I tell you what: how 'bout I take her home with me for a ring or two, and I could apologize to her all night long. Yes. In fact, I think I'll do that."

The man took a step towards Polly, as if to grab her.

But before he could get any further, Sam stepped up and shoved him hard, sending him flying through the crowd, knocking over several people with him, and finally landing on his behind.

"Sam, let's go," Polly urged in a low, hurried voice, grabbing Sam's arm, trying to pull him away. "*Please.*"

But Sam wasn't ready to walk away. A part of him, the rational part, knew that he should. But that part was quickly receding into the back of his mind. Another part came to the fore: and it was the part that wanted blood. Vengeance.

And the huge man didn't seem to be in exactly a forgiving mood, either. His face turned bright red, as he sat there, embarrassed, on his behind, looking at Sam with something like shock. It didn't help that the entire crowd was now looking down at him, howling and hooting at him, making his face turn even redder.

As he regained his feet, two other huge men suddenly came up beside him, and Sam could see that they were his friends. There was now, facing him, a pack of three of them, and as they approached Sam, they each pulled out a knife.

"Small boy," said the man, "you're going to pay for that with your life. I hope it was a good one."

The three of them lunged toward Sam.

But Sam didn't feel any fear. Instead, he felt resolve—a cold, steely resolve.

With one arm, he reached out and brushed Polly back behind him, so that he stood in front of her, offering her safety.

Then he took two steps forward, leapt into the air, meeting the huge man in the middle, kicking him in the chest with both his feet, and sending him flying backwards. In the same motion, he reached out one hand in each direction, grabbed the heads of the two other men, and smashed them together.

They collided with a sickening crack, and both collapsed to the ground.

But Sam wasn't done. He kept running forward, as the big man landed on his back once again. As he tried to regain his feet, Sam kicked him hard in the face, knocking him out cold.

Sam wheeled, looking to see if anyone else was coming after him.

But the crowd just stood there, in shock, finally silenced. Nobody dared come within feet of him.

He saw several other men come towards him, from another direction, dressed in all black. They looked like officials, all dressed in the same uniform. They were larger, meaner, more professional looking. Security, perhaps.

Five of them approached, holding clubs.

Sam felt himself pulsing with rage, and he couldn't stop it. He leaned back and roared, the rage coursing through every inch of his body.

He had never felt such rage, and as he leaned his head back and roared, the noise reverberated, louder and louder, above the din of the crowd, finally shaking the entire stadium. Within moments, the roar became louder than even the bear's.

People from every direction of the stadium stopped and turned their attention on him.

The five security guards stopped cold in their tracks, a good ten feet away, frozen in fear at the sound and the sight.

Clearly, it was evident, even for them, that Sam was not human.

Sam blinked and opened his eyes to see Polly standing before him. It was hard to focus on her in his rage, but she was now standing just inches away, holding her hands to his face. Forcing him to focus.

"Sam," she said. "It's me."

Slowly, his rage waned.

She reached out, took his hand, and led him through the parting crowd, everyone afraid to be close to them.

Within moments, they were out the door, and back outside the stadium.

Polly led him at a quick pace, gaining even more distance, walking and walking, and they were soon far from the stadium. Eventually, they reached the bank of the river. As they did, Sam slowly felt himself returning to normal.

Finally, she let go of his hand. He was so flooded with emotion, he was having a hard time remembering what had just happened.

"Don't you ever do that again," Polly snapped. "You just put us both in danger. And our entire race."

Sam felt indignant. He had just stood up for her—this was hardly the thanks he had been expecting.

"What are you talking about?" he said. "I was looking out for you. I was protecting you. That man elbowed you."

"I don't need your protection," Polly said. "I can handle myself, in case you forgot. It's not like I'm human. And I especially don't need any protection from any boys. I'm fine on my own. And besides—you weren't protecting me: you were endangering me. And just flattering your own ego."

Sam felt angry now. He had thought she'd be grateful, and couldn't understand why she was upset.

"Fine," he snapped. "I won't help you again."

"Fine," she snapped back.

Sam stood there fuming, watching her back as she walked away.

Girls, he thought. He would never understand them.

CHAPTER SEVEN

Caitlin marveled at how quickly children rebounded. Scarlet walked beside her, practically skipping with joy, laughing aloud as she played with Ruth. Ruth practically skipped, too, glued to Scarlet's side, turning her head left and right, on the lookout for any and all possible harm that might come within ten feet of Scarlet. Caitlin had never seen Ruth so protective, or so overjoyed. The two seemed like a match made in heaven, and they were already inseparable.

Scarlet smiled from ear to ear, and looking at her now, it would seem as if she had never suffered any hardship at all. It lifted Caitlin's heart. It had crushed her to see Scarlet lying there, being beaten by that cruel human being. Now, she seemed alive again.

Caitlin was thrilled to have Scarlet by her side, too. She couldn't help herself, but as she studied her, she found herself thinking of the child that she and Caleb might have had, had they remained in the 21st century. She couldn't help but wonder if their child might have turned out somewhat like Scarlet. It was strange, but

Caitlin even felt as if she could recognize some of her own facial features in the girl. Their connection felt so real, so natural, Caitlin felt, as she walked, as if she had always known her.

After the incident in the alleyway, Ruth had started whining again, and Scarlet had rightly observed that she was famished. Before Caitlin and Caleb could decide where to go next, Scarlet had insisted on leading the way to food, and had skipped off without another word, barely even asking for their approval. She had seen that Ruth was hungry and was determined to rectify that. Caitlin and Caleb smiled as they found themselves following along, twisting and turning in and out of side streets and alleyways to Scarlet's lead.

Ruth couldn't be happier. It was as if she knew she were being led to a coming meal.

"It's not too far now, Ruth," Scarlet said, stroking her head. "Just a few more blocks. Hang in there."

Ruth whined in delight, wagging her tail, as if she understood.

Scarlet turned to Caitlin as she walked.

"You see there?" asked Scarlet. "That's the river. Just at the end of this block. From there, we make a left, and that takes us along Bankside. Just past the row houses is a wharf, and there's a man there that sells strips of meat. It's not the best in town, but they're cheap. I'm afraid I haven't any money, though."

"Don't worry," Caleb said, reaching into his pocket and extracting a fistful of gold coins. Caitlin looked at them in wonder, wondering where he got them.

"They're not from this time and place," he said with a smile, "but they're gold after all. I'm sure no vendor would turn this down."

Scarlet's eyes opened wide. "My God," she exclaimed, "are you rich or something?"

Caleb smiled down. "Something like that."

Scarlet practically skipped as they continued down the street, reaching the river, just like she had said. Caitlin marveled at her sense of direction. She had been leading them, twisting them in and out of back streets, determined to show them her entire neighborhood. They were on her turf now, and she had insisted on giving them a grand tour, as if she had been waiting for them.

As they reached the waterfront, Scarlet suddenly stopped, as if frozen, and looked up to her right. Caitlin wondered what she was looking at, and assumed maybe it was a tall, passing ship.

But when Caitlin came up beside her, she saw what it was. There, in the distance, on the London Bridge, those three prisoners that had been sitting on the scaffold were now being hoisted up higher. There was a sounding of trumpets, and suddenly the platforms were removed from all three of them.

They each plummeted down, hanging and twisting by their necks.

The crowd roared.

Caitlin reached up and gently turned Scarlet's shoulders, guiding her away from the grisly sight.

"It's okay," Scarlet said. "It happens here every day."

Caitlin looked at her with concern, and couldn't even imagine what it must have been like for her to grow up in this time and place. "I'm so sorry," Caitlin said. "That must be very sad for you."

Scarlet looked sad for a moment, but then brushed it off with a shrug and turned away.

"Come on Ruth! It's not far now. Just this way."

She suddenly skipped off in the other direction, turning left along the river. "There!" she yelled, pointing. "Come on, Ruth!" she yelled, running forward.

Caitlin smiled, keeping a watchful eye on her, and realized how protective she felt of her already. She turned to Caleb, wondering what he thought of all this. She worried for a second if he was mad that they had taken her under their wing.

But he was as happy as she was. She wondered if he, too, had been contemplating if their child would have turned out like this.

He turned and smiled. "She's wonderful," he said.

"We can't just abandon her," Caitlin said. "She has no one else to watch out for her."

"I know," Caleb said.

Caleb reached out and they held hands as they walked along the bank, watching Scarlet and Ruth running. Caitlin felt her heart warm with emotion, and felt certain that, at that moment, Caleb, too, thought of her as their child. It brought tears to Caitlin's eyes.

Scarlet and Ruth ran up onto a large wooden structure along the river bank. Before it hung a sign which read "Falcon Inn." It was a large, bustling inn—and judging from the people hurrying in and out, a seedy place.

Caitlin and Caleb caught up to them, standing behind Scarlet as she walked up to a small booth in the back of the hotel, hidden from sight. There was a man wearing a greasy, bloodstained apron, slicing huge chunks of meat.

"Two please," Scarlet said to the man.

He scowled down at her. "And where do you expect to find the money to pay for that today?" he asked, mocking. "Like I told you before: no money, no meat."

Caleb cleared his throat, stepping forward. "You will, in fact, give the girl two pieces of meat, as she requested," he said sternly, glowering down at the man. "In fact, you will give her as much meat as she wants." Caleb reached out and placed a large gold coin into the man's beefy palm.

The man looked down, eyes opening wide at the large piece of shining gold. Caitlin realized that that probably represented enough money to pay for a thousand pieces of meat.

The man quickly set to cutting huge chunks of meat off his spit, handing them in rapid-fire to Scarlet. The second they hit her hand, she reached over and dangled them in front of Ruth, who jumped up and snatched them off her fingers.

Scarlet laughed with delight.

The man handed her another piece, and she did it again—and again, Ruth snatched the meat.

Scarlet screamed with laughter. "You're so hungry, Ruth!"

Ruth licked her lips. The man kept slicing meat, in bigger and bigger chunks, and Scarlet kept feeding them to her.

After six more slices, Caleb stepped forward.

"The next piece is for you, Scarlet."

She took the next piece with delight, eyes open wide, and devoured it. Clearly, she was ravenous.

"We'll each take one, too," Caleb said, and the man cut them each a slice.

Caitlin bit hard and sucked the blood out of it, and she saw Caleb do the same. She felt it trickle through her veins, and realized how famished she was—for real blood.

It took the edge off. But it also made her realize that she needed to feed—to *really* feed. She took a deep breath, forcing herself to be disciplined. There was probably a forest not far from here, and she would force herself to wait.

"Come on, Ruth, you have to see the view!"

Scarlet bounded off, zigzagging behind the hotel, and Ruth took off after her.

Caitlin and Caleb struggled to keep up. By the time Scarlet had stopped running, she had led them all to a large wooden pier, jutting out over the river, with a set of stairs sloping down right into the water. A large sign read "Paris Garden Stairs." The rickety staircase sloped right down to the water's edge, and was filled with people sitting, standing, looking out at the water, and with more people arriving in boats.

Scarlet ran right up to the water's edge and pointed at a passing boat with a huge sail rising into the sky. Ruth ran up beside her, looking out.

Caitlin stood behind her, worried that Scarlet not slip and fall into the water. She looked out at the river, and was amazed at the sight: it was like being in a painting. The sun broke through the clouds, striking the water, while tall, historic sailing ships slowly bobbed their way past.

Caleb slid his arm around her waist, looking out, too, and Caitlin breathed deeply. For the first time, she felt relaxed in this time and place.

The mission was important to her, but it felt so good having Caleb by her side. She realized that was all she really needed to feel content. That, and knowing that the people she loved and cared for were safe. She found herself thinking of Sam and Polly again. She hoped they'd made it safely out of the Notre Dame. She realized that seeing them here, safe and sound, would be all that she needed to feel complete.

At that moment, Caitlin heard a creaking on the boardwalk behind her, and her senses were on high alert. She spun around, and could not believe what she saw.

There, walking onto the stairs, looking out at the river, not even aware of her presence, were Sam and Polly.

Caitlin wondered if she were seeing things. She blinked several times, thinking she was imagining it.

She finally realized that she wasn't.

She stepped forward, barely able to catch her breath with shock and excitement.

"Sam? Polly?"

The two of them spun and looked at her.
It was really them.

*

Caitlin was overwhelmed with joy as she embraced her little brother. Tears flowed down her cheeks, as she held him tight.

She pulled back, and looked over Polly, her one time best friend, and for a moment, she hesitated. She remembered that last she had seen her, in Versailles, they had not been on the best terms. Polly had been so smitten by Sergei, and had refused to listen to Caitlin, they'd had a falling out.

But Polly stepped forward and embraced Caitlin with all she had, hugging her tightly, and Caitlin knew that whatever fight they'd had in the past was behind them. It felt so good to hug her best friend again. Caitlin was overwhelmed. Having both her brother and her best friend here, in this time and place, meant the world to her.

Caitlin stepped back, and remembered Caleb. She wondered if they had all formally met, and couldn't quite remember.

She cleared her throat. "Sam, this is Caleb."

"I remember you," Sam said, as he shook Caleb's hand.

Caleb smiled, and shook his hand back warmly. "And I you," Caleb answered. "You have really grown up. Thank you for what you did for us back in the Notre Dame."

Sam smiled proudly, and Caitlin was thrilled to see them getting along.

"And Caleb, this is Polly."

Caleb bowed his head slightly, taking her hand, and kissing it. "A pleasure," he said.

Caitlin heard a clearing of a throat, and looked down to see Scarlet standing there, a smile on her face, anxiously waiting to be introduced.

Of course. Caitlin felt terrible she had forgotten, and knelt down beside her.

"And most important of all, allow me to introduce you to Scarlet," Caitlin said. "We are her family now," Caitlin added, liking the sound of those words even as she said it.

Scarlet stepped forward and reached out a hand, polite, adult-like.

"A pleasure to meet you," Scarlet said in her best adult voice.

Sam smiled and reached out and formally shook her hand back.

Polly, though, knelt down and picked Scarlet up in a big hug.

"Oh my god, aren't you a dear?" Polly said. "And so beautiful. Look at that hair, those eyes.

I think you just might be the most beautiful little girl I've ever seen," Polly said.

Scarlet beamed back.

Ruth suddenly barked, and Polly's eyes opened wide in surprise. She knelt down and gave her a hug, too. "Oh Lord! Look at you. My how you've grown!"

Ruth licked her face, as Polly petted her.

"Oh my God," Polly said, standing, facing Caitlin. "We've been searching for you *everywhere*. I can't believe we found you. We just left the most hideous bearbaiting ring. Oh my God, it was awful. The worst place I've ever seen. And we were walking along the river, trying to figure out where on earth to go next. For a second there, I didn't know if we find you at all and—"

"Suffice it to say that we are so happy to see you," Sam said, cutting her off.

Polly looked at Sam, annoyed.

Caitlin looked back and forth between the two of them, and for a moment wondered if they were in a relationship. But she saw how irritated they looked by each other. The idea amused Caitlin.

"We were there, too," Caitlin said, "at the bearbaiting ring. But just briefly. We never actually went inside."

"That explains it," Sam said. "I thought I sensed you there. But I wasn't sure."

"What were you doing in such an awful place?" Polly asked.

"Well," Caitlin began, "we were just following clues. Or, so we thought. We found ourselves in Westminster Abbey. There were people there, our kind, and they helped us. They led us to a golden scepter, which led to this ring."

Caitlin held out her hand, displaying the ring she now wore. Sam reached out, fascinated, just as he had always been by all things relating to their father. He slowly read the inscription aloud.

Across the Bridge, Beyond the Bear,
With the Winds or the sun, we bypass London.

He furrowed his brow in silence, puzzled.

"We crossed the London Bridge," Caitlin continued, "thinking maybe that's what the bridge was. And then it mentioned the bear. And we heard about bearbaiting, so we came here, hoping. But there is nothing. I think we misread the clues. I thought we were heading in the right direction. But now, I'm not so sure."

"Across the bridge, beyond the bear," Sam repeated, as if willing himself to figure it out, "across the bridge, beyond the bear…" Finally, he exhaled. "I have no idea," he said.

"I don't either," Polly said.

Silence came over them, as the four of them stood there, stumped.

"If you read it faster it might make sense," Scarlet said.

Caitlin spun, as did the others, and stared down at Scarlet. She was beaming back, a playful smile on her lips.

"What did you say?" Caitlin asked.

"Your riddle makes sense to me."

Caitlin stared at her intently, suddenly realizing that she might have figured out something they didn't.

"How?" Caitlin asked, eager, "how does it make sense?"

"Well," Scarlet said slowly, enjoying the attention, "he read it so slowly. That's your problem. Try reading it faster. He skipped the most important part."

Caleb furrowed his brow. "What do you mean?"

"The winds or the sun," Scarlet said. "That's the important part. Read it faster."

She hesitated, then continued, "It's not the 'winds or the sun'. You need to connect the words. Not 'winds or' but 'windsor.' It's Winsdor. You know, Windsor Castle. Across the bridge is Windsor, and beyond the bear is the forest you have to cross. The Bear forest," she said, as if it were the most obvious thing in the world.

They all looked at her, mouths open in shock.

She smiled back proudly.

"The place you are looking for is Windsor Castle."

CHAPTER EIGHT

Kyle opened his eyes in a blinding rage. He sensed immediately that he had traveled back to the right time and place, the same city and year in which the despicable Caitlin, Caleb and Sam would be. He should be grateful for that.

But he wasn't.

He was sick of time travel, especially in the wrong direction; he missed his war in New York, and he resented Caitlin more with each trip back. He lay there, so overcome with rage, that he could barely even move. He thought of all the ways he'd take vengeance on her. Killing her, and torturing her, would no longer be enough. Not after this many trips back in time. And killing her beloved, Caleb, and her brother, Sam, wouldn't be enough either. He needed more. He would have to think of an even more inventive way. Like tracking down every one of her friends, any and all distant family members, and killing and torturing them slowly, too.

The thought of it relaxed him, made him even smile just a bit. Yes, maybe he could arrange something like this. He saw himself torturing everyone closest to her, while she was still alive, and in plain view of her. He thought of various ways to kill them—the acid treatment, throwing them into vats of boiling oil, feeding them slowly to sharks—and his smile widened.

He exhaled, finally feeling like himself again. Slowly, everything was becoming right in his world.

He lay in the absolute blackness, comfortable in the stone sarcophagus, and reached into his belt. He was satisfied to see his vial of bubonic plague had made the trip. He was delighted, in fact. He had enough live cultures of the plague around his waist to take out nearly the entire human population of the city, to wreak havoc, single-handedly, on an unimaginable scale. He would create so much human devastation and panic, it would surely bring Caitlin and her crew out, like rats from the sewers. Those pathetic vampires always came running to help when humans need it. It was so easy to bait them out, it was almost laughable.

Kyle liked his new strategy more and more. Why should he waste so much energy hunting her down, tracking her every step, as he had in past trips? This time, he would make her come to him. With enough devastation and chaos, she would be drawn like a magnet to save these pathetic little humans. Then he could capture her unaware, and put an end to her for good.

Plus, he didn't want to risk confrontation again. Her brother, Sam, had thrown him off guard with his shapeshifting, and his own confrontation with Caitlin had left him surprised. They had each grown powerful, as he'd feared they would. Now, they were formidable foes to be reckoned with. He was no longer so certain he could kill them all on his own, in direct conflict—especially with Caleb there, too. And he didn't want to waste energy trying.

Kyle wouldn't take any chances this time. This time, he had a backup plan, a surefire way to kill her, Caleb, and all of them.

He would track down Thor, his old friend, locked up in the Tower of London. Centuries before, the two of them had had quite a grand time torturing humans and rival vampires. It would be great fun to see him again. But more importantly, Thor held the key Kyle was looking for: a special vampire poison.

Centuries before, in the Dark Ages, Kyle had been shocked to watch it in use: it was the only weapon he'd ever seen that killed a vampire effectively. Not only did it kill them, but it made them so sick beforehand, they suffered for hours. Kyle smiled at the thought. It was perfect. He needn't confront Caitlin, or any of them. He need only free Thor, get his vampire poison, and slip it into one of their drinks. It was time, he realized, to fight smart.

Suddenly giddy, Kyle reached up and smashed the stone above him with a single blow of his fist, shattering it to pieces. He jumped out of the sarcophagus, feeling reborn.

He surveyed the room, and saw that he was exactly where he'd hoped: the lower crypt of Guildhall, right in the center of London. Hundreds of feet above him, he knew, sat Guildhall, the meeting place for politicians for centuries. All of those wicked little humans, scurrying around, plotting their devious plots to further their own ambition and power. He hated politicians.

But he knew that they were a necessary evil in spreading greed and corruption. Guildhall, in fact, reminded him very much of City Hall in New York. It was always useful to place a crypt beneath a politician's lair.

The room had low ceilings and was dimly lit, by only a few torches. He could see the rows of other sarcophagi, and knew they contained the bodies of vampires that had been sleeping here for centuries. The city had caught them and stored them here some time ago, thinking that this vault could hold them in place. And they were right.

What they hadn't counted on, was Kyle coming back in time.

Kyle broke into action, kicking over each and every sarcophagus in his sight. There was the smashing of stone on stone, again and again, and within minutes, the floor was covered in rubble. Dozens of evil-looking vampires slowly sat up, aroused from their centuries-long entrapment. As Kyle finished his destruction, he stood at the center of the room, and looked at the small army of vampires, now facing him. They were clearly grateful—and ready to take whatever orders he gave.

"BROTHERS IN ARMS!" he shouted, in his fiercest voice. "FOLLOW ME!"

There was a moaning, and a roar of excitement behind him, as Kyle turned and headed out the room. Kyle could feel them on his heels, his new loyal gang, and knew they would follow him, and execute whatever orders he wanted. They would be a useful mercenary force. He would send them all throughout the city, use them to create havoc.

For now, though, Kyle had a bone to pick with the politicians. He burst through the stone corridors, running underground through the ancient halls, his small army right behind him, and tore up flights of medieval steps, twisting and turning, flight after flight. He finally reached the upper levels of Guildhall, and with a single kick, he knocked down a huge oak door that had been there for centuries.

He burst into the main room, the medieval grand hall of Guildhall. It was a magnificent room, hundreds of feet long and high, with huge arched ceilings, built with limestone walls five feet thick. The walls and ceiling were covered with statues, gargoyles and biblical images: in one corner sat a huge statue of the mythical giant Gog, while in the other sat a huge statue of the mythical Magog. Kyle loved these mythical demon giants, right from the Bible, the very images of evil themselves. He always wondered why the humans had chosen these images to adorn this place.

But then again, looking at the hundreds of politicians gathered before him, he shouldn't have. These politicians, the most evil type of humankind, held a soft spot in his heart. But at the same time, he hated them with a passion. And now, after his time travel, he had to let his rage out on someone. Moreover, he needed to feed. And these humans were an easy target.

Kyle burst into the room, the vampires behind him, and as he did, the huge congregation of politicians screamed and began fleeing for the doors.

They didn't get very far.

Within moments, Kyle was tearing off their heads left and right, feeding on their throats, and discarding the cadavers. All around him, his small army was doing the same. None of them had drank for centuries, and they all wanted their fill.

Within minutes, the walls and floors were lined with blood. Not one of the humans made it out alive.

When they all finally finished feeding, Kyle turned and faced his now-loyal throng.

"BROTHERS!" he yelled. "You are going to help me spread the plague to every corner of this city. Stop at nothing until you've accomplished your mission," he said, handing out small vials of the plague to each one as he walked through the crowd. "When your mission is over, then you can gorge as much as you wish. But only on my command." He stopped and surveyed the crowd. "Am I understood?"

The crowd roared back in approval.

He smiled.

Oh, how he had missed London.

CHAPTER NINE

Caitlin flew over the British countryside, a smile on her face. Beside her flew Sam, Polly and Caleb, holding Ruth. Caitlin held Scarlet on her back, who clutched her tight with her small hands. Caitlin thought back to Scarlet's expression when Caitlin told her that she could fly, and that she was going to take her with her up into the air. She had never seen anyone's eyes open so wide in her life. If Scarlet had been an adult, surely she would have dismissed it as being possible. But because she was a child, Caitlin could see in her face that she believed it, and was utterly thrilled—as if Caitlin had just confirmed to her that supernatural powers really do exist.

Without hesitating, Scarlet had jumped onto Caitlin's back. Caitlin had told her to hold on tight, and a moment later they had all been up in the air. Caitlin could hear Scarlet shouting and laughing with joy as they flew off into the horizon, and could only imagine her thrilled expression.

Caitlin thought back again to how they had finally decoded the riddle, of Scarlet's quick-witted solution. She marveled once again at how intelligent this child was. She had, somehow, managed to trump four adults, had managed to decode the riddle in a fraction of a second. Caitlin had never possibly imagined that the answer to the riddle would come from a child. She had vastly underestimated her: this was a special child. Caitlin felt so fortunate to have found her, and couldn't help wondering whether they had been destined to meet, whether this had all been pre-ordained.

Windsor Castle. Of course. It was a place of legend, a place she had heard about only in textbooks. She was thrilled herself to be going there. The second Scarlet had mentioned it, it had felt right. And when Caleb then told her that Windsor Castle had been the seat of royalty for thousands of years, and had also been the place where King Arthur and his Knights of the Round Table had actually met, she knew it was meant to be. If there were more ancient clues or relics to be found, she could think of no more appropriate place than Windsor Castle.

It was only 20 miles away, just west of London. As they all flew through the air, at top speed, Caitlin looked down, and saw an endless stretch of forest pass under them, barely inhabited. She once again felt her stomach growl. But they flew so fast, there was no stopping now. It hardly took fifteen minutes from the time they'd left the river Thames until Caitlin caught her first glimpse of the castle.

The sight took her breath away. In her journeys, she had been to some pretty magnificent places, but this one was close to the top. What struck her most was that the castle so big, spread out over so much land. It must have consumed hundreds of acres, and the walkway alone, a perfectly manicured path, stretched for miles. The land sloped gently upward, and finally brought the visitor to a massive, imposing gate.

Up high, Caitlin had the benefit of flying over the gate, and from her bird's eye view, she could see what lay behind it. The castle had a huge inner courtyard, with manicured grass, and multiple structures spread out on either side. It seemed not like one castle but several, all welded together in one huge structure. At the far end it culminated in a circular building, high up on a hill, its ramparts reaching into the sky, set off from the rest of it, and surrounded by a moat.

"A castle!" Scarlet shrieked in excitement, "a real-life castle!"

Caitlin could feel her giddiness, and smiled at her enthusiasm, as Scarlet clutched her more tightly.

"Will I get to meet a real-life princess?" Scarlet asked.

Caitlin smiled wider.

"Maybe," she responded.

"That's the tower!" Caleb yelled out. "That's where King Arthur and his knights met."

He then pointed in another direction.

"And there is Saint George's Chapel. Where rulers met for hundreds of years."

They flew over the castle's grounds, circling again and again, taking it all in. Caitlin was more impressed every time they flew over it. She felt something stir within her, and knew, just knew, that whatever clue was next, it was below. She felt encouraged again, as she knew she was in exactly the right place for the mission.

"Where should we land?" Sam yelled out.

Caitlin had been wondering the same thing herself. The castle grounds were so immense, the clue, whatever was, could be anywhere. More importantly, she noticed royal guards and soldiers standing watch in every direction, and knew that if they just landed smack down in the middle of the place, it might set off a confrontation.

"Let's land outside the castle, and approach the main entrance formally."

They all seemed to like the idea, and they all dove down and landed out of sight, behind a group of trees.

Caitlin set Scarlet down and Caleb set Ruth down, and Scarlet immediately grabbed Caitlin's hand, bouncing with joy, as the group of them walked towards the main gate.

"Can we do that again!?" Scarlet asked. "I want to keep flying!"

"Soon," Caitlin smiled. "We need to see the Princess first."

"Will she be wearing a crown?" she asked. "Can I wear it, too?"

Caitlin smiled. "We'll see," she said.

The five of them, Ruth in tow, approached the main entrance. Caitlin looked up at the towering stone wall, and it was much more imposing from down here. Before them stood several guards, standing at attention, blocking the door.

Caitlin realized they must have seemed like a strange collection of people—her, Caleb, her brother, Polly, Scarlet, and Ruth. She worried for a second what the guard's reaction might be. She assumed it was not every day that a group of visitors appeared out of nowhere, and approached the royal palace.

"The castle is closed for visitors," a guard snapped firmly, looking straight ahead, blocking their way.

They stopped, and Caitlin stood there, contemplating her options. She was afraid something like this might happen. She wondered if they should have approached a different way.

"But I have business here," Caitlin said.

"What business?" the guard snapped back.

"I'm on a mission. A very important mission. And it leads me to this place," Caitlin said, not wanting to divulge too much.

"I'm sorry," the guard said. "No admittance without an invitation."

Caitlin began to feel anger burning inside her, but she breathed deep, finally able to keep her emotions in check.

But her brother, Sam, was clearly not as restrained; he stepped up and got in the guard's face.

"My sister said she wants to come in here," Sam said. "We're going in."

Sam reached out, and with a single hand, shoved the guard.

Caitlin was amazed. By barely touching the guard, Sam sent him flying several feet, stumbling off his feet, bumping into another guard, and knocking them over.

The dozen or so other guards immediately extracted their swords, and began to approach.

Caitlin was annoyed. Sam should have been more cool-headed, held his emotions in check, and let her handle it. Now they had a fight on their hands. It was the last thing she'd wanted.

Worse, Scarlet started crying, and Ruth started growling. Caitlin could feel herself tense up, and could feel the situation quickly growing out of control.

Just as the guards were getting close, just as Caitlin was debating how best to take them out without hurting them, suddenly, thankfully, the large oak door opened.

Out came strutting a single woman, dressed in the most beautiful clothing, and with the most beautiful jewelry, Caitlin had ever seen. She walked right up to them, blocking the guards' way, acting as interference between the two hostile parties, and momentarily setting the tension at ease.

She walked right up to Caitlin, stopped before her, and stared.

Caitlin could not believe it. Standing before her was a woman she loved, a woman who had once been a close friend.

It was Lily.

Lily stared back, expressionless, looking as regal as ever, and for a moment, Caitlin wondered if she remembered her.

A tense silence hung in the air, as Lily stared, everyone waiting on her command.

Finally, she broke into a smile.

"Caitlin," she said, smiling wide. "I told you we'd meet again."

CHAPTER TEN

Caitlin felt as if she were in a dream as she walked, with the others, through the sprawling courtyard of Windsor Castle. She was so happy to see Lily again, and amazed to see that a human, too, could live multiple lives. It was uncanny to see her here, and as a royal, once again.

On the one hand, everything was so different here—the time, the people, the architecture of this castle—but in other ways, nothing had changed at all. Here was Lily, still royal, still beautiful, still regal—still her old self, just living in a different place and time. It made Caitlin wonder if all of us were destined to live a similar life, over and over again, just changing our place and time, our fashions and names. Was everything in every place and time connected? Was the distance between places, the time gap between centuries, really just an illusion?

It made Caitlin feel connected to everyone and everything. And, of course, to Lily. Along with Polly, she had felt as if Lily were her closest friend, and seeing her again, here, felt like having a sister back.

Lily hadn't changed at all. She was still tall and proud and regal, with dark skin, flowing black hair, and glowing green eyes. Except now, she was dressed in a whole new fashion, and a whole new set of fineries. She still wore an incredible amount of fabric, flowing down to her feet, and she was still draped in the most lavish jewelry, from her dangling earrings, to her diamond necklace, to her emerald rings. Yet she had a different aura about her. More British this time than French.

As they walked, Caitlin could not help noticing that the grounds of Windsor were spectacular. Caitlin marveled at the size and breadth of all the buildings, spread out in a long rectangle, with the courtyard in the middle. Up in the distance, high up on a hill, was a round tower, looking down over everything.

"Windsor Castle has been home to English royalty for centuries," Lily said. They followed on her heels, rapt with attention. "That very spot was where King Arthur and his Knights met, before this castle was even built. This location was chosen for that reason. It is believed to be a very sacred place. In fact, high up on the hill, where you see that round tower, is the very place where the round table was placed."

Scarlet suddenly walked up and tugged on Lily's sleeve.

"Are you a real princess?" she asked.

Lily looked down and smiled, as she stroked Scarlet's hair. "No, my love," she said. "But I bet you are."

Scarlet's eyes opened wide, and she giggled, as she looked embarrassed.

"No I'm not," she said.

Caitlin looked down at Scarlet with all the seriousness she could muster, and said, "Yes you are, Scarlet. Don't ever forget that."

Scarlet stared back at her, wide-eyed, and slowly, Caitlin saw her fill with pride. Caitlin took her hand, and held it as they walked.

"My mission has led us here," Caitlin said to Lily, as they walked, continuing across the courtyard. "I am still searching for my father." Caitlin turned and looked at Sam. "*We* are still searching for our father," she corrected, wanting to include him. "And for the mythical shield."

"I know," Lily responded. "I've been expecting you for some time now. Vampires are usually the keepers of the relics. But in this case, I was chosen." Lily stopped, and looked at Caitlin with all seriousness. "I know exactly what it is you're looking for."

Caitlin stared back, and felt her heart beating faster. She suddenly wondered if her father could be in this place? It certainly looked grand enough to hold him.

"This way," Lily said, and suddenly turned, entering a magnificent building.

They followed her as she marched down corridor after corridor. She led them up a winding, stone staircase, down a grand hallway, up a twisting, medieval stairwell, and down another corridor. Caitlin marveled at their surroundings. They walked on the finest of rugs, and everywhere were massive crystal chandeliers.

They finally arrived at the grandest staircase Caitlin had ever seen. Unusual banisters framed either side, and as they walked down the steps, they faced an enormous marble statue, with suits of armor around it. The statue soared above them, dozens of feet high, and as they descended the red-carpeted, marble steps, Caitlin felt as if she were royalty herself.

"Queen Elizabeth lives here now," Lily said, "with her court and her servants. Hundreds of people live here at any given time—the royal staff, and all the royal advisers. This castle is like a city in and of itself."

They walked through another chamber, all stone, with high arched ceilings, stained glass in every direction, passing dozens of guards as they went. Finally, Lily led them to a grand, oak door, opened it, and stepped aside, a smile on her face.

"Saint George's Chapel," she announced formally, with a wave of her hand.

Caitlin walked in, with the others, and the sight took her breath away.

It was immediately apparent that this room was the crown jewel of the castle. It looked like it had taken hundreds of years to build. The floor was bedecked with a glorious white and black diamond-shaped marble tile, so brightly polished that the sun reflected off of it. The ceiling was hundreds of feet high, arched and coming to a point, and made of limestone. The room was long and narrow, and all along the walls were huge, arched, stained-glass windows. Before them were long wooden benches, on which sat, Caitlin assumed, the royals or politicians when they had grand meetings. It looked like an ancient parliament, from medieval times. She wondered if King Arthur and his knights had met here, too.

Up above hung rows of flags, of all shapes and sizes and colors.

"The Knights of the Garter," Lily explained. "This was once a meeting room. The Knights of the Garter were the highest chivalric order in England, the most elite and most honorable association to belong to. This was their meeting place.

"More importantly," Lily continued, "this room has also been used as a burial place for British Kings and Queens for hundreds of years. Which is why it is significant for our purposes."

Caitlin looked at her, puzzled, but Lily turned and continued walking, her heels clicking on the marble. They followed.

"Is this where the Princess lives?" asked Scarlet, as she tugged on Caitlin's pants.

Caitlin smiled down at her, and stroked her head. "I'm not sure," she answered. "I guess we're about to find out."

As they continued, the room became divided by a huge, elaborately carved mahogany divider. They walked through the doorway, and appeared on the other side of the room.

This side of the room was even more breathtaking. There, off to the side, sat dozens of sarcophagi—huge, marble, elaborately carved. Caitlin could tell right away that they were the final resting places of Kings and Queens.

And as soon as they entered this part of the chamber, Caitlin felt an electric thrill. She felt the ring on her hand heat up, and knew that they were very close to whatever it was they needed to find.

Caitlin stepped forward, allowing the ring to lead her, and found herself standing before a single, huge sarcophagus, in the corner of the room. She surveyed it closely, and saw the effigy on its lid: it was that of an ancient king, with a long, flowing beard, wearing a crown, and holding a staff. He was dressed in royal garments, and chainmail, his hands folded across his chest.

Oddly, one of his fingers was raised slightly higher than the others. Caitlin knew, she just *knew*, why.

She reached down, slipped the ring off her finger, and let her senses guide her to slip it onto the finger of the effigy.

Everyone crowded around her and watched.

The ring fit perfectly.

There was the slightest click, and in the effigy's other hand, Caitlin saw a small, marble scroll. She looked at it closely, and saw that its tip was now slightly ajar.

She reached over and pulled at it gently, and discovered that it was hollow. Inside, lying there, sat a real scroll—a real piece of parchment.

Caitlin's heart beat faster as she reached in, and slowly, gingerly, slid out the frail piece of parchment.

Everyone crowded in even closer, as she rolled open the small scroll. On it was a delicate, antique handwriting, which she immediately recognized as her father's. She felt overwhelmed with emotion, looking at it.

She cleared her throat, and read aloud:

My Dearest Caitlin and Samuel,

If the two of you have made it this far, then you're standing here together, joined on your search for me and the Shield. This scroll you are holding has been especially well hidden, so if you are here, it is only because you are meant to be. I commend you both.

You are two fruits of the same vine, the Rose and the Thorn, and you have different destinies. You are both on the same search, but you must both take different routes. And you might not be searching for the same thing.

Samuel, your road leads to Warwick, where you will begin to find the answers you seek.

Caitlin, find me on the mount of judgment.

With all my love,
Your father.

Caitlin slowly lowered the scroll, and looked over at Sam. He stood there, staring at her, wide-eyed. She could tell that he was taken aback by it all. After all, this was the first clue that was also addressed directly to him. Caitlin remembered the feeling of enormity of having a letter from the past addressed directly to her for the first time.

"Samuel," he said. "No one's called me that in forever."

Caitlin stood there, reading it again, trying to decode it. It warmed her heart that her father had left this for her, and she felt closer to him than ever. But at the same time, the idea of splitting from Sam hurt her. Why couldn't they be on the same journey together? What were their different destinies?

The mount of judgment.

She had no idea what that meant.

She looked slowly at Caleb, wondering if he knew, but he just shook his head, as did Polly, Sam and Lily.

"Warwick?" Sam asked. "What's that?"

Lily cleared her throat.

"That part's easy. It can only mean one thing. It has to be a reference to Warwick Castle. It's the oldest in that region, and it's been a stronghold for your kind for thousands of years."

"And what about the mount of judgment?" Caitlin asked.

Lily slowly shook her head. "Your guess is as good as mine."

*

Caitlin's mind reeled as she sat at the huge dining table with the others. That letter from

130

her father, which she had since read again and again, had been like a bomb dropped into her consciousness. It held so many implications, both for her future, and for Sam's. She kept going over every word in her mind, trying to figure out what it all meant.

But she didn't have time to think about it all right now. Lily had led them all to this enormous banquet, laid out so generously, under her supervision. It was indeed a lavish feast. She sat at a huge, oak table, Scarlet beside her, Caleb on her other side, and Sam, Polly and Lily across from them. Just the six of them, sitting at a table meant to hold a hundred, reclining in gilded, gold, stuffed armchairs.

Caitlin examined the silver, the delicate china plates, the fresh flowers, the huge candles, the chandeliers above, and the enormous windows on all sides of them, letting the sunset in. Before them were spread out heaps of every type of food. There were slices of the finest steak, overstuffed turkeys, breads, fruits, jams, desserts…there was no end to the food in sight. And behind them stood several waiters, ready to jump at their slightest need.

Caitlin looked over and saw Scarlet's expression, how amazed she was at the feast before her. Clearly, she had never seen anything remotely like it in her young life. Caitlin smiled wider, realizing she must think she was dreaming.

"Is this all for us?" Scarlet asked Caitlin, blinking in disbelief.

"Yes, sweetheart," Caitlin responded, "it's all for us. Dig in."

Scarlet reached over, like a kid in a candy shop, and grabbed a large piece of cheesecake to start. Caitlin smiled. Scarlet had probably not eaten this well in her entire life. She grabbed the food quickly, as if worried someone might take it away from her.

Caitlin reached out and laid a reassuring hand on top of hers.

"It's okay," Caitlin said. "You can take all the time in the world. All this food is just for you."

Scarlet looked at her with a look of complete disbelief, as if she had landed in heaven.

More relaxed, Scarlet heaped several large strips of steak on her plate, along with the cheesecake. Caitlin smiled, as the tower of food soon reached higher than her head.

Scarlet then took the top slice, reached over, and handed it to Ruth, who had been sitting patiently by her side, watching wide-eyed, smacking her lips. Ruth snatched it from her fingers, and Scarlet laughed in delight. Scarlet did it again and again, giving her an entire plate of steak.

Caitlin was amazed. Here Scarlet was, probably having never having such food in her life, and the first thing she did was give all her food to Ruth. Caitlin admired her more than ever. If she ever had a daughter, she wished she'd be like her.

Caitlin reached out and put a huge serving of steak on Scarlet's plate. "This portion is just for you, Scarlet," she said.

Scarlet looked at it wide-eyed, picked up a knife and fork, and put a big piece in her mouth. She chewed, and Caitlin could see the satisfaction in her face.

Suddenly, servants appeared, and large, bejeweled goblets were placed before Caitlin, Caleb, Sam and Polly, overflowing with a white liquid. Caitlin could already sense what it was, with every pore in her body: the finest of white blood. Every ounce of her body craved it.

They all lifted their goblets, reached forward and clicked them together. Caitlin leaned back and, finally, drank.

It was the best blood she'd ever had. She drank the entire goblet without stopping, and with every sip, she felt every ounce of her being restored. By the time she set it down, she felt like a new person.

Caitlin watched as the servants placed delicately cut strips of meat before Lily, and she remembered that, of course, Lily was human. It felt so natural having her around, Caitlin had momentarily forgotten that she was not one of hers. Lily, sitting with a perfectly straight back, ever poised, reached out and gently took her knife and fork, cut it into small pieces, and chewed. It was like watching royalty. Caitlin was amazed at how refined Lily was.

Scarlet's laughter filled the table, giving it a festive feel, as she snuck Ruth piece after piece of food off the table. Caitlin felt her heart warm at the sight, so happy to see Scarlet so well cared for here, and that Ruth was equally happy. Caitlin sat there, looking at Caleb, Sam, Polly and Lily, everyone smiling and chatting and happy, and felt so grateful. Finally, they were all together. She was with Caleb, she was with Sam, she was with Poly and Lily. They were all in this beautiful place, having this amazing meal. Finally, she felt as if there were peace and serenity in her life. It felt so good, and she wished she could freeze this moment forever.

But the letter gnawed away at her. Once her dad's voice got in her head, she found it impossible to get it out. The phrases turned in her mind, over and over again. The mount of judgment? Where could that be? Why were she and Sam being given two different paths? Would they both lead to the same place? Or would their separate journeys tear them apart forever?

And what would happen if she actually found this mount of judgment? Would her father be there? Or would she have to go back in time, yet again?

She found it hard to rest until she knew the answers to all these questions.

Caitlin needed clarity. Seeing how happy and content Scarlet and everyone else was, she slowly stood.

Everyone looked at her. "Please excuse me for a few moments," Caitlin said.

A servant hurried over and pulled back her chair.

"Of course," Lily said, "it's been a long day. The servants will show you to your room."

Caitlin leaned over and kissed Scarlet on the head, and leaned in and kissed Caleb on the lips. Then she walked out of the room, following a servant. She felt a bit bad leaving everyone there, but they all seemed content and happy, and she needed just a few minutes to herself, to get her mind clear. She found it hard to think with everyone there.

Caitlin was shown to a magnificent room, enormous, at least fifty feet in every direction, and shaped in a semi-circle, with an entire wall of glass, looking out over the grounds of Windsor Castle. It was an exquisite room, an architectural masterpiece, with moldings all over the walls and ceilings, huge rugs laid out in every direction, antique couches and chairs and bureaus and dressers, and a huge four-poster bed in the corner. It lifted Caitlin's spirits to be here, although at the same time, she sensed that she wouldn't be here long, that her journey would lead her elsewhere.

She walked over to the window and looked out, at the last fading light of the day. Where was it that her father meant for her to go? Would there ever be an end to this mission, to these clues? Would she see Sam again, after their journeys took them in different directions? She knew that Caleb would accompany her. But what about Polly? Would she go with her, or with Sam?

And what about Scarlet? Already, Caitlin felt as if she were part of her family. She could not see herself ever abandoning her. But what would that mean for the future? Would she bring Scarlet on this mission everywhere? Would that be too dangerous for her?

Caitlin spotted a small writing desk in the corner, and sat before it. She reached back, deep into one of her pant pockets, and extracted her journal. She had been carrying it all along, and it felt good to take it out and hold it.

She turned back page after page, and saw the journal was getting thicker, more used up, weather-worn. It was truly becoming an old, trusted friend.

Finally, she found an empty page, grabbed the quill off the tabletop, blotted it, and settled in to write.

What is my destiny? When am I meant to find my father? Who is he? Does he really love me? Why was I chosen for this mission? Why is it that I'm so special? And how is my mission different from Sam's?

And what will happen when I find the shield? Will all of this be over? What does that mean? Will I ever return to a normal life? When and where? Will Caleb be in it?

Caitlin stared at her entry. It surprised her. It was not her typical journal entry. She wasn't summarizing, like she usually did. She didn't feel the need to anymore. Now she felt the need to question. To question the very deepest essence of who she was. She lifted the quill again:

Should I forget the mission? Should I just stay here, forget the clues, live here happy, safe, and secure? Or should I go out there again, back on the trail and part from Sam? Is there more security in staying here? Or more security in fulfilling my mission?

"Look!" came an excited voice.

Caitlin spun around, snapped out of her reverie.

There stood Scarlet, dressed in a beautiful, small silk white gown, wearing a diamond laden tiara and small diamond necklaces and diamond bracelets. She was positively beaming.

Caitlin couldn't believe the sight. She looked like a real, small princess.

"Lily gave these to me. She said I could have them. Can I? Please?"

Caitlin smiled wide. She didn't quite know what to say. "Um…if she said so, then, um…of course."

Scarlet smiled wider than Caitlin ever thought possible, and came running over and hugged her. Caitlin hugged her back. It felt good to have her in her arms.

"I love it here," Scarlet said. "Can we stay forever?"

Caitlin stared back, thinking how uncanny it was that Scarlet should ask the very thing that was on her mind. She could see that Scarlet was a very evolved child, and wondered just how deep her powers went.

"I would love to," Caitlin said. "But if we have to leave, we will always be able to find another place that is nice."

Scarlet hugged Caitlin again. "I love you, mommy," she said.

Mommy.

The word rang through Caitlin like an electric shock. It was so unexpected, and yet it felt so good to hear it, and it brought up so many feelings, that Caitlin found herself bursting into tears, crying as she held Scarlet, feeling the hot tears pouring down her cheeks. She felt that she really did love Scarlet like her own child. And she couldn't help it, but it made her think, once again, of being pregnant, and of the child she might have had with Caleb.

Scarlet pulled back and looked at her. "What's wrong mommy?"

Caitlin quickly wiped away her tears. "Nothing, sweetheart. Everything is perfect."

Ruth came running into the room, and Scarlet wheeled, bursting into laughter as she turned and played with her. The two of them ran throughout the huge room, chasing each other.

Caitlin wiped away the last of her tears, and looked out the window, at the setting sun. She knew that she had a major decision to make. And that she had to make it soon. Would she stay here forever? Or would she pursue her destiny?

CHAPTER ELEVEN

Kyle loved watching the night fall. This was his favorite time of day, especially as he went further back in time, as he watched all the simple human folk close up their shops, board up their shutters, scurry to their homes, as if terrified of the dark. The further back in time he went, the more afraid people seemed to be of the night.

And of course, they had reason to fear.

This was the favorite time of day for people like Kyle, and for his entire race. As dusk fell, that creepy feeling that the humans began to feel was indeed the feeling of his kind awakening. Kyle never felt so energized as he did at dusk, so ready to head out there and wreak whatever damage he could.

Kyle reached down and touched the dozens of vials of plague he had stored safely in his pouch, and a reassured smile crossed his face. Standing there, in the heart of London, he looked at the bustling crowds before him, all these pathetic little humans who had no idea what was about to come, the storm that he, single-handedly, was about to bring. He felt elated, like a kid about to enter a candy shop. Everywhere, there were crowds, alleys, bars— places to spread the plague. He was so giddy, he hardly knew where to begin.

But Kyle had to control himself. He knew that if he wanted to spread this plague thoroughly and professionally, he would need to enlist not only his mercenary vampires at arms, which he already had, but also an army of critters—rats. An army of rats would be much more effective, and much faster, at spreading the plague than he ever could, and so his first task was to find and infect them. He might also, of course, try to infect humans individually, and in large gatherings, but that would just be for fun.

Kyle practically bounced through the streets, ready to have some fun. As he saw a big fat man, swaggering with a bottle of gin in his hand, Kyle reached up and patted him hard on the back—as he did, sticking a small, infected needle into his shoulder blade.

The fat man screamed out, suddenly wide awake at the pain, but Kyle just bumped him hard and kept walking, disappearing into the crowd. Kyle smiled wide. The first infected was always such a great feeling.

Kyle saw a wild dog sniffing at a mound of garbage beneath his feet, and he dropped to one knee, suddenly grabbed the dog by its mane, and stuck a small needle right into its neck. The dog yelped, and tried to turn around to bite Kyle, but Kyle was faster. He leaned back in time and kicked it, sending it back several feet. The dog yelped again, and took off. Kyle smiled, knowing the damage it would do as it carried the plague all throughout the streets.

Kyle saw a vendor's stand up ahead, with rows and rows of fruit spread out over it. He walked up to it and the vendor stared back cautiously, staring at all the scars on his face. Kyle discreetly spread the plague on his hands, then reached up, and ran his palms all along the fruit, in one great swipe.

"Hey, get your hands off my fruit!" the man screamed.

Kyle smiled, grabbed an apple, reached back and hurled it at the man's throat. It was a perfect strike; the man reached up with both hands and grabbed at his throat, struggling to breathe from the blow.

As Kyle preceded down the block, he watched several humans crowd around the fruit he had just infected, feeling it. He smiled wide.

Now it was time to get serious. Kyle spotted a rotting wharf in the distance. Perfect. He knew exactly what he would find beneath it. Rats.

He hurried off to the riverbank and slipped down the muddy slope, until he was in the blackness beneath the wharf. There, he saw exactly what he'd expected: dozens of rats, crawling into and out of the water, scurrying under the wharf. They turned and hissed at him, and most began to flee. He laughed at the irony: rats scared of him.

But Kyle was faster than they. He zoomed in, using his instincts, on the Queen rat, and darted at her, grabbing her hard on the neck, reaching up, and injecting her. The rat hissed, trying to bite him, but Kyle chucked it far from him. He then reached out and grabbed another rat, and another, and another. In a dizzying array of speed, he managed to prick at least a hundred rats before they could flee from his super-fast reflexes.

Kyle had emptied a good portion of his vials, and, satisfied, he hurried back up the slope, away from the water. He stood at the top and brushed himself off, and looking down, saw the rats scurrying in every direction. He watched as several of them slipped into a large boat, crowded with humans, and as several more scurried up the riverbank, into the crowded streets. He knew that his job was done—at least for now. Within hours, they would infect every corner of this city.

Now it was time to get really serious. The humans were taken care of, but he still had to get the poison, the special poison, to kill Caitlin. He had to get to the Tower of London, and free his old vampire friend, and get him to tell him where it was.

Before Kyle could set off, he suddenly heard a distant roar. He looked out, across the Thames, and saw, in the distance, a small circular stadium, lit up from the torchlight. He heard another roar, and suddenly realized what it was: a bearbaiting stadium.

Kyle was overcome with joy. It had been centuries since he'd seen bearbaiting, and he missed it dearly.

Without thinking, he leapt into the air and flew over the river Thames, heading right for the stadium. It would also, he realized, serve a double purpose: there, he could infect thousands more humans. And more importantly, he could enjoy wreaking havoc personally. He felt a craving for violence, and it was time to let it out on someone.

Kyle knew, as he flew over the bearbaiting stadium, that he should stay focused, proceed to the London Tower, break his friend out, and get the poison. But he wanted to have some fun. He still had plenty of time, and he was still way ahead of schedule. He figured he could afford a small distraction to wreak some havoc of his own.

Kyle flew over the stadium and looked down, in the torchlight, at the thousands of humans packed in below, screaming, betting, at the bear tied in the middle, being attacked on all sides by dogs. It was his kind of fun.

He dove down, right for the stadium, and landed right in the center of the pit. As he did, he grabbed a dog from behind, picked it up, spun it over his head, and hurled it right into the bleachers.

There was a look of shock and amazement among the thousands of humans who watched him land, right in the center of the stadium, who watched him seemingly drop out of the sky. They all stood, gasping, wondering what on earth he could be. Several of them crossed themselves.

Kyle grabbed more dogs, throwing each one over the bleachers; as they landed in the seats, all worked up, they began biting humans.

Next, he ran right to the bear. The bear, sensing something, recoiled, trying to get away from Kyle.

But Kyle wasn't done. He grabbed the bear's chain and tore it off the pole. Then he picked up the chain, and swung the bear around and around. Finally, he threw it.

It landed in the bleachers. Humans shrieked, trying to run—but it was too late. The bear landed in the bleachers in a blinding rage. It swiped its paws left and right, murdering people with a single swipe. It bit, and chewed, and swiped, and trampled, killing every human in its path.

A stampede erupted, and humans trampled humans as they tried to get away. Even more people were crushed in the melee than the bear could kill. Within moments, the entire stadium was emptying out, people running in every which direction, screaming, hoping to make it out alive.

Kyle wasn't finished. He grabbed the torches along the sides and raced through the bleachers, setting everything on fire. Then he ran outside the stadium, and quickly circled the perimeter, setting fire in all directions, and barring all the entrances.

It worked. Most humans were trapped inside, as the flames and smoke grew higher. Kyle flew up, over the edge, and hovered over the Stadium, watching as the flames grew higher, as people screamed, trapped, and as the infuriated bear tore any survivors to pieces.

Kyle couldn't ask for a better start to his night.

CHAPTER TWELVE

Caleb flew, holding Ruth, Caitlin at his side, and Scarlet on her back. Caleb marveled at how inseparable Caitlin and Scarlet had become since they'd met. It was strange looking at them, as it seemed as if they'd always been together.

The four of them flew through the breaking sky of dawn, heading north towards his castle in Leeds. It had been a solemn departure this morning, as Caitlin and Sam had parted ways. The two had embraced, tears in their eyes, as they had each decided to go their own ways, to pursue their own clues. Caleb thought that Caitlin had made the right decision. Sam clearly needed to pursue his clue, and she needed to pursue hers.

Polly had surprised them by announcing that she was going with Sam. Sam had seemed surprised by that, too. But Polly had quickly added that it was purely for professional reasons, that she thought, since Caitlin had Caleb, it would be better to balance out the numbers, and have her help Sam. After all, they were all searching for the same thing. Sam hadn't seemed to object. Caleb smiled as he thought of it. It seemed obvious to him that the two of them liked each other, but that they were both set on not showing it.

Caleb thought of his love for Caitlin. He flew so close to her now, the sky blending into a million colors, their wings nearly touching, and felt such love for her. Their time together had been magical. They had managed to come back together, had been together the entire time, and finally, it felt like nothing was left to stand in their way. There was no Sera, no Blake, no other obstacles. It was just the two of them.

This physical place and time wasn't as dramatic as Paris or Venice, and yet, their time together now felt more romantic to him than ever. It made him realize that true love wasn't about where you lived. Caleb had never felt so happy, and he felt that Caitlin never had, either.

He discreetly reached to his side, and as he felt the bulge in his pocket, his heart lifted. His mother's ring. It was still there, safe and secure, and now, finally, the time felt right. They had a lull in their search. Sam knew where he was going, but Caitlin had no idea where her clue lead. Caleb didn't either. So, since they had nowhere to go, he'd used a tiny bit of trickery, looking for an opportunity to get some time alone with Caitlin, so that he could propose. When Caitlin had decided to leave Windsor

Castle and was standing there, unsure where to go, he had suggested an idea for where they might search. Trusting him, she had went along with it.

Now they flew north, to a place where Caitlin thought might lead them to a clue. But what she didn't know was that they were actually flying to one of Caleb's castles. Leeds Castle was one of his most beautiful properties, one he had bought centuries before. He had boarded it up the last time he had been there, and hoped that it was still in good condition. He owned castles in nearly every corner of the world, but this one was his favorites. It was also his most romantic property.

It came to him that it would be the perfect place to propose to Caitlin. He thought of the hilltop that overlooked the property, the wild grass and wildflowers in every direction that afforded a commanding view of the countryside. He knew that this would be the perfect place and time.

He had not expected to propose in front of anyone else, and was a bit caught off guard that Scarlet was with them, and Ruth. He would have to figure that out when the time came, but he was sure he could find a way to get just a few moments alone with her. Regardless, he was so happy that Scarlet was in their life, he would give up anything to have her there.

As they rounded a hilltop, Caleb's castle came into view. Sprawled out in the early morning sun, it was magnificent, just as he had remembered it. Built in a white limestone, with turrets in every direction, immaculately laid out in a large square, with an inner courtyard, and a drawbridge, it sat regal and proud, dominating the otherwise empty countryside. It stood empty, just as he'd hoped it would.

For now, he didn't want to actually bring her into the castle. Instead, he wanted to take her right to the hilltop overlooking the property. Caleb suddenly dove down, pointing, and Caitlin followed him.

Moments later, they landed on a plateau, at the top of a sprawling hill. It was the highest hill in the countryside, and from this vantage point, they could see forever. Caleb set Ruth down as he landed, and Caitlin set Scarlet down.

"Why have we landed here?" Caitlin asked.

Caleb had rehearsed a thousand times in his mind what he would say when the big moment came. But now that it was actually here, he found himself getting nervous, tongue-tied. His throat suddenly went dry, his hands were sweaty, and for a moment, he forgot what he was about to say.

"Wow, look at that castle!" Scarlet shouted, staring off at the horizon, pointing.

Caleb turned to her. "Sweetheart, I think Ruth needs to use the bathroom. Maybe you can take her to that small grove of trees, right over there?"

Caleb pointed at a small grove of trees, maybe thirty yards away, on the far side of the plateau, a place where he could keep them in sight, yet still have privacy to speak to Caitlin.

Scarlet took off with Ruth, thrilled to run through the grass, Ruth skipping beside her, playing as they went.

Caitlin gave him a puzzled look.

"What's got into you?" Caitlin asked. "You're acting funny."

He cleared his throat.

"Caitlin," he said, stopping, clearing his throat again. "There is something I've been meaning to—um—to—well—to—ask you—um—for centuries now. Every time I try, something seems to get in the way. But now, the time is right."

She looked at him, puzzled, and he could tell that she had absolutely no idea what he was talking about.

"I brought you here for a reason," he continued. "It's a very special spot for me. And for my family, throughout the centuries. That castle that you see on the horizon, it was used by my family for centuries. It is mine now. A place I can call home. A place, maybe one day, we can call home together."

Caitlin turned and looked at the castle, and gasped at the sight. He reached up and held her shoulders, and she turned back to him.

Her brown eyes were so beautiful against the breaking dawn. He reached up and ran the back of his hand along her face, brushing back her delicate brown hair.

"Caitlin," he said, "I want to spend the rest of my life with you. And there is something very important I need to ask you."

He reached back, felt the ring in his pocket, and he knew the time had come.

Slowly, he took it out, held it in his hand, and got down on one knee.

The time had come to be with her forever.

CHAPTER THIRTEEN

Sam flew in the morning sky, Polly beside him, heading towards Warwick Castle. Polly kept her distance from him, and he kept his. He was surprised she had decided to join him; she had made it clear that she was only accompanying him for professional reasons, to even out the teams, two and two, in the search for the shield. She reasoned that Caitlin didn't need backup, already having Caleb with her, and that Sam just might.

Sam resented that. He didn't need backup. He felt fine on his own. But he did like having Polly's company, even though she talked too much at times, and he was glad she had chosen to accompany him. He smiled inwardly, realizing that it must have killed her to admit that she wanted to go with him, since she had been trying so hard, all along, to make such a point of keeping a distance from him.

But since then, all through the flight, for hours, she had kept a far distance from him, and hadn't said a word. He was actually now beginning to wonder if she even liked him after all.

It upset him having to part ways with Caitlin. He had been so happy to have found her again, and was becoming comfortable in Windsor Castle—especially after that feast, and those incredible rooms. The last thing he wanted to do was leave Caitlin's side, especially after all the trouble he'd had in finding her, and to have to leave Windsor Castle. But it was clear from his dad's letter that that was what was needed—that they split up, and each search for him in a different direction.

He wondered why. Did they each have a different destiny? Would they ever be put together again, searching on the same track? And if his destiny was different, how was it different than Caitlin's? On the other hand, he liked having his own clue, a clue meant just for him, and him alone. He was excited to see where his clue lead him, to see what Warwick had in store, and to find out, finally, what his side of the search entailed.

They rounded a hilltop, and there, on the horizon, sat an enormous castle, the only structure in view for hundreds of miles. Clearly, this was the fabled Warwick Castle. The early morning sun lit it a shade of orange, and even from this distance, Sam could see it looked ancient. It was sprawling, and reminded him in some ways of Windsor Castle, with its high walls, parapets, open-air inner courtyard. This castle wasn't quite as big as Windsor, but it had some things which Windsor didn't, like a huge tower soaring hundreds of feet high, built upon a hill, with parapets. And it had several smaller towers, too.

Warwick Castle, he could see, was also built right on the bank of a river, and was thus protected entirely by water on one side. Like Windsor, it was completely surrounded by nature, by farmland, as far as the eye could see. And it was the only structure for hundreds of miles, lending an even more imposing presence in the otherwise rural landscape. The dirt road that approached it stretched forever, gradually sloping up the hill, making it even more imposing.

From Sam's bird's-eye perspective, though, it wasn't quite as imposing. In fact, from up here, it was beautiful, especially in the morning light.

Polly surprised him, suddenly dipping down low, diving in for a closer look, without even giving him any warning. Typical. He followed on her heels, swooping down, getting a closer look.

The parapets were manned with soldiers in every direction, and as they approached, Sam sensed something, and he could tell that Polly did, too. These were no ordinary soldiers. They were vampire soldiers.

Sam didn't sense any danger, though. On the contrary, he sensed kinship. A thrill ran through him, as he realized they'd found the place they were supposed to be, the place that his father had intended for him. Could it be that his father was behind those gates?

As they circled the castle, Sam debated where to land. Should they land on the road, and walk up and knock on the gate? Or should they just dive right into the inner courtyard?

He was about to ask Polly what she thought, when suddenly he heard something behind him, and turned.

There, to his surprise, were dozens of vampires, behind them, flying straight up into the air, like a flock of bats, and heading right for them. It looked like an entire army of vampires, and from this distance, Sam couldn't tell if they were coming in for an attack.

"Polly!" he yelled sharply.

She spun, and saw it, too.

Sam instinctively flew in front of her, protecting her, in case they should attack. He geared himself up for battle, ready to grapple with whatever came at him, though he could already tell, by their numbers, that the odds were not in their favor.

The vampires flew right for them, then suddenly stopped, just a feet away. Sam and Polly stopped, too, hovering in mid-air, facing them. Just feet away, the lead vampire glared at them.

"Aiden has sent us to bring you in," he said.

He didn't look exactly like family, but he didn't appear to be hostile either.

Polly moved forward, brushing Sam aside. "Aiden?" she asked, hopeful.

The vampire nodded back.

Suddenly, Polly's eyes lit up. "Tyler? Is that you?" she asked.

The facial features on the vampire softened, as he suddenly seemed to recognize her. "Polly?" he asked.

The two suddenly came in and embraced in mid-air.

Despite himself, Sam felt a surge of jealousy, felt his face reddening.

"Aiden lives here? You all live here?" Polly asked, her eyes open wide with hope.

Tyler nodded back. "We've been here for centuries," he said.

Tyler turned and looked at Sam, inquisitive.

"This is Sam," Polly said finally. But she had waited too long, Sam thought, annoyed.

Tyler looked him over, also looking jealous, and simply nodded coldly back.

"Well, what are we all waiting for?" Polly asked in delight "I can't wait to see Aiden!"

She was about to dive down, but Tyler reached out a hand, stopping her.

"I'm sorry, Polly," he said. "He only wants to see Sam for now."

Polly turned and looked at Sam, shocked. Sam was shocked, too.

"But by all means, come down and join us. You can join our sparring in the courtyard while those two talk."

Polly scanned the crowd of vampires, and saw faces she recognized, and moved forward and embraced several of them in mid-air.

They all dove down together, heading towards the ground, one big happy flock.

Tyler remained behind, however, staring coldly at Sam.

"Follow me," he said, diving down, in the opposite direction, towards a lone tower at a far corner of the castle.

Sam hovered there for a moment, watching Polly go the other way.

Grudgingly, resentfully, he turned and followed Tyler.

*

Sam followed Tyler sullenly through the courtyard of the castle. A part of him was in awe at the architecture all around him, the ancient limestone. It reminded him of Windsor castle, but smaller, older.

"William the Conqueror built this place in 1066," Tyler said, as he walked. "It's been around far longer than we have."

Sam only half-listened as they walked, trailing several feet behind. They weaved in and out of trails, through medieval archways and passages, down stone corridors, as he followed Tyler. He assumed that he was being lead to Aiden. But he was only half interested.

Dominating his mind, to his surprise, were thoughts of Polly. Did she love Tyler? Did she truly not care about Sam? And why should he even care? He hadn't thought that he'd really liked her. But now, he guessed, he was starting to realize, that maybe he felt more for her than he'd thought.

He was mad at himself. He promised himself he wouldn't fall for another girl, especially anytime soon. But now, he found himself getting distracted by thoughts of her. He realized it was probably nothing, that he was probably just caught off guard. He tried to force it out of his mind, to focus on what Tyler was saying.

"Did you hear what I said?" Tyler asked.

They stopped before a huge, arched open door, with an enormous brass lion head knocker on it. Sam looked at him, and realized he hadn't been listening.

"I love her," Tyler said. "Polly."

Sam's heart pounded. So, it was true.

"But not like that. I love her like a sister. I'm already married," Tyler said.

He placed a hand on Sam's shoulder. "It's obvious that she loves you. Take care of her," he said.

With that, he turned and strode off, away from the courtyard. Sam turned and watched him go, baffled.

Sam was shocked. Polly? Loved him? What made Tyler think that? Sam hadn't realized that at all. How was it obvious? It wasn't obvious to him.

"What about Aiden?" Sam yelled out, as Tyler kept walking away.

Tyler turned and looked back, a smile on his face. "I told you. Through that door. I'm afraid it is a walk you must take alone."

Sam turned and walked through the door, and found a narrow, circular stone stairwell before him. He entered and climbed the steps, circling again and again. As he did, he passed small, narrow windows in the stone, more like slits, through which he caught glimpses of the countryside, especially as he climbed higher.

After hundreds of steps, Sam was beginning to feel winded, when finally, he reached the top.

He stepped out, and found himself on top of a white, round tower, encircled by parapets.

There, standing with his back to him, was a man in a long white robe, long silver hair and beard to match, holding a staff.

As Sam reached the top, he couldn't help but be awestruck by the view: he could see the entire countryside spreading out for miles and miles on this crystal-clear morning. He felt nervous as he stood there, Aiden with his back to him, and started to wonder why he had been summoned. What was it that Aiden had to say to him? And why was it that his father's clue had led him here, to this place?

Whatever it was, Sam, defiant as always, resented being summoned here, resented having to stand there, like a chided schoolboy, and wait for Aiden.

"Yes," came Aiden's slow voice, his back still to Sam, "you do resent me. You resent everything. I can feel your resentment coursing through your veins."

Sam was shocked at how crisply his thoughts had been read. He felt embarrassed. But also, he felt understood for the first time.

Aiden slowly turned. His large eyes were vivid, shining blue. "And that is precisely why you have not evolved in your quest," Aiden added.

As he stared at Sam, with his vivid blue eyes, Sam found it hard to concentrate. He felt his thoughts being read, even as he thought them, and felt almost hypnotized by Aiden's presence. He hardly knew what to say, or how to respond.

Several moments of silence followed, and Aiden finally sighed.

"Your problem, Samuel, is that you let yourself be run by your emotions. Your love, your lust—for Samantha, for Kendra, for Polly. Your anger. Your resentment. Your revenge. You are caught in a whirlwind of primal emotions. You have not learned to evolve above them. To control them. Like your sister has."

Aiden slowly paced, looking out over the horizon.

"When she first came to me, she was much like you. Controlled by anger, by fury, by hatred. The product of your difficult upbringing. For you both."

He stopped and turned.

"But she learned how to control it. To control herself. She learned how to become bigger than her emotions. You, though, have not. You are still reckless. You have traveled back for hundreds of years, but you are still young. Still a teenager."

Sam felt himself reddening, felt himself on the defensive, ready to argue back, to snap back at Aiden, to storm out, to do all the things he might normally do. And at that moment, he realized, for the first time, that that was exactly what Aiden was talking about. He realized that Aiden was right, that he had summed him up perfectly. That he was not in control of his emotions, or himself.

And for the first time, Sam felt determined to take control of them. To not let himself be run by them. To not be reactive. To not yell back, or storm out. Instead, to his own amazement, he stood there and listened.

Aiden must have sensed the shift in the air, because he turned and stared at Sam.

"Yes, very good," he said, slowly. "I see that you do have the potential. Of course you do: you are of the same lineage as Caitlin. But with you, it's more complicated. She was turned by Caleb. But you were turned by Samantha. A strand of darkness runs deep in your turner, and so it must in you. Caitlin requested to be turned; you did not. And Samantha was filled with blackness."

Aiden paced.

"So, unlike Caitlin, you have both in you. The light and the darkness. Good and evil. So far, you have overcome the darkness. But you must be strong to never give in to it. It gives you great benefit—it gives you more physical power than Caitlin will ever have. Than nearly any vampire could ever have. But it also gives you

163

great potential for danger, for downfall. And it gives you a vastly different mission."

"What is my mission?" Sam asked, getting out words for the first time, his throat dry. "My dad's letter sent me here. Where's the next clue?"

Aiden shook his head, as if disappointed.

"So impatient," he said. "You are interested only in what benefits you. In grabbing the next clue and moving on. But you never stop to consider that perhaps, *I* am the clue."

Sam stared back, dumbfounded. *Aiden? The clue?*

"You were, in fact, not sent here for a physical thing. You were sent here to see me. By your father. You were sent here for training. Finding your father is not your destiny. That is Caitlin's. Your destiny is to guard over Caitlin on her quest. You are not the chosen one. She is."

Sam felt devastated to hear those words. On the one hand, he would be thrilled to watch over Caitlin, to protect his sister. On the other hand, he also wanted to feel chosen, to feel special. And hearing those words crushed him. Deep down, he had always sensed that he wasn't as special as her. And now, it was confirmed.

"You *are* special," Aiden corrected, reading his thoughts, "just in a different way. You were sent to me by your father to become all that you were meant to be. To harness your emotions. To learn how to summon your true, inner power. And to learn how to properly watch over Caitlin, until she fulfills her mission. You will meet your father too, one day, but the mission is hers to fulfill."

Sam felt anger well up within him. "What if I don't want to train with you? What if I don't want to stay here? What if I don't want to watch over Caitlin? Are you saying that I don't count?"

Aiden shook his head slowly. "Life is how you perceive it to be," he answered cryptically.

And that was all he said.

Sam stood there, fuming with emotion, feeling like bursting out of there, not knowing what to do.

Aiden took a step forward and fixed his eyes on him. "You are free to leave, of course. No one holds you here. You can go, but you will never be free. Because until you learn to master your skills, your biggest enemy is yourself."

CHAPTER FOURTEEN

Kyle flew through the London night, feeling happier than he had in ages. He hadn't had that much fun in he didn't know when. It put such joy in his heart watching that bear tear apart those humans, watching them trample each other. He smiled wider and wider, as he kept flashing to the images of the people screaming, being torn to bits—and one particular image, of watching the bear tear a man's torso in half. He felt like a kid again. He was happily surprised to realize that this night, and his entire time in London, was turning out to be much better than he'd expected.

He flashed back to his infecting all those rats under the wharf, and he imagined them, even now, racing through the streets, infecting other rats, carrying the plague to the far corners of London. He could see in his mind's eye all the fleas that the rats would host, and all the people the fleas would bite. The plague, in just a matter of hours, would begin to spread like wildfire. He laughed out loud. He couldn't help himself. He just hadn't expected to have this much fun, this quickly.

And if all this weren't enough, he was now on his way to see his old friend, Thor, who he hadn't seen in centuries. Thor had been stupid enough to get himself caught by a nest of rival vampires, and trapped in a human prison inside the Tower of London. It was a very special cell, and unlike other prisons, this one was above ground, held in the highest levels of the tower. Kyle relished the idea of seeing his old friend again, and of the gratitude his friend would show him for his breaking him free.

Not that Kyle necessarily wanted to do him any favors. Thor was evil and selfish and manipulative—which was precisely why they had become fast friends—and Kyle wasn't looking to do him any favors. But Kyle knew that if he dangled freedom before him, he would have to tell Kyle where the special vampire poison was. And with that in hand, Kyle could finally kill Caitlin, and her entire crew.

Kyle sped through the air, looking back over his shoulder one last time to get a good view of the former bearbaiting ring, now up in flames, the glow becoming distant on the horizon. Even from this great distance, he could still feel the heat, could still hear the faint screams of humans being trampled to death, burned alive, and the thought filled him with a new sense of purpose.

It would only be a matter of days until the entire city below him, right now, a mass of torchlight, was slowly extinguished, would become a huge burial ground. Maybe, if he killed enough of them, he could wipe out the human race for good, while killing Caitlin and her crew at the same time.

Kyle dove low, increasing speed, flying right over the Thames River, circling over the London Bridge. He circled to his left, and saw it, sprawled out below him: the Tower of London. He circled again and again, getting a good view of it, as memories flooded back to him, from all the times he'd visited throughout the centuries.

Kyle remembered when the tower had first been built, by William the Conqueror in 1066. Back then, it had just been a single tower. Over the centuries, they had added to it, building a complex of buildings, several towers, even a palace, and had encircled it with two huge walls of defenses, along with a moat. It had been an impressive work of architecture back then, and was still impressive now, towering over everything else in London. Over time, the humans used it for many things—a treasury, a royal palace, and most famously, a prison and execution ground. It was one of Kyle's favorite places in Europe.

As he circled again, Kyle could see how heavily fortified it was. Unlike in the 21st century, when the tower was just another tourist spot, now, in the 16th century, it was an active, working fort and prison. Hundreds of soldiers surrounded it, in every direction, preventing anyone from coming near it, and preventing anyone inside from escaping. An army of British guards stood before the walls, on top of the walls, on the drawbridges, around the moat, and they patrolled the courtyards. It was a sprawling complex, and there were guards in every possible direction.

Kyle dove down lower, zooming past the parapets, using his incredible vision to zoom in on every corner of the structure. It was exactly as he remembered, with four huge towers, spread out across the four corners, built in a nearly perfect square. He circled again and again, flying past the round towers, and used his senses, trying to sense and feel were Thor might be. In ancient times, they had kept the most dangerous vampire victims far below the earth. But Kyle's sources had told him that just a century ago, they had created a new cell, high up in the highest tower, a place where no vampire would expect to break out another. He had heard rumors of a specially built silver tower, its outer walls stone, but its inner walls completely lined with silver, a foot thick, and with silver bars on its windows.

As Kyle circled again, he suddenly felt it. There it was. The tower of the Northeast wing. He could feel the silver even from this great distance, and as he got closer, he felt sure that that was it. He knew, without a doubt, that Thor was inside.

Kyle dove and landed on the parapet, directly above the tower. There was a guard standing on its edge, looking out, and when Kyle landed behind him, the guard slowly turned. He looked at Kyle in shock, dropping out of the sky, and his bayonet dropped from his hand. His eyes open wide at the sight of the enormous, disfigured Kyle, landing just a few feet away.

Kyle grinned, and before the human could react, he took two huge strides, picked him up, and hoisted him right over the edge.

The human plummeted, flailing and screaming, and Kyle leaned over and watched him hit the ground with a splat.

The guard had made too much noise: now guards from every direction turned and looked. It had been stupid of Kyle, he knew; he should've just crept up behind him and snapped his neck silently. But Kyle couldn't resist: he loved watching humans plummet to earth—it was one of his favorite hobbies—and he just couldn't resist watching this one go.

But now he would pay the price. Dozens of guards blew whistles, and were already heading in his direction.

Kyle had to act quickly. He reached back, took aim, and punched a hole into the stone beneath him.

The thick, granite walls caved in, as stone went flying everywhere.

But Kyle withdrew his hand in pain; he had struck a layer of solid silver.

He was prepared for this. He reached into his sack, pulled out a special dust, and sprinkled it on the silver. A hissing noise, along with a cloud of steam, rose up, and Kyle leaned back, getting out of the way, as the silver corroded. Finally, it ate a hole large enough for Kyle to squeeze his body through, and jump down inside.

Kyle fell ten feet below, and landed on the stone, on his feet. He wheeled, and there, before him, just feet away, was his old friend: Thor.

Thor stood there, scowling back, a large scar running across the bridge of his nose. He was as ugly and nasty as Kyle had remembered.

"What the hell took you so long?" Thor barked.

Kyle grinned. That was his friend. Nasty, ungrateful. It brought back good memories.

"You're lucky I saved your sorry ass at all," Kyle retorted.

Thor just scowled.

"What do you want?" he asked. "I know a selfish bastard like you wouldn't waste his time unless there was something on his mind."

Kyle grinned. At least Thor got right to the point.

"The poison," Kyle said. "The one you used in the Dark Ages. The one that you killed our coven leader with. The vampire poison. I need it now."

Thor broke slowly into a smile, an evil, crooked smile.

"And why should I help you? I might just sit here and rot, just for the sake of not giving you what you want. Besides," he added, "you already punched a hole in the wall—I can break out now without you. In fact, I think I will."

Thor stepped up and shoved Kyle, and Kyle felt himself go flying back through the air, smashing hard into the wall.

Kyle was shocked. He hadn't remembered Thor being that strong. Maybe all the centuries of waiting had built a tremendous strength in him.

Kyle shook it off, just in time to see Thor reaching up and about to jump up through the hole in the ceiling.

Kyle broke into action. He dove and grabbed Thor' legs at the last second, and yanked him back down. He hurled him in a circle, and smashed him hard into the opposite wall.

Now it was Thor turn to look shocked. He wiped blood from his lips, breathing hard.

"You wait any longer, they'll patch that hole," he said to Kyle. "We'll both be stuck in here."

"So be it," Kyle answered. "If I don't get what I want, then neither do you."

Thor looked back at him, sweating, in a sudden panic.

"You're bluffing," Thor said. "You wouldn't risk being jailed in here."

Kyle grinned back.

"You bastard," Thor said. "You would, wouldn't you? Just to spite me?"

Thor' expression morphed into a scowl, and he charged Kyle with an unearthly growl.

Kyle snarled back, and charged his friend, too.

The two met in the middle, like two rams meeting, with a tremendous crash. Their grunts and snarls filled the room, as the two of them tested each other, wrestling, slamming each other wall to wall, to the ground, back up onto the wall. They destroyed rock and stone in every direction, but neither one got the best of the other.

They fell and wrestled on the ground, and each held the other in a deathly grip, grunting and sweating, out of breath, neither gaining an inch.

Suddenly, a dozen guards stood over the hole, looking down, shouting at each other.

"They'll fill that hole any minute," Thor grunted.

"It's your freedom to lose," Kyle grunted back, not giving in.

They continued trying to choke each other for several more seconds; finally, losing the game of chicken, Thor released his grip.

He leaned back and shook his head. "You haven't changed," he said. "Not one drop. You're still a stubborn bastard."

"So you'll give me the poison?" Kyle asked.

"If I never see your ugly mug again."

Kyle grinned.

He suddenly jumped up into the air, breaking through the hole in the ceiling, knocking back several guards just as they were preparing to put a huge plate of silver back over it.

Thor followed, kicking several guards out of the way, and sending a few over the edge, screaming to their deaths.

Kyle grabbed one soldier by the feet and swung him like a ragdoll, knocking all the others like bowling pins off the edge. Then, with one final spin, he hurled that soldier as far as he could. Kyle watched with glee as he went flying, head over heels, through the air, and crashing down to earth with a shriek.

"Where is it?" Kyle asked Thor.

"There. In the tower."

Kyle's eyes opened wide. He'd guessed that they'd have to travel far and wide to find it; he'd never imagined that Thor would be so crafty to store his most valuable treasure right under his captors' feet.

Thor suddenly flew across the courtyard, and Kyle followed on his heels. He dove down, and landed on a far rampart of the tower.

Thor went over to an unusually large stone, bent down, scraped out the mortar, and revealed a secret opening.

Kyle leaned over, and was shocked to see a small vial of bright green liquid. He reached in to grab it.

Thor reached out and grabbed his wrist, stopping him.

"You touch that vial, and you die," Thor said. "It's porous."

Thor wrapped his sleeve around his hand, reached in, and grabbed the vial with his sleeve. He then held it up for Kyle to look at. It bubbled, glowing a bright green against the moonlight.

Kyle was shocked that Thor had just saved his life. And he was furious at himself for being so stupid to almost grab it.

"Why didn't you just let me grab it?" Kyle asked. "Why didn't you just let me die?"

Thor looked at him and grinned. "Life is just a little bit more interesting with you in it." Then his grin widened. "And after all, what else are friends for?"

CHAPTER FIFTEEN

Caitlin stood there, on the hilltop, staring back at Caleb, and she could not for the life of her figure out why he was acting so strangely. She had never seen him so nervous, so at a loss for words. She even thought she could see drops of sweat on his forehead, and she had never seen him sweat before. Why was he so nervous?

Was being back here, at his family's home, making him nervous for some reason? she wondered. And what was it that he wanted to talk to her about?

Caleb suddenly knelt down on one knee, keeping his eyes fixed on her.

"Caitlin, I have lived for centuries, but you are the one and only love of my life. If I have to live a thousand more years, there's no one else I would rather spend it with."

Suddenly, something clicked for Caitlin. He was down on one knee. He was talking about spending the rest of his life with her. He was reaching into his pocket, and as she watched, he pulled out a small, black velvet box.

Her heart leapt into her throat. She was utterly shocked. She had never expected this.

She loved Caleb with all her heart, and had always wished that they could be together forever, that she could spend eternity with him. But she had never quite known if he'd felt the same, if he'd felt as strongly about her as she had about him. And in the vampire world, forever truly meant *forever*, and she assumed that vampires rarely, if ever, proposed to each other. She had always believed that if a vampire ever proposed to another vampire, then that, more than anything, would be a sign of true love. It made human love pale in comparison. It was a love that truly meant forever.

She already felt as if she had known Caleb for lifetimes. Everything felt right when she was with him. And as he knelt there, and opened the box, and she saw the huge, magnificent sapphire and ruby ring, excitement rushed through her.

She was being proposed to. Asked to be married. To spend a life with someone. There was a man in the world who loved her enough to want to spend eternity with her. She could hardly breathe.

When she was young, a little girl, she had dreamed of a day like this. But she had never dared to imagine, even in her wildest dreams, that something like this would happen in such a miraculous, beautiful place as this, atop a hill, overlooking a beautiful countryside, a gorgeous ancient castle—and more than anything, by the man she loved. And she never dreamed she would be offered such an exquisite, magnificent ring. She felt weird even taking it.

"Caitlin," he continued, as he broke into a slow smile, "will you marry me?"

He slowly extracted the ring from its box, and held it out.

She slowly reached out her hand, which was shaking, as he slipped it onto her finger.

Caitlin was shaking so much, she could hardly speak. She wanted to scream YES, but her throat went dry, and her voice got stuck in her throat.

"Yes," she finally managed to whisper, as she started crying. "A thousand times, yes."

Caleb stood, and they embraced. It felt so good to hug him, to feel his body wrapped around hers, and she felt the tears pouring down her cheeks as he did. This was all she had ever wanted from the world. To be with a man who loved her as much as she loved him. And to be with him forever. To know that he was hers, and that he always would be.

Caitlin leaned back, as Caleb did the same, and the two stood there, faces just inches away.

She could see the love in his eyes, and they both leaned in and kissed each other. She felt her whole world melt with that kiss, which they held for seconds.

Finally, slowly, they pulled back. She reached up and placed her hand on his cheek.

"I love you," she said. "And I always will."

"Mommy?" suddenly came a voice.

They both spun and saw Scarlet and Ruth skipping towards them.

Caitlin knelt down and reached out and gave her a huge hug as she ran into her arms. She picked her up, and spun her around.

"What happened?" Scarlet asked. "Why are you crying?"

Caitlin set her down, and held her by her shoulders.

"Scarlet," she said, "we have some very good news for you. We're getting married!"

Married. It felt so unreal to say it. As she did, the word resonated through her body like a bomb. *Married. Marriage.* She couldn't believe it. Her. It was really happening to *her.* Not to one of her friends. But to *her.*

Scarlet screamed in delight, and Ruth barked by her side.

"Married married married!" she yelled.

Scarlet jumped up and down hysterically, and leapt into Caleb's arms, too.

"Can I come? Can I be the flower girl? Can I wear a pretty dress?"

After spinning her, a huge grin on his face, Caleb set her down.

"Of course you can," he said.

"Then where will we live after that? Where will our home be?"

Caitlin looked over at Caleb, who slowly looked back to her. They both knew that the time had come to make a formal decision about Scarlet. They both could read each other's minds: it was time to formally adopt Scarlet, to officially make her part of their family. They wanted her to be their child. To make official what was already unofficial, since the moment they'd met her.

Caleb nodded gravely back at Caitlin, silently giving her permission to speak for them both.

Caitlin knelt down, and brushed the hair out of Scarlet's face.

"Sweetheart," Caitlin said, beaming, "We have some even better news for you. If you'd like, we want you to be our daughter. Our *real* daughter. We want to truly be your mommy and daddy. Would you like that?"

Scarlet teared up, and tears rolled down her cheeks.

"I was hoping you'd ask me that," she said.

She went in and gave Caitlin a hug, tightly gripping her leg, then ran over, and gave Caleb one, too. Caitlin picked her up, and she and Caleb all embraced her in a single hug, each planting a kiss on her forehead.

"From the second I saw you," Scarlet said, "I never loved two people more."

CHAPTER SIXTEEN

Sam walked with Polly through along the river bank, on the outskirts of Warwick Castle. After his meeting with Aiden, he had stormed out of the castle, upset, and had run into Polly, who'd been catching up with her old coven members. Polly had seen the upset on his face, and had suggested that the two of them take a walk.

They had been walking for hours now, along the riverside, Sam barely saying a word. He knew he was being rude, and should be talking more, telling her what was on his mind—but he had been too overwhelmed by his emotions. Everything that Aiden had said was whirling through his mind, again and again, each pronouncement going off like a new bomb.

Caitlin was the chosen one, not he. His mission was only to guard Caitlin. He wasn't special. He had his own destiny. He didn't choose to be turned—Caitlin did. The person who turned him was darker, evil. He had evil blood running through his veins. He had a possibility of slipping to the dark side. He was way more powerful than nearly any vampire. But much more vulnerable to slipping. And his clue, his father's clue for him, ended here. At Warwick Castle. To train with Aiden.

Sam didn't know what to feel, as he thought through all of this. Part of him was furious, wanted to scream at Aiden, to tell him that he didn't know what he was talking about. Another part of him, though, deep down, sensed that it was all true, that he had always suspected something like this. A part of him felt like a failure, felt insignificant. Another part of him felt important, that he was so powerful. He felt tugged in all different directions.

As if all this were not enough, he also kept thinking about what Tyler had said to him, before they'd parted ways. That it was obvious that Polly loved him.

Sam stole a sideways glance at her, saw her strolling along, looking at the grass, the river, the trees, the sky. She seemed happy. But that was probably only because she had just been reunited with her friends. It didn't seem obvious at all that she loved him. In fact, it didn't even seem that he liked her much.

She had, though, invited him to go on this walk, seeing how upset he was. That meant a lot to him, and he appreciated her company. He really appreciated her respecting his need for silence, but figured he should probably say something to her now.

He cleared his throat.

"The meeting didn't quite go as I had expected," Sam began.

She looked at him, concerned.

"What do you mean?" she asked.

Sam thought about how to phrase it.

"Well, um, Aiden, he…is not exactly what I expected."

Polly seemed happy that he was talking again. "I know, he's the best, isn't he? He taught me so much. All of us. And your sister, specially. She's like a whole different person after training with him," she said in a rush, excited, as always. "What did he say to you? What did he tell you? Where will your dad's clue lead us next?"

Sam shook his head. In a somber, broken voice, he said, "The clues won't lead me anywhere else." He paused. "This visit is the end of the road for me. It led me to Aiden. That was my clue. It was a message from my father. He wants me to train with Aiden."

Polly looked at him, confused. "I don't understand," she said.

Sam stopped, and faced her. "Aiden said that my mission is different from Caitlin's. That *she's* the special one. That *she* is the one meant to find him. My mission is only to protect her."

Polly stared back at him.

"Aiden wants me to stay here. To train with him. He said I'm not ready yet. That I'm still run by my emotions. That I have a lot to learn. Do you agree?"

Polly looked at him, and her expression softened a bit.

"I think we all have a lot to learn," she said. "And you can be a little bit of a hot-head, yes," she said with a smile.

Sam couldn't help smiling back. Polly had a way of making it hard for him to stay mad at anything.

"But he also said I have a dark side. That I was turned by an evil person. That, if I'm not careful, I can slip to the dark side."

"But we all have good and dark sides," Polly said. "That's not necessarily a bad thing. It just forces us to be disciplined to stay on the right side. I think any of us, at any time, can be good or bad, can always slip."

Polly paused.

"The person that turned me wasn't the best of people," she added, softly, her expression darkening.

Sam looked at her in surprise. He never stopped to consider who had turned her.

"I was born a half-breed, to vampire and human parents, and they abandoned me on an island. But later in life, I was also turned. Fully turned. By a boy—a stupid boy. It was a dumb relationship mistake. I was in love with him for about a minute. And then I realized, too late, what a jerk he was. The first of many bad boy decisions, I guess," she said with a sigh.

Sam stared at her.

"So you see," she added, "it's not just you. I have it in me, too. And I haven't turned to the dark side. So it doesn't mean that you will, either."

Sam felt better talking to her. He didn't know what he would have done without her here.

"So you think I should stay here, and train?" he asked, hesitantly.

"You're lucky Aiden made you the offer. You should be grateful for that. Of course you should. Don't you want to become the best fighter you can be?"

Sam thought about that. She was right. He did want to become the best he could be. And until Caitlin needed his protection, he figured it was as good a place to be as any.

Sam found himself wondering if Polly would stay here, too. He felt butterflies in his stomach as he realized, finally, that he wanted her near him.

"Are you going to stay, too?" he asked, hesitant, not wanting her to hear in his voice that he cared.

But his tone must have given him away, because she suddenly broke into a big smile.

"And if I won't?" she asked. "Will you miss me?" she said, her smile widening playfully.

Sam looked away, and felt his face turning bright red.

"You're blushing," she said, with a giggle.

Sam's face reddened even more.

"I—uh—um—I—never—I never said that I would *miss* you," he said, stumbling over his words, trying desperately to sound neutral.

Polly giggled. "You don't have to. I can see it in your face."

Sam suddenly looked directly at her, and he could see that she was staring right back at him. This time, she wore a new expression. For the first time, it was finally clear to him that she liked him. They locked eyes, and neither of them looked away.

"Aiden said that I wasn't special," Sam said softly, staring into her eyes.

Polly took a step forward, and placed the back of her hand on his cheek.

"You're special to me," she said.

Sam felt his heart pounding, as he slowly leaned in towards her, and as she slowly leaned in towards him. He saw her lips approaching, and knew that they were about to have their first kiss.

Suddenly, right before their lips met, a trumpet sounded. They both, startled, wheeled and looked. A group of their coven members were sounding trumpets, and waving huge flags in their direction.

"THE GAMES BEGIN!" one of them shouted. "Aiden wants you both here!"

Their moment ruined, Sam and Polly both looked away from each other, self-conscious. They both turned and began walking back, both keeping their distance, embarrassed to even hold hands in sight of everyone else.

Sam, his heart still racing, couldn't help wondering if a moment like that would ever come for them again.

CHAPTER SEVENTEEN

Sergei opened his eyes, and quickly raised his hands to cover them, as they burned from the light. He struggled to see where he was.

He was lying in mud, on a steep slope on the bank of a river. He turned his head again away from the light, covering his eyes, which burned a hole through his skull. He looked up and saw that he was underneath some sort of rotting bridge, and he scrambled into the shadows, recessing further and further back.

Finally, he could breathe again, and slowly opened his eyes. He took stock of his surroundings, and could tell right away that he was in London. He was, in fact, under the London Bridge, a bridge he could recognize anywhere. He looked up and saw the rotting wood underneath it, saw the huge, stone foundations on the other side, saw the parade of boats passing through the Thames. He recessed further, deeper underneath the bridge, and rats scurried to get out of his way. Deeper and darker in the shadows, he was beginning to feel more like himself.

"Hey you!" came a voice. "That's my spot!"

Sergei saw a bum shuffling towards him, holding an empty flask of gin, stumbling. "You better move, if you know what's good for you!"

Sergei was in no mood for a human now. This trip back had been especially rough, and his head was still splitting, as if he had a thousand hangovers.

"Did you hear what I said?" the bum yelled. "I'm going to teach you—"

Having had enough, Sergei suddenly jumped up and lashed out. In a single move, he used his long fingernails to slice the man's throat.

The bum's eyes opened wide in shock as he dropped his flask and reached up to try to stop the blood pouring from his throat.

Sergei felt his fangs suddenly grow long, and realized how hungry he was. This bum, he realized, had come along at the perfect time.

Seeing the fangs extending from Sergei's mouth, the bum's eyes opened five times wider, and he stumbled backwards, crossing himself, trying to get away.

But it was too late. Sergei was ravenous now. He leapt forward and sank his fangs long and deep into the man's neck. The bum screamed out, and Sergei reached up with his free hand

and clamped his mouth shut, as he sucked deeper and deeper, the blood rushing through his veins.

In a few seconds, he felt the bum's struggling body go limp. He drank his fill, then let the body collapse onto the mud.

The man's blood coursing through him, Sergei felt himself again. He looked down at the lifeless corpse, and disgusted, gave it a hard kick.

It rolled several times, then landed into the Thames, and started slowly floating downstream. Sergei smiled at the sight, watching the lifeless corpse bob and float along the water. He imagined the expression of a passing fisherman who came across it, saw it floating past his boat, and his smile grew even wider. He couldn't stand humankind, and he wished that the entire river before him was filled with nothing but floating corpses.

But in the meantime, he had work to do. He had come back in time yet again to make amends to Kyle. He was still set on being Kyle's loyal servant, and on leading Kyle's army, on one day leading the war in New York, if Kyle should see fit to appoint him, and if he could find his way back. He knew that he messed up in Paris, letting Caitlin slip through his fingers. He thought that he had done his best to seduce Polly. He had used her and deceived her. He smiled at the thought. Nothing made him happier than deceiving and abusing women.

But in the end, he had not succeeded. And now, in this time, and in this place, he would make it up to Kyle. He would find Polly again. He would find a way to deceive her again. It was his favorite pastime. And since he already attracted her once, he felt confident that he could attract her again. This time, he would use Polly to get to Caitlin, and then he would present them both to Kyle as his trophy.

Sergei smiled at the thought of it. Kyle would love him forever.

The sun was close to setting, and Sergei was beginning to feel like a new man. The thought of taking advantage of Polly, yet again, filled him with a perverse joy. He was so overcome with joy, that he couldn't help himself.

He leaned back and summoned his vocal skills, and belted out an aria from a Beethoven Symphony. As he sang, in his professional voice, louder and louder, expertly hitting all the notes, the sound echoed underneath the bridge, and slowly drew a huge crowd of puzzled bystanders above, all wondering where it was coming from.

Of course, they had no idea that it was coming from right beneath them, from a singular vampire who was intent on destroying them all.

CHAPTER EIGHTEEN

Sam stood on the training ground, holding a long staff, facing off with yet another of Aiden's men. There were dozens of his warriors there, and by now, Sam had faced nearly all of them. None of them had posed even the slightest challenge.

Sam didn't know what it was, but it seemed as if everyone else were moving in slow motion next to him. He'd anticipated their every move, was always a second ahead of them, always felt when to sidestep, dodge, duck, or strike. It had been like cutting through butter, and Sam was amazed at his own skills and power.

Facing him now was Cain—large, muscular, and holding a long staff just like Sam's. He charged, scowling.

But he was no match for Sam. As Cain swung wildly, Sam blocked blow after blow. Cain couldn't get anywhere close.

When Sam was ready, he knocked Cain's staff clear out of his hands with one sharp strike, and the staff when flying over his head, and into the crowd. Sam then followed up with a hard jab in the solo plexus, knocking Cain to his knees.

An impressed groan rose up from the crowd, and Sam stood there, victorious, yet another coven member down.

Aiden stepped out of the crowd, towards Sam, facing him.

"You are losing," Aiden said, disapprovingly, slowly shaking his head in front of everyone.

Sam didn't know what he meant. He had defeated everyone who had appeared, and easily. He felt stronger than he ever had. He had listened to Aiden's lessons all morning long, and he felt as if he were following every one of them, and becoming a better warrior with each bout. How was he losing? What did he mean?

"You are still fighting from the wrong place," Aiden continued. "You fight from *here*," he reached out and touched Sam's heart. "Not from *here*," he added, reaching out and touched Sam's forehead.

"You don't know what you're talking about," Sam spat back, defiant. "Not one of your people could beat me. And you're embarrassed. That's all it is. I fought perfectly. You just refuse to admit it."

There was a startled gasp from the crowd. No one had ever spoken to Aiden that way before.

But Sam wasn't afraid. He called things as he saw them.

Aiden slowly shook his head.

"Reactive," he said. "Too reactive. Just because you win, doesn't mean that you will always win. Winning or losing doesn't matter. Fighting from the right place is what matters. Your technique is still external. Not internal. Your emotions control you."

Suddenly, Aiden extracted a staff from within his robe, swung it, and cracked Sam hard along the rib cage.

Sam yelled out in pain, feeling the bruise in his ribs. He dropped to one knee, and looked up in astonishment. He hadn't noticed Aiden holding a staff—and, more surprisingly, he had never seen a blow coming. How could Aiden have possibly moved that fast? It was like, one moment, he was standing there, and the next, he was in pain.

Sam looked up at Aiden, blind with rage. He had embarrassed him in front of all the others—and *no one* embarrassed him.

Sam leaned his head back with a primal snarl, and lunged right for Aiden's throat.

Sam leapt through the air, both hands extended, aiming right for Aiden's throat. He couldn't control the rage that was overcoming him. He knew in the back of his mind that he should control himself—but he couldn't. He was out for blood, and he didn't care who it was.

But just at the moment when Sam expected to feel his hands closing in on Aiden's throat, Sam instead felt himself go flying through the air, and land, face first, in the mud.

Sam turned, and looked up, and saw Aiden standing off to the side.

How had he done that? A second before, he had been there. Somehow, he had gotten out of the way and thrown Sam, before Sam could even reach him.

Aiden was still shaking his head.

"Reactive," he said. "Predictable. You rely on your strength. It is your biggest asset. But also your biggest weakness."

Sam leaned back and roared, a primal roar, feeling a rage course through him like never before. It shook the entire place. Without thinking, he rolled over and grabbed a spear, hoisted it and aimed it right for Aiden's heart.

The crowd gasped in horror.

Aiden managed to sidestep it, though, and it went flying past him, into a tree many yards away.

Sam would not be appeased. He grabbed whatever weapon he saw before him—a huge battle axe—held it with two hands, and charged right for Aiden. Even as he was doing it, Sam, on some level deep inside, was shocked by his own actions. It was as if an evil strain were coursing through him, one he couldn't predict or control, forcing him to do so. Deep down, he didn't want to kill Aiden. But some new, unknown, evil part of him had been sparked, and it was carrying him away on its own wings. He realized, even as he was doing it, that there was nothing he could do to control it. He realized, in some deep part of himself, that, paradoxically, Aiden had been right all along.

But it was too late. He swung down, right for Aiden's chest, ready to cut him in half.

There was another horrified gasp from the crowd, and Sam expected to feel the blade entering Aiden's flesh.

But at the last second, instead, he felt himself go flying through the air, and felt the blade plunge into the mud.

Sam, bent over, his back exposed, felt a sharp point in the small of his back.

He turned and saw Aiden standing there, unharmed, holding a sharp spear to his back.

Finally, Sam realized he was defeated, broken. The fighting spirit inside him departed, and the evil strand that had overcome him passed just as quickly. He felt emptied out, hollow, embarrassed, and remorseful.

Aiden stood there, scowling down.

All the other vampires, except Polly, started to charge towards Sam, as if to exact revenge for their leader.

"No!" Aiden shouted, and the vampires all stopped. "He's not in control of what he does. I don't want him harmed."

Aiden reached down and held out a hand. Sam felt terrible, so guilty, as he slowly reached up and took it, and allowed himself to be pulled to his feet by Aiden, the man who he had just been prepared to kill.

Sam hung his head low. "I'm sorry," he said.

"Don't apologize to me," Aiden answered. "Apologize to yourself. You are reckless. A danger to us all. This is why you were not chosen. And until you acknowledge your faults, you will never overcome them."

Sam looked up into Aiden's eyes, took a deep breath, and finally realized he was right. He realized that he did, indeed, have so much to learn.

"Will you teach me?" Sam asked. "I am ready now."

Aiden stared back, and Sam couldn't decipher the expression in his eyes. But suddenly, Aiden's eyes drifted higher, towards the sky, clearly watching something.

Sam turned, to see what it was.

Sam's heart leapt. There, on the horizon, flying towards them, was a group of vampires, flying low.

And leading them was his sister.

CHAPTER NINETEEN

Caitlin flew through the air, Scarlet on her back, Caleb beside her, holding Ruth, and Lily on Caleb's back. Coming off the proposal, Caitlin was still ecstatic, riding on cloud nine, and her life felt surreal. She had been brimming with joy the entire flight, ever since they'd left Leeds Castle, ever since the moment Caleb had proposed to her, and since they had adopted Scarlet. They had stopped only to pick up Lily at Windsor Castle, and to tell her the news.

Lily had been so ecstatic and delighted, she hadn't stop screaming for ten minutes. She'd gushed over Caitlin's ring, and embraced them both. She'd insisted on coming with them, on being there when Caitlin broke the news to Sam and Polly and Aiden's entire coven.

They had been flying for hours now, heading towards Warwick to break the big news, and all the while, Caitlin hadn't been able to stop turning over in her mind the big moment when Caleb had proposed to her. It had been so surreal, had happened so quick, out of nowhere, and she kept reliving it, again and again. Her heart filled to the brim. She felt that now, flying beside Caleb, and with Scarlet, Ruth and Lily there with them, and about to be surrounded by her brother and all their friends, she truly had all that she needed in the world. She wished that she could just freeze this moment, and that everything would stay like this forever.

In fact, she wondered if maybe it could. She had no idea where her next clue led, and no concrete leads to follow until she figured it out. Unless Sam had a new lead, she saw no reason why she couldn't stay with Aiden's people for a while, live in peace, and enjoy this moment. And, of course, plan the wedding. She figured that a vampire wedding, as rare as it was, must be an extraordinary event.

Caitlin dove down with the others as Aiden's coven came into view. She found them all, as she suspected, on the training ground, and spotted Sam in the middle, facing Aiden. She was happy to see that he was here, training, and that Polly was not far from him.

They dove in and landed, and as they did, the coven parted ways for them. She set Scarlet down, as Caleb set Ruth and Lily down.

Polly broke through the ranks and hurried over to her.

"OH MY GOD!" Polly screamed out, as she reached over and lifted her hand, holding it close, inspecting, "IS THAT A RING!?!?!?"

Polly screamed in delight as she grabbed Caitlin's hand and held it up, inspecting it, her mouth wide open, her eyes wide in excitement, bringing her hand to her mouth in shock.

Caitlin beamed, knowing that Polly lived for news like this. Polly got excited by even the smallest news—so news like this must have been like an earthquake in her world.

"Yes," Caitlin said, beaming, "it's true. We're engaged!"

A big roar of approval rose up from all the coven members, as the tension in the air seemed to break.

Polly jumped up and down like a child.

"OH MY GOD OH MY GOD OH MY GOD!!!!!" Polly screamed, over and over. She gave Caitlin a huge hug, wrapping her arms around her tight.

Caitlin smiled over her shoulder, and hugged her back.

"I'm so happy for you! I'm so excited! How did it happen!? Tell me every detail! When is the wedding? Can I be your maid of honor?!?"

Before Caitlin could respond, Polly broke away from her and ran over and hugged Caleb.

Caitlin didn't know which question to answer first. She hadn't even thought of when the wedding would be, and hadn't given any thought to a maid of honor. But as soon as Polly said it, she realized that felt right. She would be honored to have her as her maid of honor. Although she still had no idea what was involved in a vampire wedding, or what it would even look like.

All the other coven members quickly hurried over, surrounding Caitlin and Caleb, embracing them, asking them a million questions at once. Caitlin recognized so many faces from the past, and she felt very loved. She was thrilled to share the news with all of them, and delighted to see the excitement on all their faces.

Sam stepped forward slowly from the crowd, and looked at her. As he did, he looked dazed and confused, as if he had just been interrupted from something. She could not figure out his expression, or what was going on with him. She couldn't tell if he was happy for her or not. He just looked startled.

"Sam?" she asked. She truly hoped that he would be happy for her.

"Is it true?" he asked. "You guys are getting married?"

Caitlin nodded back, beaming. She reached over and held Caleb's hand. "It's true," she said.

Sam stepped up and hugged her, a strong embrace, and she could feel the power coursing through his veins.

He slowly turned and looked to Caleb, then reached over and hugged him, too.

"I've always liked you," Sam said. "Take good care of her."

"I will," Caleb said.

"When is the wedding?" Polly asked.

"Where are you guys get married?" Tyler asked.

"How many people will you invite?" asked another.

"Are you going to have an engagement party?" someone else asked.

Caitlin's mind spun with all these questions. She had always dreamed of her wedding day, and now that preparations were finally here, she felt overwhelmed by all the things that lay ahead of her.

"Can I be your flower girl?" Scarlet asked.

Everyone laughed.

Caitlin draped her arm over her shoulder, and kissed her forehead. "Of course you can."

Caitlin picked her up and held her, and suddenly turned to everyone.

"Everyone, Caleb and I have more big news: Scarlet is our daughter now."

The entire crowd shouted with excitement, running over and giving Scarlet a big hug.

"I never knew that you had such a big family," Scarlet said to Caitlin, and the crowd laughed.

Aiden stepped forward, and Caitlin turned to him. She hadn't considered what his reaction to all of this might be, and seeing him now in the flesh, she was a bit worried, wondering what he would say. He was always so serious, so focused on training, she wondered what he would think of a wedding. Would he consider it a distraction?

Behind his silver beard, she saw him break into a small smile.

"Happiness is a good thing," he said. "Very powerful. But remember: you have an important destiny in this world. Never lose focus."

He turned and disappeared into the crowd, and before she knew it, he was completely gone.

As Caitlin turned she saw Sam standing there, his head down. He had a funny expression, as he watched Aiden leave. She knew something was wrong with him, and wanted to know what it was. Was it related to her engagement? Or was it something else?

She also wanted to know what clue he had found, and why her father's letter had sent him to this place.

"Sam," she said, approaching. He looked up. "Can we talk?"

Looking despondent, he slowly nodded.

Caitlin leaned in and kissed Caleb. "Excuse me for just one moment," she said, as she took a few steps off to the side of the crowd, which was now swarming around Caleb and Scarlet.

"What is it?" Caitlin asked Sam, as soon as they were out of earshot. "Are you not happy for me?"

"No, not at all," Sam said, suddenly putting on a forced smile. "I'm thrilled for you. I'm sorry. I didn't mean for it to seem that way. It's not that at all."

"So what is it?" she asked.

"It has nothing to do with you," he said.

"Well?" she prodded. "What is it?"

Sam hesitated. Finally, he took a deep breath.

"It's Aiden. I realize it now. Everything he said is true. I'm not in control of my emotions. I behaved badly."

Caitlin understood. She had been there. It had been a long, hard struggle for her to regain control, and she still felt as if it were a daily battle, and that she were learning something new every day. She felt her journey was far from over, but she also felt she'd come a long way. She remembered what it was like in the early days, and how Sam was feeling now: emotions and passions seemed to consume you, it was so hard to control them.

She reached over and placed a conciliatory hand on his shoulder.

"It's okay," she said. "I've been there. We all make mistakes. Training is a process. It doesn't happen on day one."

Sam seemed to brighten a little. Caitlin remembered how she had always had a way of making him feel better, even growing up, even in their terrible little apartment in New York.

"Tell me about the clue," she said to him. "Warwick. Dad's letter. What did you find?"

Sam slowly shook his head.

"That's the other thing. Aiden told me that there is no clue. That *he* is the clue. That this place is the clue. My being here." Sam lowered his head. "He said that *you* are the one who's meant to find Dad. I'm only meant to protect you. My part of the mission is ended. You are the special one."

Caitlin was shocked at his words. She had never imagined that she was more special than Sam, or that their missions were different. It made her feel burdened, as if she carried the final remaining clue to whatever it was they needed to find.

"But I have no idea what my clue means," she said. "I'm been thinking about it, processing it over and over. I have no idea what the mount of judgment is. Do you?"

Sam slowly shook his head.

Caitlin sighed. "Then I'm afraid that there's nothing for me to do either, until we figure it out."

"And when you do?" Sam asked.

She paused. "Then I'll go pursue it, whatever it is. In the meantime—"

"In the meantime, there's nothing for you to do but enjoy yourself," Lily said, coming over, putting an arm around her shoulder. "It's your engagement after all. Cheer up! Celebrate. I insist that you do!"

Caitlin smiled, warmed, as always, by Lily's presence.

"In fact, I have decided that I'm going to throw you to an engagement party. Right now. We need to celebrate." She turned to the crowd. "Don't we?"

The crowd roared back in approval.

"There's a new Shakespeare play opening today at his new Globe theater," Lily continued. "Romeo and Juliet. We're all going to see it." She turned to the crowd. "Let's go celebrate these two. It's on me!"

The coven roared back in approval, and Caitlin's heart lifted, as Caleb came over and kissed her.

"Mommy?" Scarlet asked. "Can I come? Please? I've always wanted to see a Shakespeare play. Please. Please!"

Caitlin smiled. "Of course you can, sweetheart."

"Yay!" Scarlet jumped up and down, Ruth barking beside her.

Caitlin was blown away. *Romeo and Juliet.* She couldn't fathom its being called "new." Or hearing Shakespeare being called a "new playwright." Or his "Globe" being called a "new theater."

But it was 1599, after all, and everything that was old was new again.

Caitlin's heart filled with delight. Her entire life, she had wanted to go to a Shakespeare play. And now, she would be going to actually see one of the first productions of *Romeo and Juliet*, in Shakespeare's theater, while Shakespeare was alive—and who knows, maybe even there himself.

CHAPTER TWENTY

Caitlin flew through the air, her entire coven beside her. They had all left Warwick together, heading towards London, to Shakespeare's theater, to celebrate. Caitlin had never been more excited. Here she was, with everyone she loved dearly, heading to celebrate her engagement with a new play by Shakespeare. She could hardly imagine what it could be like to actually see a play of his in the time and place that it was set. She felt herself bristling with excitement.

It felt so good to have everyone together, and she was still riding high from being proposed to. She was overflowing with joy. Finally, everything seemed perfect in the world. For the first time, she saw such a bright future ahead of her. Finally, she could have it all—a happy life, surrounded by people she loved, and a time and place in which she could settle down.

Best of all, she didn't have to feel guilty about not pursuing her search for her father. She had no idea how to decode the riddle, and neither did anyone else. There was literally nothing else she could do. So she felt okay to take some time to enjoy herself. After all, how often in a girl's life did she get proposed to?

If things should change, if she should decode the riddle, then she would do what she had to, and continue on the search. But a part of her secretly hoped that it did not come to that. She was so happy and content here, she truly wished things would never change.

As they flew over the city of London, it now felt like an entirely new city, experiencing it with all of her friends and loved ones at her side. It was less shocking to her this time, having already been through it once before. It was, in some strange ways, beginning to feel familiar.

They all flew over the river Thames, then, seeing the London Bridge off in the distance, veered off to the right side of the river, to Southwark. As they approached, Caitlin spotted below the circular structures of several theaters, bullbaiting rings, and bearbaiting rings. She was puzzled to see that the bearbaiting ring she had visited days before now seemed to be damaged by fire. She wondered when that fire could have broken out.

They dove lower, circling over the neighborhood that held Shakespeare's theater. Down below, thousands of people were crammed together, all packed together on this warm September day, walking in the unpaved, muddy streets that were also filled with wild dogs, chickens, livestock, and an abundance of rats, visible even from up here.

Caitlin smiled wider as Caleb, flying beside her, squeezed her hand, looked at her and grinned. She could see how proud he was to have her by his side, and nothing made her happier. She looked down at her ring again, and again felt how lucky she was to be with him.

They all landed behind a building, out of sight of the crowd, not far from Shakespeare's theater. Caitlin set down Scarlet, as Tyler set down Lily, and they all walked out from behind a building, and right into the bustling crowd of humanity.

Caitlin found herself jostled back and forth, as did the others, and she held Scarlet's hand tight so that they would not get separated. She tried to stick together with the others, as they all pushed their way through the endless masses, trying to make it across the open square, to the packed entrance of the globe. These crowds reminded Caitlin of a time when she was young, when she went to Disneyland, and there were so many people crammed in that it'd taken her nearly an hour just to go a few feet.

As they approached the theater, Caitlin looked up at it in awe. It appeared just as she had seen in the history books, and seeing it in person was incredible. It was a large, round theater, built very steeply straight up, made entirely of wood, its exterior painted in a bright white, with dark wooden beams interlacing it, and a sharply slanted, dark roof made of straw.

As they funneled their way with the masses towards the main entrance, the energy became more and more vibrant. Lily stepped up and paid the attendant, and turned to Caitlin and the others.

"We have a choice," she said. "We can either sit in our own private box, off to the side, or stand in the middle, with the masses, and be closer to the stage. We'd be standing on the ground the entire time, but we'd be closer."

Caitlin thought, and looked to Caleb, who didn't seem to have any preference. Caitlin didn't want to sit in a fancy box off to the side.

"I'd like to stand," Caitlin said, "with all the others, right on the ground, close to the stage. I want to experience it the way the masses do."

"You got it," Lily said. "That's fine with me. You just saved me a bunch of money anyway— groundling tickets are only a penny! It can be a bit of a rough crowd, though. Is that okay?"

Caitlin smiled. "That's great," she said. "I want to see the real London."

Lily smiled back. "It's *your* engagement party," she said, with a large smile, "whatever you want."

As Lily paid, they all walked through the ramp-like entrance, and right into the theater.

"Can I sit on your shoulders?" Scarlet asked, yanking Caitlin's hand.

Caitlin smiled. "Of course," she said, hoisting her up, onto her shoulders. Scarlet squealed with delight, kicking her legs, as she looked every which way.

Caleb came up beside her and held her hand.

As they entered the theater, the electricity in the air was palpable, and the sight took Caitlin's breath away. She looked up, all around, at the wooden seating, the rows of benches on all sides, rising steeply into the air. In the center of the theater was a circular pit, a ground floor made of dirt, on which thousands of people milled, huddled together.

The wooden stage was raised about fifteen feet off the ground, and so wide, it stretched about a hundred feet across, and about forty feet deep. It was framed by columns all across. She was surprised to see how simple the stage was, hardly adorned by any sets, and of course, not having any lighting. She remembered that nighttime shows hadn't existed yet in this century, and that all plays still had to be performed in the sunlight. Indoor theaters were an invention yet to come.

"GET YOUR GIN HERE, ONE PINT! GIN HERE, ONE PINT!" a man yelled out over and over again, carrying a pouch slung over his stomach, dozens of small bottles in it.

Their group made its way slowly through the huge crowd of groundlings, gently but firmly making their way as close to the stage as they could.

"Excuse me! Excuse me!" Scarlet kept saying to the people in front of them.

It worked like a charm. People everywhere turned and made way for her, smiling when they saw her, and she managed to make their way nearly to the lip of the stage.

"Can't wait to see what Will has this time," Caitlin overheard one crowd member say.

"I hear it's a tragedy," one of them responded.

"No. It's a romance," another said.

"You're both wrong," another said, "it's a comedy."

Caitlin smiled to herself. It shocked her that these people had never seen it. Once again, she felt so fortunate to be here at this moment, in this time and place, right when it was first happening.

As she looked around, trying to take the entire scene in, she also realized that she was a bit surprised: this was not how she'd pictured a Shakespeare crowd. She'd pictured it to be more refined, more elitist, more snobbish. But the opposite was true. The people here were just ordinary masses, hard-working people. In fact, many of them didn't even seem to be respectable enough to be hard-working people—the majority of them, to her surprise, seemed to be rough looking types—drunks, scoundrels, and various unsavory characters. If Caitlin hadn't known better, she could have easily mistaken this crowd for a group of convicts.

Caitlin was shocked that they would all come to see a Shakespeare play. And she was also shocked that, in this time and place, even the most uneducated person could grasp a Shakespeare play at first glance. It made her sad to think how far the 21st century had fallen behind.

Suddenly, a rush of excitement spread throughout the crowd. The chatter began to die down, and the vendors selling products began to quiet, too. The jostling and shuffling for position began to slow, as well. Caitlin felt herself bristle with excitement, as she sensed the play was about to begin.

Moments later, a lone actor stepped forward, out to the center of the stage, walking dramatically right to the front, just feet away from Caitlin. Caitlin could hear Scarlet gasp up above her, on her shoulders. The entire crowd became deathly silent. In fact, Caitlin could not believe how silent it became so quickly, at how much respect these people gave to the theater: there were thousands and thousands of unruly people here, and yet now, at this moment, she could not hear a peep. There were certainly no cellphones or beepers to go off, either. That was another thing that made Caitlin appreciate this time.

The actor proudly lifted his chin, commanding their attention, and spoke the opening lines of the play:

Two households, both alike in dignity,
In fair Verona, where we lay our scene,
From ancient grudge break to new mutiny,
Where civil blood makes civil hands unclean.

As the actor continued his long monologue, introducing the play, Caitlin was overwhelmed by his clarity of voice, by his precision, by how the actors performed in this day and time. It was truly an art form.

The play unfolded, the narrator followed by a large, rowdy group of actors, who played out an opening fight scene in a crowded marketplace, quickly establishing the rivalry between the two families in the play: the Montagues and the Capulets.

One scene followed the next, and Caitlin found herself becoming completely entranced, losing all sense of space and time. She had never experienced theater like this—so real, so alive. It truly felt like the first time *Romeo and Juliet* had ever been performed. As she got lost in it, Caitlin found herself forgetting what actually happened in the play, and found herself riveted to every word, wondering what would happen next.

The scenes raced by until they came to an elaborate dance scene, a formal dance hosted by the house of Capulet, which Romeo had snuck into. Caitlin found herself riveted as she watched Romeo see Juliet for the first time:

ROMEO
What lady is that, which doth enrich the hand
Of yonder knight?

SERVANT
I know not, sir.

ROMEO
O, she doth teach the torches to burn bright!
It seems she hangs upon the cheek of night
Like a rich jewel in an Ethiope's ear;
Beauty too rich for use, for earth too dear!
….
Did my heart love till now? forswear it, sight!
For I ne'er saw true beauty till this night.

Caitlin could not help thinking of the first time she had seen Caleb, of her instant love for him. It also, briefly, made her think of Blake. It made her wonder how love at first sight works, what it was, exactly, that made one person feel attracted to another.

Caitlin watched Romeo sneak onto the dance floor, steal a dance with Juliet, and speak to her for the first time:

ROMEO
If I profane with my unworthiest hand
This holy shrine, the gentle fine is this:
My lips, two blushing pilgrims, ready stand
To smooth that rough touch with a tender kiss.

JULIET
Good pilgrim, you do wrong your hand too much,
Which mannerly devotion shows in this;
For saints have hands that pilgrims' hands do touch,
And palm to palm is holy palmers' kiss.

Caitlin was riveted as she watched Romeo lean in, and the two kiss each other for the first time. It made her think of her first kiss with Caleb, and then made her think of their incredible night together in Edgartown. She found herself more and more deeply identifying with Juliet, feeling that Caleb was her Romeo, that they had come from two different houses, from forbidden loves. She found herself losing all sense of time and place as she became engrossed in the scenes playing out before her.

There soon came the balcony scene, and Caitlin watched, riveted, as Romeo crept up to Juliet's balcony and watched her, speaking to himself before he was detected:

ROMEO
But, soft! what light through yonder window breaks?
It is the east, and Juliet is the sun.
Arise, fair sun, and kill the envious moon,
Who is already sick and pale with grief,
That thou her maid art far more fair than she:
...
The brightness of her cheek would shame those stars,
As daylight doth a lamp; her eyes in heaven
Would through the airy region stream so bright
That birds would sing and think it were not night.
See, how she leans her cheek upon her hand!
O, that I were a glove upon that hand,
That I might touch that cheek!

JULIET
O Romeo, Romeo! wherefore art thou Romeo?
Deny thy father and refuse thy name;
Or, if thou wilt not, be but sworn my love,
And I'll no longer be a Capulet.

Romeo stepped forward on the large, wide stage, and Juliet, up high in a balcony, looked down at Romeo in shock:

JULIET
How camest thou hither, tell me, and wherefore?
The orchard walls are high and hard to climb,
And the place death, considering who thou art,
If any of my kinsmen find thee here.

ROMEO
With love's light wings did I o'er-perch these walls;
For stony limits cannot hold love out,

Caitlin felt her heart soar, as they expressed their love for each other for minutes on end. Finally, slowly, the scene came to an end:

ROMEO

O blessed, blessed night! I am afeard.
Being in night, all this is but a dream,
Too flattering-sweet to be substantial.

JULIET
Three words, dear Romeo, and good night
indeed.
If that thy bent of love be honourable,
Thy purpose marriage, send me word to-
morrow,
By one that I'll procure to come to thee,
Where and what time thou wilt perform the rite;
And all my fortunes at thy foot I'll lay
And follow thee my lord throughout the world.
…
Good night, good night! parting is such
sweet sorrow,
That I shall say good night till it be morrow.

Caitlin could not help but think of Caleb, of his proposal to her, of their upcoming marriage. She felt as if she were Juliet, as Juliet stood there, hoping for Romeo to come back, to propose to her, to make her his forever.

As the play went on, some scenes blurred in her mind, while others stood out more prominently. She was captivated as Romeo approached the Friar, asking for his permission to marry Juliet:

ROMEO
Come what sorrow can,
It cannot countervail the exchange of joy
That one short minute gives me in her sight:
Do thou but close our hands with holy words,
Then love-devouring death do what he dare;
It is enough I may but call her mine.

FRIAR
These violent delights have violent ends
And in their triumph die, like fire and
powder....

She was captivated as Romeo held his best
friend, Mercutio, in his arms, having been
stabbed to death on Romeo's behalf. She
watched Romeo pick up the sword and stab his
rival, Tybalt, killing him in revenge. Caitlin
thought back to New York, when Caleb died in
her own arms, as the result of Sam tricking her.
And worse, she felt a tear roll down her cheek
as she remembered Blake being stabbed in the
Roman Coliseum, taking the wound for her, and
dying in her arms.

BENVOLIO
Romeo, away, be gone!
The citizens are up, and Tybalt slain.

Stand not amazed: the prince will doom thee death,
If thou art taken: hence, be gone, away!

ROMEO
O, I am fortune's fool!

She watched as Juliet stood there, on her balcony, waiting for Romeo, who had just been banished, and who could never come back to her. Her heart broke, as it made her think of all those times Caleb had left her, as she stood there, waiting for him herself.

JULIET
Come, night; come, Romeo; come, thou day in night;
For thou wilt lie upon the wings of night
Whiter than new snow on a raven's back.
Come, gentle night, come, loving, black-brow'd night,
Give me my Romeo; and, when he shall die,
Take him and cut him out in little stars,
And he will make the face of heaven so fine
That all the world will be in love with night
And pay no worship to the garish sun.

She was breathless as she watched a desperate Juliet run to the Friar, desperate for any possible solution that could bring her and Romeo together again, that could end his banishment. It made her think of Aiden, of Pollepel, of her begging him to bring Caleb back, her promising that she would do anything, even risk her unborn child, to travel back in time and save Caleb.

FRIAR

Take thou this vial, being then in bed,
And this distilled liquor drink thou off;
When presently through all thy veins shall run
A cold and drowsy humour, for no pulse
Shall keep his native progress, but surcease:
No warmth, no breath, shall testify thou livest;
The roses in thy lips and cheeks shall fade
To paly ashes, thy eyes' windows fall,
Like death, when he shuts up the day of life;
Each part, deprived of supple government,
Shall, stiff and stark and cold, appear like death:
And in this borrow'd likeness of shrunk death
Thou shalt continue two and forty hours,
And then awake as from a pleasant sleep.

JULIET

Love give me strength! and strength shall help afford.

There was not a peep in the house, the entire crowd riveted, as Juliet sat alone in her bedroom, took out the vial of sleeping liquid the Friar had given her, and prepared to drink it— knowing full well that drinking it could result in death:

JULIET
Farewell! God knows when we shall meet again.
I have a faint cold fear thrills through my veins,
That almost freezes up the heat of life:
….
Come, vial.
What if this mixture do not work at all?
Shall I be married then to-morrow morning?
….
Romeo, I come! this do I drink to thee.

She watched as Juliet's nurse and parents stormed into the room, finding her sleeping and thinking her dead.

NURSE
O lamentable day!

LADY CAPULET
What is the matter?

NURSE
Look, look! O heavy day!

LADY CAPULET
O me, O me! My child, my only life,
Revive, look up, or I will die with thee!
Help, help! Call help.

CAPULET
For shame, bring Juliet forth; her lord is come.

NURSE
She's dead, deceased, she's dead; alack the day!

LADY CAPULET
Alack the day, she's dead, she's dead, she's dead!

CAPULET
Ha! let me see her: out, alas! she's cold:
Her blood is settled, and her joints are stiff;
Life and these lips have long been separated:
Death lies on her like an untimely frost
Upon the sweetest flower of all the field.

NURSE
O lamentable day!

LADY CAPULET
O woeful time!

CAPULET
Death, that hath ta'en her hence to make me wail,
Ties up my tongue, and will not let me speak.

FRIAR
Come, is the bride ready to go to church?

CAPULET
Ready to go, but never to return.
O son! the night before thy wedding-day
Hath Death lain with thy wife. There she lies,
Flower as she was, deflowered by him.
Death is my son-in-law, Death is my heir;
My daughter he hath wedded: I will die,
And leave him all; life, living, all is Death's.

She felt heartbroken as she watched Romeo in his own world, still ignorant of what happened with Juliet, and as she sensed the impending doom to come.

ROMEO
I dreamt my lady came and found me dead--
Strange dream, that gives a dead man leave to think!--
And breathed such life with kisses in my lips,
That I revived, and was an emperor.

Time passed in the blink of an eye as the play came to a close. As it nearly ended, Caitlin could not believe that hours had already passed. It felt like the play had just begun. She had stood there, not moving an inch, the entire crowd not moving an inch, with no intermission, no break—even Scarlet, on her shoulders, hadn't moved the entire play. They had all been completely riveted, from start to finish.

And as the play reached its final scenes, its climactic ending, Caitlin felt tears pouring down her cheeks, so enmeshed in the story, feeling as if it had all just happened to her. She couldn't help thinking of the time in the King's Chapel in Boston, when she was dying, and when Caleb had held her in his arms, and had brought her back from death. All of it, everything, came flooding back to her, all the loves, all the lifetimes, all the centuries. She felt completely overwhelmed, felt as if she were one with Juliet as she watched Romeo stand over her, in the mausoleum, and assume that she was dead.

ROMEO
O my love! my wife!
Death, that hath suck'd the honey of thy breath,
Hath had no power yet upon thy beauty:
Thou art not conquer'd; beauty's ensign yet

Is crimson in thy lips and in thy cheeks,
And death's pale flag is not advanced there.
...Ah, dear Juliet,
Why art thou yet so fair? shall I believe
That unsubstantial death is amorous,
And that the lean abhorred monster keeps
Thee here in dark to be his paramour?
For fear of that, I still will stay with thee;
And never from this palace of dim night
Depart again: here, here will I remain
With worms that are thy chamber-maids; O, here
Will I set up my everlasting rest,
And shake the yoke of inauspicious stars
From this world-wearied flesh.

Caitlin could hear people sobbing all around her, as they all watched in horror, as Romeo drank a vial of true poison, assuming Juliet to be dead.

ROMEO
O true apothecary!
Thy drugs are quick. Thus with a kiss I die.

And then the horror deepened, as Juliet awoke from her sleep to find Romeo dead, truly dead, beside her, having just killed himself because he thought, tragically, that she was dead:

JULIET
What's here? a cup, closed in my true love's hand?
Poison, I see, hath been his timeless end:
O churl! drunk all, and left no friendly drop
To help me after? I will kiss thy lips;
Haply some poison yet doth hang on them,
To make die with a restorative.
  She kisses him.
Thy lips are warm.
…
then I'll be brief. O happy dagger!
This is thy sheath;

The entire crowd – thousands of people, visibly gassed as Juliet took the knife and plunged into her own stomach, killing herself.

JULIET
There rust, and let me die.

Caitlin found herself completely lost as the play came to its conclusion and the actors disappeared behind the curtain.

She slowly looked around the audience, and she could tell, from their tears, their horrified expressions, their wide eyes, that these people had truly just seen this for the first time. They look stunned, and horrified, and yet inspired. They were all completely silent.

Finally, the actors made their way back out onto the stage, bowing, and the silence broke into applause, roaring, screaming, hooting, as people clapped louder and longer than Caitlin had ever heard in her life. Scarlet clapped above her, as did Caleb, Polly, Sam, Lily, and all her coven members.

Slowly, Caitlin felt herself coming back into her world, to her reality. She reached up and clapped, letting the tears roll down her cheeks.

Finally, after the actors had taken several bows, they parted ways for a long figure, who walked out onto the stage. Caitlin's heart stopped, as she realized who it was.

It was Shakespeare.

William Shakespeare was standing before her, just feet away, dressed in a traditional Elizabethan wardrobe. He bowed, and the applause deepened even further.

Caitlin was speechless.

"Would you like to meet him?" came a voice.

Caitlin turned and saw Lily standing there, smiling.

"After all, it's your party. I know where they go to drink. I'm friends with several of them. I can get us in—all of us. We'd have to go now."

Caitlin couldn't possibly think of a better engagement present than a chance to meet Shakespeare himself—and his actors. She barely had words to respond.

"Uh—yes!" she stuttered.

Lily smiled wide as she rounded up the others, and they all began to make their way through the crowd. Caleb grabbed her hand and led her. She couldn't believe it. As if witnessing *Romeo and Juliet* performed for the first time were not enough, she was now on her way to meet William Shakespeare.

CHAPTER TWENTY ONE

Caitlin felt as if she were in a dream as she found herself being led through the thick crowd, down a crowded, muddy alleyway, and across the street to a small tavern. She could see actors from the play filing in there, some still dressed in their extravagant wardrobes. They looked relieved, and were laughing, cheering, patting each other on the back. The mood was festive, and she marveled at how jovial these actors were, despite having just performed such a tragic play. She figured that was just the nature of actors: able to change their moods at whim.

She held Scarlet's hand tight as they wound their way through the crowd, Caleb holding her other hand, and Lily in front of her. Sam and Polly joined them, along with the rest of their coven members.

Lily ducked into a small, stone tavern, heading down the steps, ducking her head as she went, and they all followed.

The tavern was comprised of one small room, with stone floors, and long, well-worn wooden benches. It was crowded and cheery in here, brightly lit by several torches affixed to the walls. There must have been close to a hundred people crammed in, sitting and standing. The mood was jovial. Everyone seem relaxed, as if a great tension had been broken, and most already had a drink in hand.

Of all the differences between the 21st and 16th centuries, Caitlin was amazed to see that bars had hardly changed at all: they still looked mostly the same, down to the drinking glasses, the long, well-worn slab of wood that made up the bar, the busy bartender behind it, pouring drafts of beer. At least one thing hadn't changed over the centuries: people still loved to drink, and they still loved taverns.

Caitlin felt a glass thrust into her hand by a passing waiter, who was handing out a dozen glasses to a large group. A frothy liquid, the head of a beer, flowed over it and down over her hand and wrist. She tried to step back, to prevent the froth from running over her shoes, but she was jostled from every direction, and had no room to maneuver.

"To Will Shakespeare!" yelled someone from the crowd.

"To Will Shakespeare!" the crowd roared back, and everyone raised their glasses and drank.

Caitlin tried to catch a glimpse of him, but it was hard to see in the thick crowd.

"Would you like to meet him?" Lily asked.

Caitlin looked at her, amazed that she was close enough to make an introduction. She didn't know what to say, and only managed to nod in return.

Lily took her by the arm, and led her through the thick crowd. As they pushed their way through, passing one person at a time, Caitlin noticed the rows of actors sitting side-by-side, laughing with each other. The room broke out into song, as they began singing a festive tune that Caitlin didn't know.

She recognized many of the actors from the play in here, including Romeo, Mercutio and Tybalt. It was funny to see them there, all now sitting happy, laughing together, sharing a beer—while just moments before they'd been killing one another on stage.

"Will, I'd like you to meet someone," Lily said.

Caitlin turned, her heart pounding.

There, standing before her, was Shakespeare. He looked to be in his late 30s, with long-ish black hair, a goatee, intelligent, brown eyes which stared back at her, and dark circles beneath them, as if he had been up all night. There were worry lines etched into his forehead, and he already looked older than his age. Sweat dripped from his forehead in the hot and crowded room, but nonetheless, he seemed relieved, as if happy his play had been so well received.

He smiled back at her.

"Caitlin," he repeated, "a fine name. Do you know its origin?"

Caitlin shook her head, put on the spot, and embarrassed to be at a loss for words. What could she possibly say back to Shakespeare that could make her sound even remotely intelligent?

"It is Greek, of course. Meaning 'pure.' I could see that about you. They say that people's faces reflect their names. Don't you agree?"

She only nodded back dumbly, afraid to even speak. She couldn't remember ever feeling so self-conscious. She, of course, had had no idea of her name's origin.

"Of course," he continued, a mischievous smile on his lips, "the Greeks stole it, as they do everything. The true origin of Caitlin is actually Irish. It's a Gaelic variation of the old French name, which was derived from Catherine, which in turn, was derived from the ancient Greek. So there you go—full circle. Some people would attribute it to the Greek goddess, Hecate. She, of course, is associated with magic, witchcraft, necromancy, and crossroads.

"I'm working on a new play, actually, that features Hecate—the original Caitlin, if you will. I'm thinking of calling it *Macbeth*. Are you a player?"

"I'm sorry," Caitlin said, not understanding.

"An actor?" Lily clarified.

A *player*. Meaning, *actor*. Of course, Caitlin realized. The old usage of the word. She felt even more embarrassed.

"Um…no," she said.

She didn't know what else to say. Was William Shakespeare truly asking her if she acted? Was he offering to put her in one of his plays?

"WILL!" shouted someone, a large beefy man, who suddenly reached over his huge arm and draped it around his shoulder. He hugged Shakespeare tight, and the two of them clinked glasses, as their bills beer spilled over. "You owe me a drink," the man continued. "We had a wager, remember? And I didn't forget a single line!"

"You did," Shakespeare responded.

The man furrowed his brow. "Which one?"

"Well, not a line, but a phrase within that line. You skipped a word. But I'll forgive you. Bartender, give him that beer!"

A small cheer arose among the actors.

Shakespeare was then dragged off, yanked in several different directions, and before Caitlin could say another word, there were already a dozen people between them.

Caitlin turned and looked at Lily, feeling stupid, as if she had just missed a great opportunity. But still, even now, she didn't know what to really say to him. That she loved his work? Wouldn't that seem so obvious, so common? Or should she have tried to say something smart in return? Or should she have told him that she came from 500 years in the future, and that he was a huge success in the 21st century?

He probably would have thought she was crazy. She could have told him that she had seen several movie versions of *Romeo and Juliet*. But then, he would have asked her what a "movie" is.

"Was it what you expected?" Lily asked.

Caitlin simply nodded, not knowing what else to say. Meeting him had, indeed, been overwhelming. He had a certain presence, an aura, an energy—intelligent, but also fun, and filled with energy. She could now see how he could write so many plays so quickly: he had a larger-than-life persona.

"I know," Lily said, understanding. "I was like that the first time I met him, too. It's a bit overwhelming. What's most overwhelming of all is that he doesn't even realize his star is beginning to shine. He still clearly thinks of himself as just an ordinary writer, an ordinary actor, just one of the boys, just like everybody else."

Lily shook her head slowly, as if amazed.

Caitlin made her way back to the others, happy to see that they'd found an empty table. She sat beside Caleb and Scarlet, and Polly and Sam, and Lily joined them, with several of their coven members. They all had drinks before them.

"Can I taste one?" Scarlet asked.

Caitlin exchanged a look with Caleb.

"I'm sorry, sweetheart," she said, "this is only a drink for adults."

Caitlin suddenly thought of Scarlet's being in here, and looked around, at all the rough types, and suddenly realized that maybe this wasn't the best place to bring a child. She wondered why she hadn't considered that before. She just wasn't used to being in the mindset of a parent. She realized that she should probably take her out of here soon. Caitlin was feeling a little tired herself, anyway. The energy in the room was relentless. Watching the play had been one of the deepest experiences of her life, and she felt she needed some quiet time to process it all.

Caitlin leaned forward and took Caleb's hand, and he smiled back at her, a beer in hand, drinking with all the others. Just as she was about to suggest him that she leave with Scarlet and that he catch up later, suddenly, a voice rose up over the din.

"Caleb? Is that you?"

It was a woman's voice, and Caitlin turned, immediately on edge.

The table seemed to quiet down, as they all stopped and looked.

There, standing at the head of it, looking down on them, was one of the most beautiful women Caitlin had ever seen. She was tall and blonde, well proportioned, with glowing green eyes, and wearing an outfit that was nearly skintight, surprisingly revealing for this time and place. She was dressed in all black, and Caitlin could immediately sense that she was one of hers: a vampire.

Caitlin looked at Caleb, gauging his expression. She could tell that he was shocked, and saw how flustered he became, and Caitlin began to worry. She could sense that something had happened between these two.

"Violet?" Caleb asked back.

She smiled down at him.

"I always thought that we'd run into each other again, in some time and place," she said with a smile. "Some things are destined, I guess."

Caitlin's heart started to pound as she could sense with even more power the strength of the bond between these two.

Who was this woman? she wondered. She had never heard of her before. Why hadn't Caleb told her? Could this be another one of his ex-wives?

Caitlin felt her mouth become dry with upset and worry. She had thought they'd finally put Caleb's ex-loves behind her, after all she went through with Sera. And now this?

She had assumed, had been *sure*, that there was no one else out there who could possibly get in their way. And with Caleb's ring on her finger, she had felt more sure than ever that their destiny as a married couple was just ahead of them.

And now this.

As if reading her thoughts, Violet suddenly turned and fixed her startling green eyes directly on Caitlin. She slowly looked down at Caitlin's ring, as if in recognition, then looked back up.

"Who is she?" Violet asked Caleb slowly, a bit disdainfully.

Their table quieted completely, the jovial mood broken. Sam, Polly, Lily and the others all looked from Violet to Caitlin to Caleb, and she could feel all the eyes on her. She was beginning to feel embarrassed, not knowing what to make of all this.

"This is...um..." Caleb began, stuttering, "um...Caitlin," he finished, clearly nervous, looking back and forth between the two.

"And who is that?" Caitlin asked Caleb, now looking directly at him. She could feel herself beginning to tremble with fear and upset.

He cleared his throat. "Violet," he said.

"I know," Caitlin said, annoyed. "I already caught her name. I'm asking you *who* that is."

The table became silent, the tension thick in the air, as all eyes turned to Caleb.

Caitlin could feel her heart pounding in her throat. Clearly, there was something he was hesitant to tell her. What on earth could it be?

Caleb looked down at the table, then slowly looked up at Caitlin, with guilty eyes.

"Violet is the one who turned me."

CHAPTER TWENTY TWO

Kyle pushed and elbowed his way through the thick crowd inside Shakespeare's Globe theater. He had stood there for hours, on the outskirts, throughout the interminably long play, waiting for his chance. Romeo and Juliet. What terrible stuff. He had despised every word, stupid stuff of poetry, a waste of his precious time. The only parts he had liked were watching Romeo and Juliet die. He only wished they had died right away. Too bad he, Kyle, wasn't a playwright, he thought—he could teach Shakespeare a thing or two.

But he wasn't there for such trivial matters. He was here for business, *real* business. He had been waiting forever for the play to end and the crowd to disperse. Vampire poison deep in his pocket, he had been relentlessly tracking Caitlin, and her entire crew, ever since they had arrived. He'd watched their every move, had watched them watching the play, and had bided his time.

He was proud of himself. This was the new Kyle. No longer did he waste precious energy by confronting them head on. He had learned his lesson enough times. Now, he was fighting a new way. With stealth and treachery. Poison was a trusted device, and it was time to try something new.

But he had to get as close to them as he could, and he had to wait until they had a drink in hand. In the meantime, he had stood there, waiting forever. At least he had made himself useful: throughout the play, he had drifted along the outskirts, releasing dozens of more rats, and packages of fleas, setting them free all throughout the audience. At least, when he left this place, thousands more humans would be infected with the plague. He smiled at the thought: he had brought down the bearbaiting ring with fire, and he would bring down Shakespeare's theater with a simple little flea.

Finally, the play ended and the crowd dispersed, and Kyle had followed Caitlin, keeping a good distance. He followed as they'd crossed the street, and entered that tavern. He waited a good time, so that they wouldn't sense they were being followed, knowing that the thick crowds would dilute their psychic ability.

Finally, Kyle felt the moment was right, and he slipped into the bar. Wearing a cloak and hood, pulled tight over his face, he slipped between the crowd, creeping towards Caitlin's table. He saw her sitting there, next to all of her stupid little friends. He wanted to kill them all, and he would if he could.

But this time, he forced himself to stay focused. He clutched the poison vial in his hand, using his sleeve to hold it, determined to kill her for good this time.

Kyle crept behind Caitlin, and just as he did, a strange woman, who introduced herself as Violet, appeared at the head of the table. Kyle got lucky: he hadn't planned for this, and it was the perfect distraction.

He moved quick. When everyone was looking away, he quickly emptied the vial of poison into her drink. Then he slipped out of there, thrilled that it had gone so smoothly.

In just minutes, Caitlin would drink. And when she did, she would be dead within days— if not hours. It would be a cruel, agonizing death.

This time, Kyle would leave nothing to chance. He would track them, wherever she went, and watch her final moments in death.

CHAPTER TWENTY THREE

As Caitlin sat there, staring back and forth between Caleb and Violet, she could not believe what she was seeing. She felt her entire body start to shake. How could this be happening? And why now, of all times? When things were finally looking so bright? When all the obstacles for their relationship seemed to have finally disappeared?

Like a thunderbolt out of the sky, this woman had appeared, ruining the high of their engagement party. It wasn't fair. It just wasn't fair.

Worse, Caitlin could see in Caleb's eyes, could sense deep down, that these two had a special relationship. The one who had turned him? She had never even considered such a thing.

Of course, now that she thought about it, she should have. *Someone* had turned him, at some point. But she had never considered it would be a woman. And a gorgeous woman at that. Or that, possibly, the two might still have feelings for each other.

Caitlin remembered once being told that the strongest relationship you could have in the vampire world was to the person who turned you. It was something that ran deep in your blood and soul, something that you could never shake. It helped make you what you were, as that person's blood ran through you.

Caitlin knew that to be true. She felt that with Caleb. After having been turned by him, she felt as if he were always there with her, a part of her. It felt deeper than love, deeper than a connection. It truly felt like they were one.

Now, as she examined Violet, Caitlin wondered if Caleb had the same feelings for her. Was she always there, somewhere inside of him? Did he ever think of her? From the way he was stammering, and from the nervous look on his face, Caitlin suspected that he did. Maybe, she realized, deep within his consciousness, there was another woman lurking there.

It was too much for Caitlin to think of. She didn't want to do or say anything rash, especially after having learned her lesson back in France. And she desperately didn't want to assume the worst, as she had before.

But at the same time, she just couldn't bear to sit there and watch this unfold before her eyes any longer. Whatever game fate was playing on her, she didn't want any part of it. She had to get out of this place, this loud drinking hall, to clear her mind, to get fresh air. She had to leave before she did anything rash, or jumped to any conclusions, or said anything she might regret.

Caitlin stood abruptly, taking Scarlet's hand.

Caleb stood, too, a concerned look on his face. "Where are you going?" he asked her.

Caitlin didn't trust herself to answer him, didn't trust herself to say the right thing. So instead, she silently took Scarlet and pushed her way out through the crowd.

"Caitlin, you don't understand!" Caleb yelled out after her, "It's not like that. It was centuries ago!"

Caitlin grabbed Scarlet's hand more firmly, and parting the crowd, finally made it to the staircase, and up the steps.

"Mommy? Where are we going?" Scarlet asked.

But she was distracted by Caleb's words, which rang through her mind. *Centuries ago.* She desperately wanted to believe that there was nothing there. She breathed deeply, willing herself to believe it.

She made it outside, and standing there, she began to feel better already. She breathed deeply, trying to get a hold of herself. She willed herself to believe Caleb. She had made the mistake in the past of not giving him the benefit of the doubt. And she felt that now she had to grow, to become a better person, to learn from that. She *had* to believe him.

Rationally, she knew that she did. But deep down, emotionally, it was hard. She saw the look in Caleb's eye. And the look in Violet's eye. The way they looked at each other. As a woman, she knew there was something there.

Caitlin stood there, feeling at a crossroads. She didn't know which way to go. A part of her wanted to flee, like she had in the past, to get far away from Caleb, and everyone.

But another part of her, a part that was evolving under her eyes, knew that she had to be more mature. Patient. To hear everyone out. To think things through. To allow everyone the benefit of the doubt. She had to be the bigger person.

"Mommy, I'm not feeling so well," Scarlet suddenly said.

Caitlin snapped out of it. She knelt down and looked at her, and brushed the hair out of her eyes. As she did, she noticed how clammy her forehead was. She already knew Scarlet well enough to see that she was not herself. In fact, she looked extremely pale and sick.

Scarlet reached down, and scratched her ankles with both hands.

Caitlin looked down, and her heart dropped as she saw that they were covered with welts. Bites.

At the same time, Caitlin noticed several rats, scurrying past them in the mud.

Bites. Around the ankles. Large, red welts.

Caitlin's breathing stopped, as she realized what they were. Flea bites.

Caitlin tried to push the thought of her mind. Flea bites didn't necessarily mean the Plague. But she knew it didn't bode well.

"Mommy, I feel really sick," Scarlet said again. And then, as she said it, Scarlet suddenly fainted.

Caitlin's lightning fast reflexes allowed her to catch Scarlet in mid-air, in her arms.

"Scarlet? SCARLET!?" Caitlin screamed, frantic.

But she didn't respond.

Scarlet opened her eyes, gently. She looked deathly ill.

"Mommy, can we go home?"

"Of course, sweetheart," Caitlin answered, repressing tears.

Scarlet closed her eyes again. As she did, Caitlin picked her up, and took off into the air, flying with more speed than she ever had. She knew where she had to go: to the one person in the world she knew who could help someone who was deathly ill.

Aiden.

CHAPTER TWENTY FOUR

Caleb sat there, watching Caitlin leave the tavern, in total shock. He could not believe that this was all happening. Just moments before, it had been a high point for them, one of their very best days, an incredible engagement party, an incredible play, and they were having an amazing time with everyone. It had seemed like things could never get better.

And then, moments later, it all came crashing down, and so unexpectedly. Caleb had been absolutely shocked to see Violet, someone who hadn't even entered his consciousness for hundreds of years, and he was at a complete loss for words. He didn't know what to say to her, and he didn't know what to say to Caitlin. It had happened so fast, he was so caught off guard, and before he knew it, Caitlin was leaving.

"Caitlin!" he had called after her again.

But it was no use. She had already pushed her way through the thick crowd, Scarlet in hand, and was already heading out the bar.

Caleb wanted to go after her. And he would. But he figured it was best to first let her get some air, to clear her head and calm down. He planned on giving her a few minutes, then he would go out and talk to her.

In the meantime, he wanted to know what Violet was doing here—and he didn't want to be rude by walking out on her.

"She's a touchy one," Violet said, looking down and smiling at Caleb.

Caleb was not amused, and did not smile back.

"How did you find me here?" he asked. "And what are you doing here? Last I heard, you were living in Sweden."

She smiled back. "That was five hundred years ago," she said. "People move around. London is my home now. It has been for the last 200 years."

"Did you follow me here?" Caleb asked. "Is there something you want from me?"

Caleb felt nervous that perhaps she was stalking him, wanting to ruin his relationship—maybe wanting to get back together.

But he was also a bit baffled, because Violet had never been that type. She had always been a loner, and when they had broken up, hundreds of years ago, she had never once tried to contact him.

"Don't flatter yourself," Violet shot back. "You're not the only reason that someone lives in London, or goes to a Shakespeare play. This is a very popular tavern. The world does not revolve around you. I happened to be here. And I happened to see you. That's all there is to it. Nothing more."

Caleb sighed, feeling the tension leave his body, and the table seemed to relax, too, the tension visibly reduced.

"I'm just leaving," she said. "I suppose I shouldn't even have stopped to say hello. But I presume you'd be more courteous than you were."

Caleb now felt badly. She was right. She had done nothing wrong, and he owed her at least a tiny bit of cordiality. He should have been more polite to her.

"I'm sorry," he said. "Just bad timing. Caitlin I just got engaged, and this was our engagement party. She doesn't know about you, so your appearing here out of the blue—"

Violet held up a palm. "I get it," she said. "Sorry. I wish you both well."

With that, she turned, and disappeared into the crowd. That was the Violet he remembered. Always quick to leave, not to stalk. Which was why seeing her in the first place had so surprised him.

The table seemed to breathe a sigh of relief as she left, and slowly, the chattering resumed.

"Don't feel bad," Sam said to Caleb, "Caitlin's always been that way. She can be hotheaded. Territorial. It's not your fault," he said.

Caleb nodded back, grateful.

"I should go and check on her," Caleb said, rising.

"Polly already went out to check," Sam said. "She'll be fine."

"I think I should check myself," he said, and rose from the table and pushed his way through the crowd.

Caleb headed out into the sunlight, and looked everywhere for Caitlin and Scarlet. The crowd was thick, and swarmed in every direction. But he could not see her anywhere. And he did not sense her presence, either.

He saw Polly standing there, looking around, too.

"Where is she?" he asked Polly.

"Your guess is as good as mine," she said, looking worried. "It seems that your girlfriend, Violet, scared her away. I don't blame her."

"Polly, she's not my girlfriend. I didn't do anything wrong."

Probably merely shrugged and looked away, and Caleb could tell that she was mad at him, too.

Girls, he thought.

Caleb stormed back into the bar, needing a drink. He went back to the table and sat back across from Sam. He saw all the empty glasses and noticed that Sam had been drinking too much, and he realized again what a wildcard Sam seemed to be. A fresh round of drinks came, and Sam grabbed two for himself, and handed a glass to Caleb.

Caleb drank the whole thing in just a couple of gulps.

"Is Polly still out there?" Sam asked.

Caleb nodded back. "She's pissed at me, too."

Sam shook his head. "Girls," he said. "I better go talk to her," Sam added, and got up from the table, seeming a little bit drunk. Caleb watched him push his way through the crowd.

Caleb felt the beer go to his head, and it felt good.

He wanted another drink, but the waiter was nowhere in sight, and he could tell that, with the thick crowd, it would take forever to get served.

He scanned the table for any leftover beer, and saw, across from him, Caitlin's untouched drink, still filled to the rim. She was gone now, and so she wouldn't be drinking it. He didn't see the harm. It was a shame to let it go to waste. And after all that happened, he really could use just one more drink.

Caleb reached over and grabbed her glass, and drank it all down. He couldn't help noticing that it tasted a little bit funny going down, not like the normal beer. He wondered if maybe her beer had gone sour, or came from a bad batch.

But he didn't care. He wanted to drown out his woman troubles, and make it all go away.

*

Polly was upset as she stood outside the bar, searching everywhere for Caitlin and Scarlet. She knew that Caitlin could handle herself, but it bothered her that she was nowhere to be found. That could only mean one thing: she had left. Gone somewhere. And that she must have been really upset with Caleb.

And Polly could understand. If it were Polly's engagement party, she surely wouldn't wish for some ex-girlfriend to show up. It was annoying, to say the least. Not that Caleb could be blamed, necessarily. But still. It wasn't what any bride-to-be wanted.

Polly knew how emotional Caitlin could be, and only hoped that she would stay clear-headed, and not let this affect things between her and Caleb. She thought they were the perfect couple, and hated to see all these things constantly get between them.

As Polly turned, preparing to go back into the bar, she suddenly felt a cold hand grip her arm. The grip was firm—too firm to be Caitlin's, and she wondered who it could be, as she spun to look.

Polly was aghast.

There, just feet away from her, stood Sergei.

He looked much like he had back in France, even wearing the same regal outfit he'd had on back then. She couldn't believe that he was here, that he had traveled back in time. And that he had tracked her down.

She still felt a burning hatred towards him. He had tricked her, back in Versailles, into revealing where Caitlin was. He had used her all along. He had duped her, made a fool of her; he had played with her heart, and broken it. She felt ashamed and embarrassed at how deeply she had fallen for him, at how blind and stupid she had been.

Now, seeing him here, back in the flesh, all of her emotions burned fresh. She felt a new wave of anger towards him, as if it had all just happened yesterday. What audacity he had to come back in time, to try to talk to her. He stood there with a stupid smile on his face, as if nothing had ever happened between them, and Polly felt her anger grow even more.

"Polly," he said, "I came back for you. To find you. I miss you."

Polly shook her arm roughly, throwing his hand off of it, and stared back at him.

"Don't you dare put your hand on me," she snarled at him. "Don't you ever put your hand on me again."

His face seemed to collapse with sorrow.

"I'm so sorry, Polly. I behaved badly. I recognize that now. I made a huge mistake. I was under such pressures—I wasn't myself. That wasn't really me. I really loved you, all along. I still do."

Polly felt such a wave of anger, she couldn't help herself. She reached up and smacked him hard across the face, the noise so loud that several passersby turned to look. It felt good to hit him, to release a fraction of her anger.

Sergei looked shocked, as if he hadn't expected that.

"You lied to me," she said, her voice cold and steely. "You used me. You're a liar. I'll never trust you again. No matter what you say. I can't believe you even came back here. You're pathetic. And you're just wasting your time if you think I'll ever so much as like you again."

He lowered his eyes.

"I deserved that. I know. And I'm so sorry. I can't say it enough. Can't you ever find it in your heart to forgive me?"

Polly could hear how broken his voice sounded. It certainly sounded genuine. And it felt good to hear those words, especially after what he had put her through. And she did have to admit that somewhere, deep down, she still felt a tiny twinge of affection for him.

But Polly quickly pushed those feelings away, forcing herself to remember what he had done. And forcing herself to think of Sam, who she genuinely liked.

"If you come near me again," Polly said, "I won't be so kind. You and I are enemies now. I will never forgive you. No matter what you say."

"I came back in time because I *love* you!" he pleaded. "And I know that you still love me too. I want to hear those words. Please, tell me that you love me, Polly. Just like you used to. Say it again. Tell me that you love me again."

Polly turned, as she sensed someone approach.

Just a few feet away, watching them, was Sam. He looked wide-eyed, a little drunk, and very, very jealous.

CHAPTER TWENTY FIVE

As Sam exited the bar, having had a little bit too much to drink, he took several steps, then ran smack into Polly and Sergei. He stopped short in his tracks, completely shocked at the sight before him: there stood Polly and Sergei. And he was asking her to tell him again how much she loved him.

Sam felt jealousy and anger well up within him. There was Sergei, who had clearly traveled back in time to win back Polly. And there was Polly, who must have just declared her love for him. Why else would he ask her to "say it again?" To *Sergei*, the creature who had betrayed Polly once, and who had betrayed his sister. The man who had tried to kill them both in the Notre Dame.

And now here they were, standing, talking together. And talking about love.

Sam felt an overwhelming rage well up in him.

Sergei turned and looked at Sam, and for a flash, Sam could see fear in his eyes.

He should be afraid, Sam thought.

"Sam," Polly said. She must have seen the look in his eyes, too.

But it was too late. Nothing she said could stop Sam's swirling emotions.

He lowered his shoulder and lunged at Sergei, tackling him hard, and driving him all the way back through the crowd.

People screamed, carts were overturned, and bodies went flying, as Sam threw Sergei across the road with such force that he went flying, dozens of feet into the air, and into a huge cart of fruits and vegetables, knocking it over.

The entire cart went crashing to the ground, collapsing onto Sergei, who lay there, looking stunned.

"Sam, stop!" Polly yelled.

Sam couldn't understand why she was being protective of Sergei. That only proved that she did care about Sergei. That she still loved him.

And that just made Sam feel even more rage.

Sam charged Sergei again as he lay on the ground, ready to finish him off.

But Sergei quickly jumped to his feet, and suddenly took off into the air, flying away, to the shock and screams of passersby. Sam had almost forgotten that Sergei was one of his, able to fly, and with reflexes nearly as fast.

Sam stood there and watched Sergei fly away, the coward that he was, afraid to fight him. Sam stood there, breathing hard, and could feel the shocked stares of all the people around him.

For now, he would let him fly away. If Sergei was too much of a coward to stand and fight, then he didn't deserve to fight Sam anyway.

Slowly, Sam's anger began to calm.

"Sam, what are you doing!?" Polly yelled.

She was standing next to him, and looked pissed, hands on her hips.

"What do you mean, what was I doing?" he snapped back. "He tried to kill my sister. He tried to kill both of us! The better question is: what were *you* doing? Why was he here? And why were you talking about how much you love him?"

Sam saw Polly's face darken. He'd never seen her look so mad before.

"I was NOT talking to him about love. You misheard us. I would have hoped that you would think better of me than that."

"Well that's not the way it looked," Sam snapped back.

"Well then," she said, "if you don't trust me, then let's just go our separate ways. We're not even together!"

Sam felt himself torn apart by his emotions—anger, jealousy, betrayal.

"Fine," he snapped.

"Fine," she snapped back.

Sam turned and stormed away from her, elbowing his way through the crowd, feeling hollowed out. His rage was leaving him, and was being replaced by something else. Sadness. He had felt that he and Polly were really getting close. And now, this. He wasn't quite sure what had just happened, but he felt that whatever it was, it had ruined things between them.

Sam hurried back down into the tavern, back to his table, and sat across from Caleb, needing a drink more than ever.

As he looked up at Caleb, who sat there, looking woozy, Sam could commiserate with him.

"Girls," Sam said, shaking his head. "I know how you feel now," he said. "It just isn't fair."

Suddenly, Sam watched as Caleb reached for his own throat, as if choking. His eyes opened wide, and he began to quiver.

"Caleb?" Sam asked, concerned. "Are you okay?"

Caleb's eyes rolled back in his head, and he began to slump over, about to collapse.

Sam, with his lightning quick reflexes, jumped around the table and caught Caleb in mid-air, right before he hit the ground. He held Caleb's limp body in his arms, as the other coven members began to crowd around.

"Caleb?" Sam prodded, frantic, as he shook him. "Caleb?"

Caleb did not respond, and his already-pale skin looked as if it were turning blue.

"We need a doctor!" Sam yelled, into the crowd.

But even as he screamed it, as the startled crowd began to gather around him, Sam knew it would be useless. After all, Caleb was a vampire. And only one person he knew of knew how to heal a vampire.

Aiden.

Sam picked up Caleb's limp body and burst through the bar, running up the steps, out the door, and with three strong leaps, jumping up into the air, carrying Caleb. He flew as fast as he could towards the only help he knew.

He only hoped that it wasn't already too late.

CHAPTER TWENTY SIX

Caitlin flew down towards Warwick Castle in a panic. She was the first of her coven members to return from London, and she held Scarlet in her arms, clutching her tight. Scarlet had been in and out of consciousness for most of the trip, and over the last hour or so, Caitlin had seen welts begin to form on her face. She was out of her mind with grief and anxiety. She was certain now that Scarlet had caught the Plague.

She dove down, behind the inner walls of the castle, into the courtyard, and landed softly. She ran with Scarlet through the large oak door, and down the stone hallways.

"Aiden!" she screamed, her voice echoing in the empty corridors.

"AIDEN!"

But he was nowhere to be found, and she did not sense his presence anywhere on the property. *Where was he?* she thought. Now, of all times, when she needed him most.

Caitlin hurried down a corridor, kicking a door open, and hurrying up a flight of steps. She knew that this wing of the castle held the bedrooms, and her first order of business was making Scarlet comfortable.

She kicked open another door, and found herself in a beautiful bedroom, with a large four-poster bed, enormous windows overlooking the river, and acres of rolling hills. It was peaceful in here, and the bedding was clean and luxurious. It would be a perfect place for Scarlet to rest.

She hurried over to the bed and draped Scarlet down, laying her head gently on the pillow. She reached over and brushed Scarlet's hair, now sticky, off her forehead. But Scarlet's eyes still hadn't opened.

Caitlin was beginning to feel overwhelmed with panic. If it had been her, Caitlin, who was injured or sick, she wouldn't be worried—and if it had been a fellow vampire, she wouldn't be worried, either. But it was someone else, and someone she loved so dearly—and a human. She felt so helpless, and had no idea what to do.

She knew the horrible twists and turns the Plague could take. She knew, from her history books, that it had wiped out nearly a third of Europe. And she knew that once you got it, your chances of survival were not good. She also knew that the pain and suffering was intolerable, even for an adult. Her heart broke, as she thought of the pain Scarlet might have to go through while the plague reached its worse over the next few days.

Caitlin ran across the room, grabbed a washcloth, dumped it in a bucket of cold water and squeezed it out. She hurried back to Scarlet's side, reached up and wiped her forehead with it. It was burning hot.

As she did, Scarlet's eyes fluttered open a tiny bit. Sleepily, she looked over at Caitlin.

"Mommy, I'm so hot," Scarlet said. "It hurts so bad. Can you make it go away?"

Caitlin's heart broke. She wished that now, more than ever, she was in the 21st century, that she could take Scarlet into a modern hospital, have them give her modern antibiotics, pain reducers, anti-inflammatories. Whatever they could to make her feel comfortable.

But here, in this time and place, there was little she could do except sit by her side, and watch it take its course.

"It's okay, sweetheart," Caitlin said. "It will go away."

"Do you promise?" Scarlet asked.

Caitlin swallowed hard.

"I promise," she said.

Caitlin felt her heart breaking inside. She couldn't believe how much had happened so fast. Just hours ago she'd been having one of the greatest times of her life. Watching Romeo and

Juliet. Meeting Shakespeare. Celebrating her engagement party, all of her family and friends so close. She had felt truly happy and secure, as if nothing could ever change.

And then, it was as if a storm had hit.

First, Violet.

Then, Scarlet.

Scarlet's illness had taken Caitlin's mind off of Violet and Caleb. But now, she thought of him.

Where was Caleb? Why wasn't he here?

Caitlin became angry now. Did he linger behind, with Violet? Why hadn't he come back to Warwick? Hadn't he realized that Scarlet was sick?

As Caitlin thought about it, she realized that Caleb didn't know that Scarlet was sick, since it had happened outside the tavern. Still, she couldn't help but feeling mad at him. She wanted him to be there, right now, at her side, helping with Scarlet. Telling her that everything would be okay.

Because deep down, Caitlin felt that it would not. That her beautiful, incredible life had just taken a very, very bad turn for the worse. And that it would never turn back around. In fact, Caitlin couldn't imagine how things could possibly get any worse.

Until suddenly, the door crashed open. Sam rushed into the room, holding Caleb in his arms, and Caitlin's heart stopped.

She couldn't believe it. Caleb looked blue, lifeless. Her heart, already broken, broke again. She was wrong about one thing: things could indeed get much, much worse.

*

Caitlin helped Sam drape Caleb on the bed, laying him down beside Scarlet. The bed was so large, it held both of them easily, one on each side.

As Caitlin looked down at the sight, she couldn't believe it: lying there, side by side, were two people she loved most in the world, both draped out next to each other, both deathly ill. Scarlet, she could understand, even if she could not accept it. She had seen the flea bites. She knew what the Plague could do. And she was human.

But Caleb? She could not conceive what could be wrong with him. He was a vampire after all. Immortal.

Wasn't he?

"What happened?" she asked Sam, frantic. She felt her heart pounding in her mouth. She had never seen Caleb look so ill.

"I don't know," Sam said. "One minute he was sitting there, the next he collapsed. I flew him back here. The others are right behind me."

As if on cue, the door burst open, and in rushed Polly, Lily, Tyler, and a dozen coven members, along with Ruth, who ran up to the bed, jumped up on it, and curled up beside Scarlet. She licked Scarlet's face repeatedly, to no avail, then laid her nose on her chest and whined.

"But it's not possible," Caitlin repeated. "Caleb—" she said, then stopped, not knowing what to say. "He's one of us. How could he be sick like this?"

"I don't know," Sam said answered, solemnly.

Polly hurried over and knelt by Scarlet's side, taking her limp hand.

"What happened to *her*?" she asked, filled with alarm.

As she looked, she saw ever-rising welts growing all over Scarlet's face. There was nothing else it could be. "The Plague," Caitlin pronounced grimly.

Sam stood and paced with anger.

"Maybe this was a coordinated attack," he said. "Both of them sick at the same time—it's too strange. But why them? And what could make a vampire sick?"

"Maybe it was an attack meant for someone else," Caitlin found herself saying aloud. Waves of guilt overcame her. Could it have been an attack meant for her?

"But what kind of attack?" Polly asked. "I don't know of anything that could do something like this to a vampire."

"Neither do I," Tyler said, coming over and standing by the bed.

Caitlin found herself becoming overwhelmed with panic. She placed both hands on Caleb's shoulders, and slowly shook him. She felt so guilty now for having left when she did. Perhaps if she had stayed, it might have somehow prevented whatever had happened to him.

"Caleb," she whispered urgently. "Caleb, please, answer me."

But he didn't respond.

"Go find Aiden!" Caitlin suddenly found herself screaming, frantic. She turned to the crowd, who stood there, gaping. "Go! All of you! Find him!" she shrieked.

The entire group hurried its way out of the room, as if scared of her, closing the door behind them.

Caitlin now found herself alone in the room, with just Ruth and Scarlet and Caleb. She lay her head across Caleb's chest, and she couldn't help herself: she began weeping.

She reached over and grabbed his hand.

"Caleb. I'm so sorry. Please forgive me."

Slowly, Caleb opened his eyes.

Caitlin's heart leapt, and she looked at him with new hope. His eyes were so glazed over, she almost didn't recognize them.

"Caleb? Can you hear me?"

He slowly nodded, squeezing her hand gently.

"I'm so sorry," she repeated. "For leaving when I did."

He struggled to speak. "There is nothing between Violet and I…."

"I know," Caitlin said, crying. "I know that, Caleb. And I'm sorry for leaving."

Caleb nodded back, seeming to be satisfied, and closed his eyes again.

"Caleb?" she asked, trying to rouse him again. "Who did this to you? Were you attacked? Were you poisoned?"

But Caleb's eyes closed tight, and he didn't respond.

Finally, after what felt like an eternity, Caleb slowly opened his lips.

"Jade. Don't worry. Daddy will be home soon."

Caleb's heart fell. Jade. His son. He was hallucinating. And talking of leaving this earth.

Caitlin felt more frantic than ever.

"Caleb!" she screamed, shaking his shoulders violently.

But it didn't do any good. His eyes closed, and didn't open again.

CHAPTER TWENTY SEVEN

Caitlin ran. A huge, blood-red sun sat on the horizon, and she ran right for it, through a field of mud. She looked down, and saw that the field was alive, and was completely blanketed with rats.

Thousands and thousands of rats squealed as she ran through them, and as she did, she saw fleas jumping off of them in every direction. A swarm of fleas hovered in the air, and they climbed up and down her legs, covering her entire body, biting her like crazy. She felt her skin on fire from all the bites; she swatted them, but she couldn't get them off.

On the horizon she saw her father, silhouetted against the sun. And she knew that if she could only reach him, she would be safe.

But this time, his face was obscured. And the more she ran, the further away he became.

She slowly sank into the mud as she went, getting lower with each step. Finally, she couldn't run any further, completely stuck, and completely covered by fleas, and then rats, all biting her in every direction.

She saw before her two coffins. One was large, and the other the size for a child. Caleb lay in one, and Scarlet in the other. They were both covered with welts, and they were both dead.

Caitlin reached out, one hand touching one coffin and one the other, as she screamed. She was trying desperately to reach them, to bring them back. But she herself was being sucked into the earth.

As she flailed, about to be completely swallowed by the mud and rats and fleas, she reached out and grabbed onto one last thing. She looked up, and saw that she was holding a large, golden key. It was attached to a rope, which hung from a tree. She grabbed it with both hands, and slowly pulled herself up.

Suddenly, her father stood over her, still a silhouette against the sun.

"The key, Caitlin," he said slowly. "It can save you. Find it on the mount of judgment. Saint Michael's Mount."

Caitlin woke with a fright, sitting straight up. She looked around, disoriented, and finally realized that it had all been a dream. She was breathing hard, and covered in sweat. She slowly brushed the damp hair out of her face and looked around, trying to get her bearings.

It was nighttime now, and she was still in the room with Caleb and Scarlet. She had fallen asleep lying on top of them, draped across their bed.

She looked up at them, and saw that they were both fast asleep, neither moving, Ruth draped across Scarlet's chest.

She sensed a presence and suddenly turned.

There, on the opposite side of the room, stood a lone figure. Still disoriented, for a second she thought it was her father.

But as she blinked several times, she realized it was not. She was really awake this time. And it was not her father. It was Aiden.

He studied her, concern etched across his face.

Caitlin stood and faced him.

"Please," she pleaded. "Can you help them?" She hurried over and grabbed both his hands. "Please."

Aiden slowly stepped forward, past her, to the bedside.

He looked down at them both grimly, as Caitlin crowded behind him.

First, he went over to Scarlet's side, reached out, and laid a hand on her forehead. He closed his eyes for several seconds.

Finally, he opened them.

He looked grimly at Caitlin.

"It's not good," he said. "As you suspected, the Plague. She is human. She is frail. It can go either way."

Caitlin felt her heart sink.

"Is there anything we can do? Anything at all?"

Aiden slowly shook his head. "She is human," was all he said.

Caitlin felt her heart tearing in two. She couldn't bear the thought of Scarlet dying. And she didn't know how she could go on without her.

Aiden walked over to Caleb's side, and laid a hand on his forehead. After several seconds, Aiden opened his eyes. This time though, he retracted his hand quickly, as if bit by a snake. He turned and looked at Caitlin with a look of shock.

She had never seen him surprised before.

"He has been poisoned," he pronounced.

Caitlin was shocked.

"Poisoned? By who? What kind of poison? Aren't vampires immune?"

"It is a very special type of poison. One I haven't seen in a thousand years. One meant for vampires. This was an attack. A murder attempt, definitely."

Caitlin fell her heart falling, afraid to ask the next question.

"Will he live?"

But she already saw the defeated look on Aiden's face.

"There is no cure for a poison like this," he finally said, softly. "I'm afraid he hasn't long left."

"No," Caitlin wailed, breaking into tears. "I refuse to allow that!"

Aiden looked back at her, sadly.

"Do you remember that night, back in Pollepel?" he asked. "When you asked to be sent back? I warned you. I told you that time travel was risky. Dangerous. That anything could happen. You knew this, yet you chose to go back. I'm sorry, but you have to be prepared to let go at some point."

"No!" Caitlin screamed. "Not now. We're about to start a life together. We're about to get married! I can't allow it! It can't be!"

Caitlin sobbed, throwing her head on Caleb's chest.

She turned and looked up at Aiden, with a new ferocity, and stared into his eyes.

"Back in Pollepel," she said, "you found a way. So there has to be a way now. There MUST be a way. And if anyone knows it, it's you. Tell me. Please. Think hard. Anything!"

Aiden got up and paced. He went to the window, looking out.

After several moments, he sighed, looking grim.

"There is one possibility," he said.

Caitlin's eyes lit up with hope. She ran over to his side, hanging onto his every word.

He faced her.

"But it is risky," he continued, "It could very likely kill you in the process, even if it saved him."

"Tell me," she said without hesitation. "Whatever it is. Please, tell me. I'll do it."

He stared at her, and his eyes burned right through her.

"Yes, you would do it, wouldn't you? You would kill yourself for him. You truly love him, don't you?"

Caitlin cried.

"Yes, I do." She wiped away her tears. "Please, tell me."

"His maker," Aiden finally said. "The one who turned him. There is an ancient vampire legend that if one vampire is dying, there is one last way to save them: to find the vampire who turned him. You would need to extract a vial of the turner's blood, then feed it to the vampire who is sick. Then maybe, just maybe, it could heal him."

Caitlin's eyes started to brighten with optimism.

"Wait," Aiden snapped, pessimistic. "It's not that simple. That is just the first step. Once the sick person is fed the blood, he must then feed on the blood of a healthy vampire—a vampire that truly loves him. You see, the sick vampire is supported by two spirits—the one who turned him, and the one he loves now. Then, and only then, will he have a chance for revival."

Aiden sighed, pacing again.

"But it brings considerable risk," he added. "The vampire he feeds on, the one he loves, will almost certainly die in the process. She gives up her life for the one she loves."

The words went off like a bomb in Caitlin's mind. She would have to find his turner. Violet. She would have to go to her and ask for her help. Then she would have to allow Caleb to feed on her, Caitlin. In the process, Caleb may or may not live. And Caitlin would likely die.

"I'll do it," she said, deciding on the spot.

Aiden shook his head.

"Foolish," he said. "Rash. Impetuous. He will likely die anyway. And you will likely die, too. And then you will both be wasted."

"And if I do nothing?" Caitlin asked.

Aiden looked grim. "Then he will certainly die."

Caitlin was resolved.

"How do I do it?" she asked.

Aiden looked at her, disapproving.

"And what of your quest?" he asked. "Your search? Your father? The shield? The entire vampire and human races? Are you that selfish, to sacrifice all of it for one man?"

Caitlin suddenly remembered her dream.

"I dreamt of him last night. My father. He held a key. And he told me to find him on St. Michael's Mount. What does that mean?"

Aiden's eyes opened wide.

"The mount of judgment. Of course. Saint Michael was the angel of judgment. Your father is telling you to find the key on St. Michael's Mount. It is an ancient vampire stronghold. It makes perfect sense. Yes, that is exactly where the key must be."

He stepped forward and held her shoulders and stared at her intently.

"You must go there immediately," he said.

"I can't," she replied. "I have to save Caleb first. I have to find Violet."

"Listen to me very carefully: once the location of the key is revealed to you, you must go immediately. If you don't, a great calamity will befall us, in which case Caleb will not live at all. You have no choice. You must get the key first. Afterwards, if you must, you can go to Violet."

Caitlin thought hard, and it felt right to her. "I promise."

Suddenly, the door to the room burst open, and in rushed Sam, Polly and Lily.

Aiden turned and walked out, before Caitlin could say another word.

"What did he say?" Sam asked.

Caitlin stood there, shaking inside, knowing what she had to do, but feeling so anxious about leaving them. She knew she had to go, first find the key, and then get the antidote—but she felt so torn over the idea of leaving Caleb and Scarlet alone, especially when they were so sick.

"There might be a cure," Caitlin said. "I have to find it. But I can't leave them alone. Will you promise—will the three of you promise me—that you'll stay here, that you'll watch them, that you won't leave their bedside? I can't leave unless I know you are here."

"But I want to protect you," Sam said. "I want to go with you. That's my mission."

"I can't go unless I know you are here," she said. "This is where I need you. Will you promise?"

They all looked at each other, then back at her.

"We promise," they said, as one.

Caitlin embraced each of them, turned and kissed Caleb and Scarlet, then, determined not to waste another precious second, she took three running steps and leapt right out the open window, flying as fast as she could into the night.

CHAPTER TWENTY EIGHT

Polly knelt beside Scarlet's side, dipping a cloth continuously into a bucket of cold water, wringing it out, and running it over her forehead and cheeks. Polly's heart was breaking. This poor child was burning up with fever. Several times in the last hours, she had awakened, screaming for Caitlin. Polly had tried to reassure her that she would be back soon, but Scarlet seem inconsolable.

Ruth, too, seemed on edge. She wouldn't leave Scarlet's side, and she spent most of the time whining, laying her chin on her chest, and snarling at anyone other than Polly, Sam or Lily who came close. Ruth was acting as if it were her own child on the bed.

Polly felt increasingly worried as she tended to Scarlet's sores. There were huge welts all over her face, now oozing pus. Every time Polly rubbed one down with cool water, another one acted up. She felt terrible for the child, and she was so impressed by how brave she was, given how painful it looked.

Polly ran her hand through Scarlet's hair again and again.

"Did I tell you that you're the bravest little girl in the world?" Polly said, trying to get her to smile.

But Scarlet wasn't smiling. She was alternately writhing in pain, and passed out.

On the other side of the bed, Lily knelt by Caleb's side, running a cool cloth over his forehead. Caleb, though, was completely unresponsive.

Sam paced the room, like a wild, caged animal.

"I feel useless," Sam said. "I wish there was something I could do. I wish I could find out who did this to them. I wish we could—"

"Please stop already," Polly snapped at him.

Sam stopped in his tracks.

"All you're doing is making things worse," she said. "Beating someone up is not going to change the situation."

Polly was at her wit's end, overstrained by the horrible situation, and still mad at Sam for his behavior back outside the Globe—for accusing her of loving Sergei.

"Well, what else am I supposed to do?" Sam snapped back.

"Why don't you try making yourself useful," Polly snapped. She walked over to him and thrust the wet rag into his palm. "Take care of Scarlet. I'm getting some air."

Polly stormed past him and out the door, closing it behind her.

Polly breathed deep. It felt good to get outside. She really needed a break from all the gloom and misery. And she needed to get away from Sam. She was feeling such mixed emotions towards him, and that, on top of everything, was really putting her on edge. On the one hand, she wanted to be with him. On the other hand, she was still upset with him. She was confused, and didn't know what to think or feel.

"There you are," came a voice.

Polly spun and looked. To her shock, standing there, just a few feet away, was Sergei. She couldn't believe it.

She was gearing up to scream at him, but before she could get a word out, he held up a hand and spoke quickly, "I know you're furious at me. And you have a right to be. And if you're not interested anymore, that's okay. I didn't come here to try again. I got the message. I just came to make amends. And to help."

Polly stared at him, not knowing what to believe.

"And how do you propose to do that?" she snapped.

Sergei took a half step forward, tentatively. "The plague that Scarlet has, and that Caleb has," he said, "I know a cure for it. I know who poisoned them. It was Kyle. And I know where the antidote is. I can lead you to it."

"And why would you do that?" Polly snapped, still not trusting him. "You love Kyle."

"Kyle and I parted ways. He is my enemy now. And like I said, I want to make amends. I'm truly ashamed for how I behaved back in France. Please, give me one chance to make it up to you. Let me help. Let me give you the antidote. You can save everyone."

Polly thought. He sounded so convincing, so genuine. And why would he offer this, unless he meant it? The idea of her helping everyone filled her with a new sense of hope. The sight of Scarlet and Caleb was almost too much for her to bear. If there was a chance, any chance, for a cure, she would have to explore it.

"How far is it?" she asked.

Sergei smiled.

"Not far at all. Fly with me. I'll show you. Please," he said, pleading, "trust me. I want to help. You can save both their lives."

Polly looked him up and down, trying to use all her senses to detect if he was telling the truth. But her senses were obscured. She desperately wanted to believe him, to believe that there was a cure. She tried to reason with herself that there was.

And with Caleb and Scarlet on death's door, what choice did she have?

"I still hate you," Polly said, "but I'll follow you to the cure. And that's it. And then I'm never talking to you again."

Sergei smiled. "That's all I ask."

CHAPTER TWENTY NINE

Caitlin flew through the night, flying faster than she ever had, using her wings to try to gain maximum speed, as she flew alone in the darkness. The night sky was filled with stars, and the rural landscape of England lay far beneath her.

She felt so alone. After having flown so much recently with large groups of people—Caleb, Scarlet, Ruth, Sam, Polly, Lily and Aiden's coven members—now, she felt the loneliness. She felt as if she were traveling a path meant only for only her to travel, deep into the universe.

She reflected back on all of the places she'd seen, the times she'd lived, and she remembered what she'd learned, time and again: that the path of the warrior was always one that had to be traveled alone. When she was truly alone, carving out new territory, that was when she knew that she was leading, not following. That was when she was becoming a warrior. That was what Aiden had taught her. And now, it felt more true than ever.

Every bone in her body wanted to race to get the antidote for Caleb, and, hopefully, Scarlet, too. Although he had only said it works for vampires, she hoped, prayed, that she could also find some way to revive Scarlet, too. But Aiden had been firm on the point that she had to visit St. Michael's Mount and get the key first, or else endanger them all. She had never seen him so firm on anything, and given his particularly dire warning that if she didn't, then Caleb would not live, she felt that she had to heed his advice.

As she continued to fly, heading, as instructed, to the farthest southwestern point of England, to the very tip of the entire island, slowly, dawn began to break. The soft sky lit up with thousands of muted shades of yellow and orange, as the stars slowly melted away. The rural landscape, the soft rolling hills, the occasional farmhouse, the smoke rising from chimneys, all slowly became visible beneath her again.

As Caitlin flew, her heart began to beat faster with the anticipation of possibly seeing her father. Could it be that he might be here? On the Mount of Judgment? Waiting for her? Her dream had seemed so real. If not, could this be the place where she would find the third key, get that much closer to finding him? She was excited to have finally decoded the riddle, and excited that her father had given her the answer in her dream. She felt he was with her more than ever, and she felt determined to find the key—especially if that was the first step in saving Caleb and Scarlet.

Caitlin brushed back her tears as she flew, trying to push her sadness to the back of her mind. The thought of losing Caleb and Scarlet was too much to bear, and she couldn't allow herself to go there right now. She had to be tough, for them all.

She finally rounded a bend, and the most incredible sight unfolded before her. She had never seen anything like it in her life, in any place on the planet: there, on the horizon, was a small island, sticking out into the ocean. The mainland of England finally ended, meeting the ocean, waves crashing all around it, and there, out in the ocean, maybe five hundred yards from the mainland, sat a small island. The island had its own small mountain, and on top of that mountain, sat a huge, fortified castle.

It was magnificent, the most dark and dramatic thing she had ever seen. It rose up out of the ocean like some primordial creation, as if the castle had been built out of the rock itself. It looked ancient, powerful, the stuff of dreams and legends.

As if all that were not enough, as she dove lower, circling the island, taking it all in, she noticed a narrow cobblestone walkway connecting the island to the mainland. The walkway stretched for hundreds of yards, and as the tides rolled in and out, she could see that the stones were just barely submerged in the water. She could see from the ebb and flow that at certain tides, at certain times of day, the island would be completely inaccessible, reachable only by boat. At other times of day, when the tide receded, one could walk there from the mainland. It was a positively magical pathway, a disappearing walkway heading right into the sea, leading to a mystical island, with a huge mountain and castle on top.

This must definitely be the place, she thought.

As Caitlin dove lower, taking it in from every angle, she could feel the energy coming off it. Clearly, this was a powerful place. And she felt certain that it either held her father, or the key to getting to him.

Caitlin debated where to land. She could have just flown right down and landed inside the castle itself. But somehow that didn't feel right to her. She felt certain that her father's coven would require formality and respect, that they would appreciate her formal entrance through their main entryway. Caitlin also felt she needed to walk towards the castle, to truly grasp its approach and the secrets it might hold.

Caitlin circled around, and landed on the mainland of England, on the sandy beach, right before the entrance to the walkway. At this time of day, in early dawn, there was not a human in sight. The only company she had was the occasional seagull and sandpiper walking along the beach, squawking at her, and the crashing of the waves.

Caitlin took off her shoes, barefoot on the sand, and walked onto the cobblestone path. It was already covered in a few inches of water, and the cold water relaxed her, as did the feel of the smooth stones beneath her bare feet.

As she walked, heading slowly out into the ocean, she had the surreal experience of feeling as if she were walking on water, the waves coming and going on either side of her, gently rolling along the walkway, ebbing and flowing. The walkway was covered in an inch or two of water, and occasionally the water rose up to her shins, then receded again.

As she approached the island, she looked up and saw the mountain looming large before her. Atop that, the castle loomed even larger, with parapets in every direction. The water was already climbing higher, now reaching her shins, and she realized that by the time she reached the island, the walkway would probably be impassible. She appreciated being a vampire: luckily for her, she could fly.

She finally reached the island, stepping on its rocky shore, and began her ascent up the mountain, towards the castle.

After a rough, steep incline, she reached a massive gate, built out of the stone, with huge iron bars. She stood before it, examining it, wondering if someone would come out to greet her.

As she stood there, the gate suddenly, mystically, opened, parting just a little bit, enough for her to walk through. Someone, she realized, must have been observing her from somewhere, possibly expecting her.

Caitlin entered through the gates and continued on, all the way to the top of the mountain.

When she reached the top, there was a broad plateau, and a wide courtyard with a magnificent, arched castle gate.

She walked towards it, and before that gate stood a single vampire, dressed in an all-white robe, a white hood covering his face, so she could not get a good look at him. She approached slowly, and as she did, the vampire pulled back its hood, and looked at her. It was a woman, with long blonde hair and glowing blue eyes. She smiled back at Caitlin.

"Sister," she said. "We have been expecting you."

Before Caitlin could respond, the vampire turned, and opened the gate. She walked right through the huge, arched entrance, and as Caitlin followed, the gate closed behind them.

Caitlin walked a few steps behind this vampire, who didn't offer any more conversation, and as she did, she felt as if she were being led to a very important place.

Soon, the long walkway opened up into an inner courtyard, lit up by the soft red glow of the early morning. There, to Caitlin's surprise, were at least a hundred vampires, all standing at quiet attention along the sides of the courtyard, lined up in a perfect row, all dressed in white robes and white hoods.

In the center of the courtyard stood a single, lone figure, a tall vampire, dressed as the others, his hood pulled back, with large amber eyes. He was expressionless.

Caitlin stepped forward, heading right to him. Caitlin felt self-conscious as she stood there, facing this man, just feet away, hundreds of vampires watching. But she also felt comfortable, reassured in his presence.

"We are very proud of you, Caitlin," he said, "and your father is, too. You have come far in your journey, and are closer than you realize to finding him, and delivering us all from a terrible evil. We are all counting on you."

He reached into his robe and extracted a small, silver chest, covered in jewels, sparkling.

"Your key," he said.

Caitlin looked back at him, momentarily puzzled. But then he saw her looking at her neck, and realized. Her necklace.

Caitlin gingerly removed her necklace, holding up the small, antique cross. She inserted it into the chest, turned the lock, and it opened with a soft click.

There, before her, nestled in a red, velvet lining, was a single, shining key. It looked just like the others.

The third key. Caleb could hardly believe it.

He nodded back, and she lifted it slowly, almost afraid to touch it. She held it in her hands. It was heavier than it looked.

"The third key," he said. "Just one more, and you will be with your father. You have done what no other vampire has been able to do. Now, we all look to you to finish the job."

He took a deep breath.

"The fourth and final key waits for you back in time. You must go back now. Without delay. Your father waits for you, and the matter is urgent."

As he finished speaking, he reached out and held up a golden goblet, overflowing with a white liquid.

"Drink," he said, "and we will send you back."

Caitlin was caught off guard. She hadn't expected this. She certainly didn't want to let anyone down, but she couldn't do it.

She slowly shook her head.

"I'm sorry," she said. "But I can't go back now. Caleb and Scarlet—my loved ones—they are very ill. They need me. I must help them. I could never go back without them."

He shook his head gravely.

"You must not delay," he said. "You may not delay once you have the key. If you do, it could jeopardize the mission for all of us. And for yourself."

"I'm sorry," Caitlin said, adamant, "but I cannot go back without them."

"Don't you realize? There is great danger ahead of you in this time and place. To stay here now is to risk your life. Permanently. And you may not be able to save them. You risk it all for the slightest possibility. Would you really risk losing it all over this?"

Caitlin stood there, torn. She certainly didn't want to upset her father, or his coven, or endanger anyone. But she felt deep down that there was just no way she could go back without them.

"I'm sorry," Caitlin said. "My mind is made up."

He sighed.

"Would you like the key back?" Caitlin asked.

He slowly shook his head, looking gravely concerned.

"No. They key is yours now. I only pray that you live long enough to use it."

CHAPTER THIRTY

Polly flew behind Sergei, following him as they sped through the night. It felt to her like they'd been flying for hours, and she had an increasingly bad feeling as they went.

As dawn finally broke, a structure became apparent in the distance. He suddenly dove down low, and she followed.

Polly's eyes open wide in surprise, as the structure came into view. There, spread before them, was a magnificent castle, one of the largest she had ever seen, shaped in a huge horseshoe pattern, with high walls, and parapets crowning each of them. In the center, was a semicircular courtyard, with a circle in the middle, atop a knoll, and a grass hill at its far end.

"Arundel Castle," Sergei announced. "It is where I live."

Without a word, he dove down low, right into the courtyard, and Polly hesitated for a moment. She was beginning to feel inside of her that something was wrong. She wondered once again whether she could trust him. But once again, a part of her desperately wanted to try anything for an antidote for Scarlet and Caleb. She would do whatever she had to, take whatever risk she needed to, even it involved this.

Polly dove down and landed beside Sergei in the courtyard, then followed him as he strutted across the perfectly-manicured pebbled path, towards a huge oak door. He yanked it open, creaking as he did, and stood to the side, waiting for her to enter.

He smiled at her, and Polly scowled back.

"I didn't come here for a visit of your home," she said. "I came here for the antidote. Where is it?" she demanded, standing before the door, hands on her hips.

"So impatient," Sergei replied. "Just relax. We are going to get your antidote. I don't keep it outside, obviously. It is safely secured inside."

Polly stood before the open door, debating. She felt such dark energy coming from inside, and a part of her wanted to flee.

But a different part refused to listen to reason, as her emotions told her she needed to find a cure.

Polly stepped inside, into the darkened space, barely lit by a small stained-glass window.

As she did, the huge oak door slammed behind her, Sergei standing just a foot away, and she flinched at the sound.

She heard Sergei's dark laughter in the darkness.

"So jumpy," he said.

And then he reached up, and she suddenly felt his icy cold hands on her shoulders.

She spun around, and brushed them off of her.

She was appalled to see that he still had feelings for her, and that he was obviously still trying to seduce her. If he didn't show her where the antidote was soon, she was going to leave.

But he just grinned back down at her, an evil grin.

"You are still so naïve, aren't you?" he said darkly.

Polly felt her heart drop at his words. Where was this going?

"Did you truly think I would lead you to an antidote? And why? I hate all of your friends. And I would enjoy nothing more than to watch all of them die slowly and painfully."

Polly's heart pounded in her chest. It was a trick. All of it. She had been tricked. Once again.

Now, she was furious.

Polly reached back, made a fist, and threw it, aiming right for Sergei's face.

But he was much faster than she thought, and he raised a single hand casually and caught her punch in mid-air.

With his open palm, he squeezed her knuckles with such strength, that she felt herself crying out, as her knuckles were squeezed in agony from his grip. She had never known he was that strong. Polly dropped to her knees in pain from his grip.

He continued to smile down at her.

"I brought you here because I enjoy playing with you. I brought you here to make you mine. Forever, this time. My slave. So you can make up for the way you treated me back in France. For making a fool of me, for making me lose Caitlin. Having you here, as my prisoner, will bring Caitlin and her crew here like a lamb to slaughter, and then I can present them all as my gift to Kyle."

She looked up and saw how ugly and evil Sergei was as he stared down at her and revealed his true self. Just as she had remembered. She felt so furious at herself for believing him a second time.

"And if they don't come for you, if they never come for you, then I shall just keep you here, as my slave forever."

At that moment, several other girls stepped out of adjoining rooms, and Polly was shocked to see that they looked similar to her. They all walked slowly, their hands and feet bound in silver chains.

As if under a trance, obediently following Sergei's orders, they all went to the large oak door and barred it shut with a huge silver post. Polly gulped as she watched her only way out barred and blocked by a dozen female vampire slaves.

"Don't worry," Sergei said, laughing. "You will get used to being my slave. After several centuries, you won't even remember that you lived any other way."

CHAPTER THIRTY ONE

Sam kept his vigil at Caleb and Scarlet's bedside, crisscrossing the room as he squeezed out a cloth in a bucket of cold water and applied it to Caleb's forehead. Lily did the same for Scarlet.

Sam was beginning to feel more and more anxious that Polly had not returned. She had said that she was stepping out of the room for just a moment, and he'd expected her to be back at least an hour ago. He was finding himself increasingly impatient, and was no longer able to contain his worry for her.

Sitting in this room, watching Caleb and Scarlet so sick, did not help to relieve his anxiety, either. Nor did the fact that he was still worried about his sister, and longed to be out there, protecting her. He didn't want to be sitting here, acting as a nurse. He felt that he could be put to better use, and his impatience was building.

He looked up at Lily, who was kneeling on the far side of the bed and applying a cloth to Scarlet's head.

"Can you watch them both for a few minutes?" he asked. "I want to check on Polly."

Lily nodded, looking tired and solemn.

Sam turned and hurried through the room, strutting across the ancient stone, heading for the oak door. As he did, he wondered why he was so concerned for Polly? Indeed, he wondered why he felt such strong feelings for her at all. Whenever he was around her, he felt as if he were caught up in a storm of emotions—happiness, joy, love, jealousy, anger, sadness… He had a hard time admitting to himself that he cared for her. But he was beginning to recognize that that was obvious. Was he falling for her?

Sam strutted through the large oak door, and was startled as soon as he stepped outside. There, before him, were dozens of Aiden's men, sprinting across the courtyard and leaping up into flight. It looked as if the entire coven were mobilizing for war. The excitement in the air was palpable.

Sam reached out and grabbed one of the vampires. "What's going on? Where are you going?"

"Haven't you heard?" he asked, stopping for just a moment, his eyes wide open in agitation.

"London is besieged. Fires have started everywhere. The plague has spread to all four corners. And someone has unleashed a rival vampire coven from the crypts—they are now attacking the humans. The entire human population is under a coordinated attack. We sense that it's the work of a rival vampire coven. We have to save the humans before the city disappears."

With that, he shook off Sam's grip and leapt into the air, flying with the others. The sky darkened with all the bodies, looking like a swarm of bats launching into the sky.

Sam looked up and saw Aiden, walking behind them all, watching the sky. He turned and looked at Sam.

"There is a great calamity among the human race. I must join this battle," he announced. "You are alone here now. I trust you to watch over our castle."

Sam didn't know what to make of it.

"I want to go, too," he said. "I want to fight with you. I don't want to just sit here."

"We don't only always do what we want. We do what is needed of us," Aiden responded. Then he turned to go.

"Wait!" Sam yelled out.

Aiden turned.

"Where is Polly? Did she go with you?"

Sam sensed deep down that something was off.

Aiden slowly shook his head, staring intently at Sam.

"Polly left hours ago. Before us. With Sergei."

Sam's heart dropped. *With Sergei?*

"She is in grave danger," Aiden added.

And with that, he turned and suddenly disappeared. Sam looked everywhere for him, but he was gone. Vanished.

Aiden's final words lingered, like a dagger thrust into Sam's heart.

In grave danger? With Sergei?

Sam closed his eyes and tuned in, and suddenly, he sensed it. He could feel that it was true. He could feel, on some level, Polly calling out to him. In danger. Trapped.

Sam opened his eyes suddenly, feeling Polly's desperation. He couldn't bear it one second longer.

Without thinking, he took three running steps and leapt high into the air, flying faster than he ever thought he could, letting his body guide him in the direction in which he felt Polly was. He didn't have a choice. She was trapped, and he must save her.

In his haste, he didn't even give a second's thought to the fact that Lily was now the only one left behind, a mere human, to guard to their castle, and two people on their deathbed.

CHAPTER THIRTY TWO

Caitlin flew from St. Michael's Mount, holding the third key in her hand, the vampire's final words still ringing in her head. She felt a sense of ominousness as she flew through the morning, through thick, black storm clouds, racing to find Violet.

Aiden had told her about Violet's castle—Bodium Castle—located in the far northern corner of England, and she raced towards it with all she had. Thunder erupted in the warm September sky, as she flew right into thick, black storm clouds. But she didn't slow. She had to get there, for all she was worth.

Caitlin felt her father's three keys in her pocket, and felt so torn. On the one hand, she felt as if she were shirking her duties to him, and to her race. On the other hand, she knew there was no way she could go back in time without Caleb and Scarlet. She would rather forgo the mission than do that.

Caitlin would do whatever it took to get the antidote. But her heart was pounding at the thought of having to go and meet Caleb's ex-lover and ask for her help. Caitlin was proud and jealous, and she would have given anything to never have to see Violet's face again. To have to seek her out, and to have to humble herself before her and ask for her help, was almost more than Caitlin could bear. But for Caleb, and for Scarlet, she would do it.

Caitlin swallowed her pride and dove down lower, as she finally sensed she was close. As she dipped down beneath the clouds, she was taken aback by the sight: there, on the horizon, was a castle that could only be Bodium. It was a small castle, but one of the most dramatic she had ever seen. Built in the middle of a lake, completely surrounded by water, accessible only by a narrow, wooden bridge that reached out for hundreds of yards from the mainland, the small castle was built in a perfect circle. It had ancient parapets in every direction, and lying perfectly still in the water, it looked as if it were one with nature, as if it had been there since the beginning of time.

It was the perfect setting, Caitlin realized, for a vampire home, secluded, surrounded by water for protection against one's enemies, and barely accessible.

This time, Caitlin decided to forego approaching formally. There wasn't time. Instead, she dove straight down, swooping in unannounced to the interior courtyard.

She landed and looked around, and was surprised to see that it seemed much bigger from down here. It was large enough to hold to a small coven of vampires. As a home for just one, it must be, she realized, a very lonely place. A place for a true loner. It made her wonder what Violet was really like.

"HELLO!" Caitlin screamed out.

Her voice echoed off the empty stone walls.

"KEIRA!" Caitlin called out.

Her voice echoed again and again, coming back, as if mocking her. It was so empty and desolate here, Caitlin felt as if she were the last person on earth.

She suddenly heard a noise, a faint musical noise, in the distance. She listened closely, and could just begin to hear it. She couldn't believe it. It was organ music, coming from somewhere inside the castle.

Caitlin crossed the courtyard and entered through one of the large, arched doors.

Inside, in the dark stone corridor, the music was louder. It was definitely an organ, filling the halls, reverberating off of them. It was creepy, and all-encompassing, and magical.

Caitlin followed it, as if in a trance, trying to find the source. As she turned down corridor after corridor, it finally became louder, more intense.

Finally, she came to a large, open room which looked like a chapel, all stone, with high ceilings and arched windows made of stained glass. The room was completely empty save for a single organ, placed against the far wall. And there, seated before it, her back to her, playing, was Violet.

She was in the middle of a song, and Caitlin stood and listened, not wanting to interrupt her. It was the most beautiful—and darkest—music that Caitlin had ever heard. It was mesmerizing, haunting. It was the sound of death coming, and yet of new life being reborn at the same time.

Caitlin felt it go through every bone in her body. It went on for she didn't know how long, and then finally, dramatically, it ended.

Violet slowly turned and faced Caitlin, standing. She was exactly as Caitlin had remembered: tall, aloof, proud, and beautiful.

"Did Caleb send you?" Violet asked flatly.

Caitlin swallowed hard, not sure how to phrase it.

"No, he didn't," she answered. "I came on my own."

"What is it, then?" Violet asked, abrupt. "I don't like receiving visitors, especially unannounced. Have you come to tell me how jealous you are? If so, you're wasting your time. Caleb and I have no interest in each other. He's all yours. I'm happy for you both."

Caitlin shook her head. "That's not why I'm here," she said.

Caitlin breathed deep, feeling overwhelmed with sadness. She felt as if she wanted to cry, but held back her tears.

"Caleb…" she began. "He's…deathly ill," she said, looking down at the ground. She looked up. "He's been poisoned. Aiden says he hasn't long to live."

Violet's eyes opened wide, and Caitlin could see how shocked she was. She visibly relaxed her guard.

"Who did this?" she asked.

Caitlin shook her head. "I don't know. But I am guessing it was Kyle, of the Blacktide Coven. And that he came back in time to do this."

Violet's eyes narrowed. "Kyle. Yes, I know of him. That is exactly the sort of thing he would do. But why Caleb?"

"Kyle was after me. I think Caleb got in the way."

Violet glowered at her, and Caitlin felt overwhelmed with guilt.

"Can you help me?" Caitlin finally asked. "Can you help Caleb?"

"How? I'm not a doctor."

"Aiden said there was one chance for him. If I had blood. From his maker. That that might save him."

Violet snorted. "You're wasting your time. That's an old wives' tale. I've never seen that work."

Caitlin was determined. "It's the only chance we have. Please. I have nothing else to try."

Violet stared at Caitlin, and several moments of silence followed.

"You really love him, don't you?" Violet asked.

Caitlin felt tears welling up, this time rolling down her cheeks.

"Yes, I do," she answered. "Very much. We are engaged to be married. We are *going* to be married."

Violet stared at her, and Caitlin felt as if she were summing her up, staring through her soul.

"Very well, then. I'll do it for you. To humor you. But you are wasting your time. You have to let him go."

She turned and strutted away.

Caitlin followed her through the castle, down a dark corridor, twisting and turning.

"What was it?" Caitlin asked. "That music you were playing?"

"Bach," Violet answered flatly. "His Toccata and Fugue in D minor."

"It was beautiful," Caitlin said. "But very dark."

"So am I," Violet answered.

They finally entered an alcove area with a small counter, on top of which sat several vials.

Violet suddenly reached out, took a small knife from her waistband, and sliced her wrist.

She then reached over, grabbed a vial, and let her blood drip into it. When it was filled, she sealed it with a stopper.

She bandaged her wrist with a rag, then held up the vial, examining it in the fading afternoon light.

"You are putting your faith for his entire life in this one vial," Violet said. "And if it doesn't work?"

Caitlin reached out, took it, and examined it.

"If it doesn't work," she said, sadly, "then I have nothing left to live for."

CHAPTER THIRTY THREE

"Daddy, wake up!"

Caleb slowly opened his eyes. They were so heavy. They had never felt so heavy, and it took all the effort of the world to open them.

There, standing over his bed, was his son. Jade.

Jade was smiling down, and filled with light. There was light all around him, and a shining light behind him, and Jade had the most angelic smile on his face.

"Daddy," he said, "it's time for you to come play with me!"

Caleb slowly sat up in bed, every muscle in his body aching, and he reached out his hand, to touch Jade. Jade's hand felt warm, and his smile widened. It felt so good to touch Jade again, to see his son in the flesh. Caleb was overwhelmed with emotion.

"Jade? I thought you were dead?"

Jade simply smiled back.

"It's time for us to be together again," he said.

Caleb closed his eyes and felt a sense of peace, of comfort. He felt his whole world slowly beginning to drift away, becoming brighter and brighter, slowly enveloped in a white light.

To see Jade again. Yes. He would like that very much.

But at the same time, he wasn't quite ready to go. He sensed that somewhere, deep inside, there was something left unresolved. That something was holding him there.

Caitlin.

"Come on, Daddy!" Jade urged, tugging on his hand.

"Soon," Caleb answered, as Jade slowly let go of his hand. "Very, very soon."

CHAPTER THIRTY FOUR

Kyle had never been so elated. His plan was working perfectly. He had put his crew of vampires to good work, and had managed to spark fires all throughout London; he had also managed to spread the plague himself, causing chaos, havoc and devastation beyond what he had even hoped for. He grinned widely.

It was so easy, in this primitive time, to cause destruction. There were no fire departments, there was no organized police force, there was no internet, and everything was built to be flammable. It was almost too easy, like dropping a match inside a pile of hay. He loved watching the expressions on the faces of the countless humans burned alive, running to and fro, spreading the fire even further.

As if all that weren't enough, the ones who survived the fire were scratching their ankles from flea bites and covered with welts from head to toe. One way or another, nearly all of humanity down there was suffering. Kyle felt like a little kid all over again.

It had served his purpose well. It was the perfect diversion. He had managed, as he had hoped, to get Aiden and all his people out of their castle, scurrying to help the pathetic humans. He had hoped they would be that stupid, and of course, they were. Which now left Warwick wide open for him to breach.

The only thing that remained to be seen was the poison. He had dropped it into Caitlin's drink perfectly, but had snuck out before he could watch her drink it. He assumed she had drank it, and was lying in Warwick right now, all alone, dead or slowly dying. But this time he wouldn't take any chances—he would head there himself and make sure she was dead. And if not, he would kill her himself.

Kyle nearly screamed with laughter and delight. Things hadn't gone this smoothly in centuries, and now he finally saw the end of his plans on the horizon. Within hours, Caitlin would be dead, and he would finally, *finally*, be done with all of them. Kyle breathed deeply as he flew through the nighttime air.

There, in the distance, he spotted Warwick Castle, wide open, completely unprotected from his visit. Kyle dove down, aiming right for it.

Kyle kicked open the wooden door, and marched into the room. It was dim in here, lit only by a few torches along the walls. There was a large four-poster bed, on which lay two bodies—an adult and a child. Kyle could smell the death in the air, the illness hanging over the room.

He approached, expecting to see Caitlin lying there, and was shocked to discover that it was not her, but Caleb. For a moment, he was furious: she had evaded him once again, and her stupid boyfriend had drank instead. Now he would still have to find her.

But then he relaxed. He realized that, with Caleb lying here, deathly ill, Caitlin would come soon, here, right to him, and he could kill her then. And at least he had poisoned one of them.

He looked at Caleb and Scarlet, and could tell right away that they were deathly ill, and hadn't long to live. He smiled more widely. He hadn't expected to kill off Scarlet, too. That was a bonus.

But he could also see that, for now at least, they were both still alive. That annoyed him. He loved the idea of all the suffering they must have gone through. But he loved even more the idea of them dead. And now was time to finish them off.

Kyle approached the bed. Caleb didn't react, and clearly, he was unconscious. It would almost be too easy to kill him. So Kyle decided he would start with the little girl first. At least she was squirming, semi-conscious.

Kyle walked around to her side of the bed, and as he did, he suddenly stopped in his tracks as he heard a vicious snarl. He looked down.

Standing there, facing him, was a wolf. He was shocked, because he could have sworn he had already killed this wolf, back in Venice, when he had killed Caleb's son, Jade. He couldn't understand how it was here again.

Before Kyle could react, the wolf suddenly lunged, landing with all fours on Kyle's chest, and sinking its sharp fangs into Kyle's throat.

The animal was much faster than Kyle had anticipated, and Kyle screamed out in pain, as the sharp fangs cut into his throat, sending blood everywhere

The wolf would not let go. Kyle grabbed and pulled, trying to extract it, but no matter which way he tugged, it simply refused to open its jaws. Blood sprayed everywhere, as the pain grew deeper and deeper for Kyle.

Finally, Kyle jammed his fingers into the wolf's mouth, feeling the pain as it tore through his flesh, and pried open the jaws. He then took the animal by its jaw, spun it around, and threw it across the room. It landed into the wall with a thud, and collapsed to the ground, unconscious.

Kyle, in a rage, walked across the room to finish it off.

But before he could reach it, he was distracted by voice.

"Leave my wolf alone."

Kyle spun in his tracks, and stared at the bed. He could not believe it.

There, sitting propped up, was Scarlet. She raised her neck as much as she could, and scowled back at Kyle, defiant.

Kyle grinned. He turned and marched right for her.

"You are a brash little girl, aren't you?" he asked. "Well, you're going to pay for that. Now I'm going to kill you, just as I killed Caleb's son."

To Kyle's surprise, the girl did not retreat in fear, or hide under the covers, or try to run or even squirm. Instead, to his shock, she didn't even look afraid. She sat up even more, and scowled back at him.

"I'm not afraid of you," she snapped back. "And you couldn't kill me if you tried."

Kyle stopped in his tracks, shocked at her audacity, her fearlessness. He burst into laughter, leaning back with a deep belly laugh. He liked this one. She had spirit. In fact, if he ever had a daughter, he would want her to be just like this. Fearless in the face of her own death.

"I like your style," Kyle answered. "Just for that, as a favor, I will kill you quickly."

Kyle took several steps towards her, reaching out his hands, ready to suffocate her.

But as he approached, he suddenly felt a searing pain slicing through his finger.

He screamed out in pain, and looked down, and was shocked to see that the girl had been hiding a small, silver dagger underneath the covers. As he approached, she'd somehow managed to slice off his index finger.

Kyle screamed in horror and shock, as he looked down to see himself now missing an index finger, blood gushing everywhere. He reached up and grabbed a corner of the sheet, staunched the blood, then reached back with his other hand, and backhanded the little girl so hard that it knocked her back onto her pillow, unconscious, and sent her little knife flying across the room.

Now Kyle was furious. He couldn't believe she'd managed to hurt him. Now, she would pay for that. No more mister nice guy. Now he would not kill her quickly. Rather, he would torture her all night long.

Kyle came in, this time, to strangle her for good. He reached out, his hand just inches away, when suddenly, he heard a thud, and felt a terrible pain on the back of his head.

Kyle staggered and crashed into the end table, then turned around to see what it was.

He was shocked. Standing there was a black girl, dressed in some kind of royal outfit, holding a candelabra, covered in blood. Kyle's blood. She had just whacked Kyle hard on the back of the head, hard enough to send him stumbling. And it hurt like hell.

"Whoever you are, you're going to suffer for that," Kyle snarled.

But to Kyle's surprise, she wasn't scared, either. Rather, she was defiant, too.

"My name is Lily, and I will pay for nothing," she answered.

Kyle suddenly let out a roar of fury, and jumped up and kicked her with both feet on her chest, sending her flying back across the room, and crashing into the far wall, unconscious.

Clearly, this woman, Lily, whoever she was, was a dear friend of Caitlin's and Caleb's—the only one that they had trusted to watch over them. A stupid idea, leaving a human to watch over vampires.

But a good idea was forming in Kyle's mind. If this Lily was that important to them, then what better way to make Caitlin pay, than to go after her friend?

Kyle marched slowly across the room, his eyes fixating on Lily's throat. Kyle could use another slave to do his bidding. And as he looked at her throat, he licked his lips, and realized he was hungry, and would like nothing more than to feed.

Kyle marched across the room, picked up her limp body, and without hesitating, plunged his sharp fangs deep into her throat. She screamed out as he did, suddenly conscious, but Kyle held her writhing body tight, sucking in deeper and deeper.

He felt her entire life stealing out from her, as she was being slowly, darkly, turned.

It had been centuries since Kyle had turned a human, and the feeling was thrilling. He would make this one in his own image, a true vampire slave, and would turn Caitlin's own friend against her.

CHAPTER THIRTY FIVE

Caitlin flew through the night sky, racing for all she was worth. In one hand, she clutched the three keys, feeling her father's presence with her strongly. In the other, she clutched the vial holding Violet's blood, feeling the energy pulsing through it, praying, hoping beyond hope that this small vial of blood could save Caleb's life. And praying that then, somehow, they could figure out how to save Scarlet's life, too.

On her way from Bodium Castle to Warwick, Caitlin had to fly over London, and as she approached it, she was completely caught off guard. On the horizon, even from this great distance, she could tell something was terribly wrong. Huge clouds of fire rose up into the sky, and as she got closer, she could already feel the heat.

The sight below her took her breath away. The entire city seemed to be a great ball of fire. The few survivors she could spot ran through the streets, screaming, shouting. Others lay in the streets, lifeless, looking as if they had been infected by the Plague. Caitlin could sense that a great evil had been perpetrated here, and she could sense that it had been done by Kyle and his people. She felt sick to her stomach, and more intent than ever on killing him, if she should ever find him.

Caitlin also sensed Aiden's presence here, and the presence of his coven members. It must have been very bad, if Aiden and his men all mobilized to save the humans in the city. But she didn't sense Sam or Polly's presence here, and she prayed that they were back at Warwick, defending Caleb and Scarlet, should anyone attack.

Caitlin desperately want to dive down below, and help the others. But she knew she didn't have time. She clutched the vial more tightly, and continued on, speeding through the air, knowing she had to get to Warwick as soon as possible, that Caleb's and Scarlet's lives hung in the balance.

Caitlin closed her eyes and flew past the horrible landscape, breathing short to prevent the huge clouds of black smoke from entering her lungs. Within moments, the sight was behind her, even as images of humans on fire flashed through her mind. She felt sick to her stomach. But she had to focus on saving the people that she could.

*

Caitlin dove for Warwick, and had a sense of dread as she swooped down low. She landed in the courtyard, at a running clip, and sprinted for Caleb's and Scarlet's room. She sensed immediately that this place was empty. She could not understand how that could be possible. How could Sam, Polly and Lily not be here? How could they possibly leave Caleb and Scarlet unprotected, when she had specifically asked them only for that?

She prayed that her senses were misleading her, and that they would be there, in the room, waiting as she entered.

Caitlin burst into the room, and a pit grew in her stomach. As she feared, Sam and Polly were not there. And neither was Lily.

Caitlin's heart dropped, as she walked slowly into the darkened room. She saw Caleb and Scarlet still lying there, on their beds. From here, she could sense they were both still alive, although they both looked deathly ill, and the sight felt like a knife going through her.

Caitlin could not conceive what could have happened. Where could Sam and Polly be? Where was Lily? And where was Ruth?

Caitlin looked around more carefully, and as she did, her heart stopped. There, lying against the far wall, unconscious, was Ruth.

Caitlin walked over to her, knelt down, and felt her rib cage. Ruth was breathing, but in a shallow way. Caitlin looked up and saw signs of blood, of a struggle.

Suddenly, she realized someone had been here, had hurt Ruth. But who? How? And if so, why were Caleb and Scarlet unhurt?

Before she could figure out the answers, she heard a shriek and a snarl, and out of the corner of her eye, saw something plunging for her.

Caitlin was so caught off guard, she could barely react in time, as Lily lunged at her, fangs extended, snarling, and threw her.

Caitlin went flying across room and crashed into a far wall, hard enough to shake the entire room. She slipped to the ground, dazed, and looked up to see Lily charging her again.

Caitlin couldn't process what she was seeing. It was definitely Lily. But Lily was a vampire. And was attacking her. And was stronger than nearly any vampire she'd ever fought.

She had been turned, Caitlin suddenly realized.

And by an evil vampire.

Kyle.

"Yes, that's right," Lily said, in a deep, guttural voice. "Kyle is my master now."

Lily lunged again, but this time, Caitlin was ready. She rolled at the last second, and Lily went head first, right into the wall, and Caitlin turned around and elbowed her hard in the small of her back.

Lily screamed out in pain, as she collapsed to the floor. Caitlin saw her chance to really hurt her, but she couldn't bring herself to. This was still Lily. Her old friend. Who had been turned by an evil, monstrous vampire. It was not Lily's fault.

Caitlin could sense that deep down, the good was still in Lily. And that she could break free of this.

So, instead, Caitlin jumped on Lily from behind, and held her in a deadly lock, keeping her from moving, from hurting anyone, or herself. Lily writhed and squirmed for all she was worth, but Caitlin held her tight, as if trying to hold a demon in place.

"Get off of me!" Lily screamed.

"Lily, it's me! Caitlin! You've been turned. By an evil vampire. I know that the good Lily is still inside. It is still with you. Release the evil strain. Become the Lily that I know."

Lily writhed and squirmed and screamed, and Caitlin sensed a tremendous battle going on within her. It was as if Lily were battling with herself, as if she were possessed.

"Caitlin," came a voice, a new voice, from within Lily. "Free me. Please. I don't want to hurt you."

Caitlin slowly got up, and took several steps back, watching carefully.

Lily turned and looked at her, breathing deep, guttural breaths, like that of a wounded animal. Lily stared at her, and as she did, her eyes glazed over, turning colors, from brown to black to green. For a flash, Caitlin recognized the old Lily. She sensed the epic struggle happening within her.

Lily suddenly reached over, grabbed a silver knife off the floor, raised it high and began to plunge.

But she wasn't trying to attack Caitlin.

Rather, she was trying to plunge it into her own heart. To kill herself, Caitlin realized.

Caitlin jumped out and grabbed Lily's hand, just before the knife could reach her heart. She held her grip with all she had, but Lily's grip was so strong, it was an epic struggle just to hold it back.

Their struggle seemed to go on forever, both of their hands shaking, until finally, Caitlin squeezed as hard as she could, and got Lily to drop the knife.

Lily leaned her head back and roared, as if trying to exorcise the demon within her.

Suddenly, Lily turned and sprinted across the room. She headed right for the huge stained-glass windows, and without pausing, leapt right through them, glass shattering everywhere.

Caitlin watched as Lily flew out into the night, her huge wings flapping, flying as fast as she could to get away from this place.

"She disappointed me," came a dark, guttural voice.

Caitlin slowly turned, knowing whose voice that was.

Kyle.

He stepped from out of the shadows, missing one eye, his skin charred, and now, Caitlin could see, missing a finger.

He was a grotesque monster, from the depths of hell

He walked slowly towards Caitlin, facing her head on.

"You are a sick, evil creature," Caitlin said. "And you're going to pay for what you did to my friend with your life."

Kyle smiled back at her.

"You couldn't kill me the first time: what makes you think you can kill me now?"

Caitlin fearlessly took two steps towards Kyle, squaring off with him.

"And you couldn't kill me the first time: what makes you think *you* can kill me now?"

Kyle snarled and roared, the roar of an animal in its fury—and Caitlin did the same.

Two adversaries, squaring off, neither willing to give an inch, they lunged for each other, both aiming right for each other's throats.

This time, it would be life or death.

CHAPTER THIRTY SIX

Sam dove down low in the night sky, aiming right for Arundel Castle. It was exactly where he had sensed it would be, and he could feel Polly's energy strongly. He felt Polly in distress, and the feeling coursed through his entire body; he was surprised by the intensity with which it had struck him. He was surprised to recognize how deeply he felt for Polly, almost as if she were a part of him.

At first, he been angry, jealous, and resentful to hear that she had flown off with Sergei. He'd had a hard time getting over the fact, and at first assumed that it could only mean that she still had feelings for him.

But the more he dwelt on it, and the more he felt her true feelings of distress, the more he began to realize that maybe it was something else. That maybe she had been duped. Or captured.

Sam had felt nervous to leave Caleb and Scarlet alone with Lily, but he reasoned he'd be back in just a few hours, and that they were safe, and that Polly's life was in definite, immediate danger.

Sam dove down right into the interior courtyard of Arundel and stopped, both feet planted on the ground. He looked around warily in every direction. It was quiet, empty. The September night air had grown colder, and a cold breeze came in off the moat.

This castle was a strange place, shaped like a horseshoe, with a circular, grass lawn in the middle, and a hill on the far end. Its stone edifice was lit only by torches, spread out all along the exterior. He could sense danger here.

"POLLY!" Sam screamed.

His voice echoed off the stone.

Sam turned, chose a door, and raced straight for it. It was solid, looked to be a foot thick, but he didn't slow down. He leapt into the air, using his full vampire strength, and kicked it open with both feet. It went flying off its hinges, shattering, and Sam ran right into the castle.

Sam sprinted down the empty, stone corridors, screaming Polly's name. He could sense how much danger she was in, and realized he'd made the right choice to come here.

"POLLY!" he screamed again, turning down yet another corridor.

As he entered a grand room, suddenly, doors slammed closed all around him. They were silver gates, and as Sam wheeled in every direction, he saw there were a dozen of them, each slammed shut by another vampire. They were vampire women, all carrying deadly weapons, all facing him.

Standing in the center of the room was Sergei. He smiled back with an evil, victorious smile.

"Your Polly is now my play thing," he said. "A slave to me. Like all the others here. She will be in my service for the next thousand years."

Sam could feel his anger heating up, rising through his veins. But he didn't try to suppress it this time. Instead, he let it boil and bubble, let it grow bigger and bigger, feeling it about to explode. He *wanted* to explode, wanted to unleash a rage unlike any he had ever known.

"She was stupid enough to listen to me," Sergei said, "not just once, but a second time. And now, she's paid the price. And so will you. And so will your sister."

Sergei nodded darkly, and the dozens of vampire women encircled Sam from every direction, wielding their weapons—huge battle axes, maces, spears, long swords.

Sam's rage finally let loose, and as they all charged him, he jumped up in the air, higher than all of them, and as he flew, reach out and grabbed the shafts of all their weapons. He flew in the air, holding them, and stripped each weapon from each vampire as he went, one at a time, right down the middle. Then, as he reached the final vampire, he grabbed the huge silver battle axe from her hand, swung it back, and flew right for Sergei.

Sergei's eyes opened wide. Before he could react, Sam flew at full speed, right at Sergei, and swung the axe down hard.

It was a clean shot. Within a fraction of a second, Sam had decapitated Sergei, his head rolling off his body, and his body collapsing to the floor.

It was as if a spell had been broken. Suddenly, the dozens of vampire women, who had just seconds before been enemies to Sam, now all seemed to be freed from a trance. They retreated from Sam, and milled about the room, giving each other solace. Sam could see in their eyes, and in their expressions, that they were no longer hostile to him.

"Please, forgive us," one of them pleaded. "We never meant to harm you."

"Where is Polly?" Sam asked.

One of the vampires stepped forward.

"I will lead you to her."

She ran and took out a set of skeleton keys, to unlock the iron gate.

But Sam had no time to lose. He stepped up, tore the huge door off its hinges with both

338

hands, and set it to the side. The girl looked up at him, shocked.

"Which way?" he asked, forcefully.

She pointed, her hand still shaking, down a corridor.

Sam followed it, and as he did, he could hear Polly's voice, screaming and pounding from behind a door. He stopped before it.

"Stand back!" he screamed.

He then leaned back and kicked the door open, sending it flying off its hinges. He ran into the stone cell, and as he did, Polly was standing there, shaking, crying.

She ran into his arms, and hugged him tightly.

He hugged her back.

"Sam," she said. "I was so stupid. Thank you. Thank you. You saved my life."

She hugged him even more tightly, and he hugged her back. He couldn't help noticing how good it felt to have her in his arms.

And that he never wanted to let her go.

CHAPTER THIRTY SEVEN

Kyle and Caitlin dove for each other, each in a murderous rage.

Caitlin met him head-on, and they crashed together like a pair of charging rams. They grappled, grabbing onto each other's shoulders. They tore and clawed at each other, and it was a tremendous meeting of strength. Kyle was twice her size, but Caitlin could feel a strength burning through her beyond what she'd ever known. And strangely enough, even in the midst of such a heated battle, she no longer felt overwhelmed by her emotions. She felt calm, clearheaded. In control. She focused on her breathing, on her inner strength, on the life force coursing through her.

Caitlin could sense Kyle's hatred, his fury. But she was surprised that she could also, as she turned in, sense something deeper underneath: fear. She was shocked to sense that Kyle was afraid. Of *her*.

After minutes of grappling, Caitlin got the upper hand. She turned and threw him, and he went flying across the room, slamming into a stone wall.

Kyle stood there, staring back at her, wide-eyed, looking shocked.

He snarled as he charged her again, as if to tackle her. But as he did, Caitlin jumped straight up into the air and kicked him right beneath his jaw, sending his chin flying back, and sending him landing flat on his back.

Caitlin then lifted her foot, aiming to crush his throat. At the last second, though, he rolled out of the way, and her foot went into the floor with such force that it put a hole in it. For a second, she was stuck. Kyle elbowed her hard in the back, sending her flying across the room, and head-first into the wall.

Caitlin fell burning pain in her back, and in her head, and momentarily, was dizzy.

Kyle charged her again, this time grabbing a huge desk, bringing it up high, and getting ready to smash Caitlin over the head with it.

Caitlin rolled out of the way just in time, sweeping out Kyle's feet as she did, forcing him to fall flat on his face, banging his head into the edge of the desk. She wheeled, tore the metal arm off the desk, raised it, and brought it down hard on the back of Kyle's head.

He rolled several times, across the room, and finally came to a stop on the ground, groaning, barely conscious.

Caitlin walked over to him slowly, raised the metal bar high, and prepared to plunge it into his chest, and finish him off for good.

Barely conscious, he looked up to her, and grinned an evil grin, blood coming from his mouth.

"Do it," he said.

Caitlin raised it high, and was about to plunge it into his chest—as revenge for everyone she loved dearly—when, at the last second, she heard a voice.

"Mommy?"

Caitlin spun at the noise, the sound of Scarlet's words coursing through her.

She saw Scarlet sitting up in bed, reaching out for her.

Caitlin spun back, to finish off Kyle, but it was too late.

He was already running for the open window, and with two huge steps, he leapt out.

All Caitlin could do was watch, as he flew into the night sky.

"We'll meet again!" he screamed out, his words echoing through the night sky as he flew away, his body disappearing into the full moon.

Caitlin dropped her weapon and ran to Scarlet's side.

She gave her a huge hug, and held her, as she was crying and shaking. She leaned back and brushed the hair out of her face, and kissed her all over her forehead. Her welts look much worse than before, and she could feel her burning up.

"I'm so sorry, sweetheart," Caitlin said. "I'm so sorry mommy left you."

Scarlet hugged her again, holding her tight, crying.

"It hurts so bad, mommy. Please, make it go away."

Caitlin's heart was breaking.

"I will," Caitlin said. "It's all going to be okay. I promise."

Caitlin ran around the other side of the bed, to Caleb's side, and knelt there, holding his hand in both of hers as she leaned in close and whispered in his ear.

"Caleb," she said.

Nothing.

She squeezed him harder, with both of her hands, and could feel the tears rolling down her cheeks. She could sense that he was still alive, but barely.

"Caleb, please," she wept. "Open your eyes. Just one last time."

Slowly, very slowly, Caleb's eyelids fluttered just the tiniest bit.

"I love you Caleb, "she said. "I want you to know that. I will always love you. And I will always be your wife."

Caleb seemed to stir. He opened his eyes just the tiniest bit more, and Caitlin slid one hand beneath the back of his head. She gently lifted his head, and with her other hand, reached over, and took out the vial of Violet's blood.

"Caleb, I need you to do one last thing for me," she said. "You must drink this. Can you do that?"

He didn't respond.

"Caleb. Please. Do this for me. Just this one last thing. *Please.*"

He looked at her, his eyelids fluttering, and seemed to nod just the tiniest bit.

Caitlin took a deep breath, reached over, unstopped the vial, and held it to his lips. She lifted his head a bit more, and forced his lips open. And then, she suddenly emptied the entire vial into his throat, closing his mouth, forcing his head back.

Caleb coughed and gagged as the blood went down the back of his throat. He was coughing and coughing, trying to catch his breath.

It did something to him, clearly, because, for just a moment, his eyes opened wide.

"And now, feed on me," she said, crying.

Caleb slowly shook his head.

344

"I can't," he whispered. "It could kill you."

Caitlin shook her head firmly.

"No. It's okay. I promise. Everything will be okay."

Caleb shook his head again and again, as his eyes began to close.

Caitlin shook him by the shoulders.

"Caleb, please, listen to me. You have to do this. Not just for me. But for Scarlet. Listen to me. I have the key. You have to try this. It might work. It might just send us all back."

Caleb shook his head, again and again.

"Mommy?" came the voice from across the bed. "I'm scared. I'm seeing things."

Caitlin jumped up onto the bed, between the two, and dragged Caleb over, next to Scarlet. She reached over and grabbed Scarlet's hand with one hand, and grabbed Caleb's hand with the other.

"I hereby lay thee down to rest," Caitlin said aloud, initiating the funeral ritual herself. "Caitlin, Caleb, and Scarlet, to resurrect another day, in God's ultimate grace."

She repeated it a second time. As she did, Caleb's eyes fluttered. She held the two of them even tighter, and then leaned over, putting her exposed throat right before Caleb's lips.

She then slipped one hand beneath his head and lifted it, forcing his teeth towards her throat.

She repeated it a third time.

As she did, Caleb's eyes opened wide, and Scarlet clutched her firmly. She squeezed the back of Caleb's head, pushing him closer and closer towards her throat, urging him.

"Caleb, please!" she pleaded. "Feed on me. I demand it!"

And then finally, as she began to feel her world spin, becoming lighter, her father's key heating up in her pocket, she saw Caleb open his lips wide. She felt his fangs protract, and with his very last bit of energy, he suddenly leaned forward, plunging his long teeth deep into her throat.

She let out a little cry, as she felt the pain of the teeth puncturing, entering her throat.

As his teeth sank deeper and deeper, Caitlin felt the room spinning, felt her world turning white. She started to lose sense of her body, and she could have sworn that she saw Jade, standing over them all, watching, smiling.

Her world slowly, inevitably, turned white, and all she could think of, as she held them all tight, was that, finally, she was betrothed.

COMING SOON...
Book #7 in the Vampire Journals

Please visit Morgan's site, where you can join the mailing list, hear the latest news, see additional images, and find links to stay in touch with Morgan on Facebook, Twitter, Goodreads and elsewhere:

www.morganricebooks.com

Also by Morgan Rice

turned
(book #1 in the Vampire Journals)

loved
(Book #2 in the Vampire Journals)

betrayed
(Book #3 in the Vampire Journals)

destined
(Book #4 in the Vampire Journals)

desired
(Book #5 in the Vampire Journals)

CPSIA information can be obtained at www.ICGtesting.com
Printed in the USA
LVOW121649230812

295668LV00001B/12/P